Love & Adventure After 40

Pecan Pie *for* Breakfast

An Azalea Lake Sweet Romance Book 1

USA TODAY BESTSELLING AUTHOR

SUSAN SCHILD

Pecan Pie for Breakfast
(An Azalea Lake Sweet Romance Book 1)

For more about this author please visit https://www.susanschild.com/

Editing by The Pro Book Editor
Interior and Cover Design by IAPS.rocks

ISBN: 978-1-7328249-8-0

1. Main category—Fiction>General
2. Other category—Fiction>Women's

First Edition

BOOKS BY SUSAN SCHILD

An Azalea Lake Sweet Romance Series

Pecan Pie for Breakfast (Book 1)

A Front Porch Sunday (Book 2) Arriving September 2021

The Lakeside Resort Series

Christmas at the Lakeside Resort (Book 1)

Summer at the Lakeside Resort (Book 2)

Mistletoe at the Lakeside Resort (Book 3)

Wedding at the Lakeside Resort (Book 4)

A Willow Hill Novel Series

Linny's Sweet Dream List (Book 1)

Sweet Carolina Morning (Book 2)

Sweet Southern Hearts (Book 3)

CHAPTER 1

CRICKET TOOK A TOO-LARGE GULP of ice water after eating a piece of spicy fish that lit up her mouth and made her eyes water. She looked across the table of the *Senegal Siren*, Azalea's hot new African restaurant. She eyed Clayton. He was the first man she'd been out with since her divorce had become final eleven and a half months ago. Men at mid-life made her twitchy ever since her husband of thirteen years went MIA. Poof. Gone with the wind. Cricket put her finger on an artery that pulsed in her temple.

Taking a tentative bite of millet that her date, Clayton, had rhapsodized about, Cricket tried not to gag. It tasted the way the moldy seed in the bottom of her bird feeder looked. Taking another swig of ice water, Cricket tried to wash it down.

With a waving hand, Clayton continued deconstructing the indie movie they'd just seen. "Many directors are heavy-handed; however, Dubois avoided clichés in presenting the existential quandaries..."

Cricket's mind wandered. She hadn't really *gotten* the movie. She watched the DIY shows and light comedies on Prime and Netflix—the ones with no subtitles and happy endings. Maybe she wasn't a deep person. That could be why Knox had left. She'd write that down on her "Possible Reasons Husband Left Me" list that she kept hidden in a file called "Household Expenses" on her laptop at home.

Clayton must have noticed her meandering attention. Trailing off, he grimaced ruefully. "Sorry, Cricket. I'm talking too much. For me, film is a passion."

Cricket's face reddened when he said "passion." Good grief. She wasn't a fifteen-year-old girl. She was a forty-five-year-old woman with a few gray hairs, iffy eyesight, and a vein going funny on her calf. She took a long swallow of her Flag Spéciale, the tasty lager he'd encouraged her to try, and shot Clayton a surreptitious glance. The man was alarmingly good-looking. With a cleft in his chin, eyes that matched the denim of his shirt, and topped by a full head of wavy brown hair, she guessed some students signed up for his sociology courses just to look at the professor.

Clayton's phone rang. Looking apologetic, he held up a finger and took the call. "Hello?" Catching her eye, he pointed to the door. Rising, he talked softly as he walked outside to continue his conversation.

Cricket felt her face flame. Who took a call during

dinner out? Wryly, she wondered if it was a sociology emergency.

Pretending to study the menu, Cricket watched him through the plate glass window as he chuckled at something the caller said. Raking a hand through his luxuriant brown hair in an almost caressing way, he threw back his head in laughter. She narrowed her eyes. This was no business call. Clayton appeared to be flirting.

Her date looked like he was winding up his conversation. Two could play at this game. Cricket reached in her purse for her phone. As he pulled open the door, she made a show of staring intently at the screen. Frowning, she scrolled through her new messages, trying to look like a hotshot businesswoman on the go.

Cricket's eyes widened. Her breath caught when she saw the subject line of a new email that read, "Cancel Service." Christine Bowden, who'd just verbally agreed yesterday to hire Cricket's company to provide forty hours a week of caregiver services to her parents, had written a brief note canceling because they'd "decided to make other arrangements." Baffled, Cricket re-read the note twice as Clayton slid into his seat.

"Sorry about that—" he began.

Cricket held up a finger. She re-read the email.

The interviews had gone so well. She had genuinely liked both the daughter as well as her parents. Scowling, Cricket remembered another client who had discontinued services with an unexpected email not long ago. Sure, her little company was bringing in new business left and right, but if they kept losing existing business in a slow bleed, she'd be back at square one.

Cricket would have to lay off staff. Going back to being the sole caregiver would be depressing. She recalled her finances in shambles, only being able to put five dollars' worth of gas in her SUV at the pump. She'd be back to the bad old days, eating a lot of beans and rice. Cricket shuddered inwardly. Looking up, she was almost startled as she saw her date gazing at her.

His amazing blue eyes glinted, and he had a look of heightened interest on his face.

For Pete's sake. He was intrigued because he'd given her the "hold on" finger, and she'd given it right back. Cricket gave herself a mental pat on the back, reminding herself that he seemed like a nice guy. He'd come highly recommended to her by the friend in her business networking group who'd set her up. Sitting up straighter, Cricket tried to shake off the bad news email she'd gotten. She'd deal with it later.

Clayton leaned forward. "Tell me about your work. You're with a hospital, right?"

"I own a small business called Cricket's Caregivers—we provide home health care to older clients…" Clayton looked like he was drifting, so she tried to sound peppier. "If your mama started to have trouble getting around or grocery shopping or cooking, we can send a caregiver to help keep her in her home instead of going to assisted living."

Her date bobbed his head vehemently as if she'd made a good point but jumped in. "The medical-industrial complex preys on people when they are most vulnerable."

Cricket blinked, confused at the transition.

With a sage look, he went on. "Last year, I co-authored an article called "The Big Rip-Off: Who Pays the Bill for Five Hundred Dollar Pills?" We shed light on the victimization of the disenfranchised by Big Pharma."

She felt her neck prickle with defensiveness. Was he talking about her business? Headquartered in her kitchen, running on a shoestring budget, Cricket's Caregivers wasn't victimizing anybody.

After making a few more points that he emphasized by making small karate chop motions in the air, Clayton chewed on the stem of his reading glasses and looked away thoughtfully.

"Interesting," Cricket offered lamely.

The silence spun out. Why hadn't she just met him for coffee instead of letting herself be talked into a movie along with dinner?

In a too-bright voice, Cricket said, "I'm going to powder my nose."

It had been so long since she had a date. Did women even say things like "powder my nose?"

Flushing, Cricket carefully stepped across the parquet floor to the ladies' room.

The two-inch heels of the new, boho fringy boots she had bought especially for that night were trickier to steer than the comfy, eco-soul shoes she usually wore. Inside, she'd call her best friend, Honey, whose well-meaning lectures that bordered on badgering—more like stressing the absolute necessity of "getting back out there" or "climbing right back on the horse that threw you" – were part of the reason she'd agreed to this blind date.

Honey would know how to handle this date that was limping along. Back in college before she married Sanders, she'd been a bona fide *femme fatale*. So thrilled that Cricket agreed to a date, Honey had dramatically sworn, "I'll hold my phone in my hand all night long in case you need dating assistance."

Standing in a corner by the baby changing station, Cricket punched in Honey's number, willing her friend to pick up.

"Dating hotline." Honey sounded crisp, efficient, and all business.

Cricket spoke softly. "Help! I'm not even sure I like this man. I'm having a hard time talking to him." Her voice was sliding up octaves. She tried to lower it. "He actually took a call during dinner. Isn't that a bad sign?"

Honey sighed. "People have no manners these days with their phones. I wouldn't rule him out for that. Just keep an eye on him."

"Okay."

"Is he smart, good-looking, or nice?" she shot out, the hardened detective on the case.

"Yes on the first two, not sure about the nice." Cricket nibbled a cuticle.

"If he's not nice, he's not your guy. Let's at least give him a chance. He's probably nervous, too." Honey paused. "Just think of this as practice. Try flirting. Laugh gaily, and act impressed with him. Let your eyes linger on his. Oh, flick your hair. Men love that."

"Okay," Cricket said doubtfully, trying to remember all the moves.

"Just do one or two. Too many of those at the same time will make you look crazy," Honey warned. "You can do this, shug."

"Thanks." Cricket blew out a sigh as she dropped the phone back in her purse. The advice sounded far-fetched. Still, she'd grasp any life ring thrown to her.

Glancing at the mirror, she brushed back her auburn hair and reapplied her Captivating Claret lipstick. She practiced a gay laugh until she noticed loafer-clad feet under the stall behind her. She groaned inwardly.

Shake it off, she told herself. *Act confident so you'll feel confident.* Cricket walked out with a cool expression on her face, trying out a swing to her hips that she'd seen on the show, *Supermodel Discovery!*

As Cricket gave the hair flick a try, her heel caught on the threshold between the wood floor and the carpet. She hurtled into the lap of a man about to pop a bite of plantain into his mouth. Her fall softened by the cushion of him and the plush leather booth, and he caught her as gracefully as if he'd expected her arrival.

Cricket heard the gasp and murmur of the other diners as her face wedged inside his leather bomber jacket, in the vicinity of his armpit. Mortified, she paused for a moment before trying to extricate herself. The man's chest was so warm and strong. He smelled of citrus, wood smoke, and leather. She inhaled and sighed, fighting a crazy urge to burrow in.

He gently righted her. "Are you all right?"

Blushing, Cricket gave an experimental wiggle of her fingers, then her toes. "I'm okay."

Clayton strode toward her, his brow furrowed with concern.

Smoothing her skirt, Cricket glanced at the man's face, inches from hers. Her breath caught. His amber-brown eyes looked back at her steadily. His boyish grin was dazzling. Goodness.

She murmured gratefully, "I'm so sorry."

The man tipped his head toward the spot where she'd tripped. "The flooring was installed wrong. Trip hazard. Glad you didn't hit your head on the table."

Feeling less embarrassed, Cricket gave him a shaky grin. "Still, thanks again."

"Glad I was here." The man gave her a half-smile.

As Clayton walked her back to their table with his arm looped protectively around her shoulder, she stole a glance back at the man she'd just met up close. Watching her, his gaze held hers for a long moment, and Cricket shivered. He gave a two-fingered salute, looped his jacket over his shoulder, and ambled toward the cashier.

Thankfully, the date was drawing to a close. As the waiter handed Clayton the check, Cricket tried to thrust money at him. He refused gallantly. Cricket thanked him, thinking about how much energy it took to talk with a man who was a stranger. All that searching for common ground as she tried to size men up. Maybe she wasn't cut out for dating.

Clayton walked her to her car. As Cricket unlocked the door, she wasn't sure how to handle the moment.

She stuck out her hand. "I enjoyed myself. Thank you."

Instead of shaking her hand, Clayton clasped it in both of his, giving her a soulful look. "I'm smitten with you, Cricket. You're smart, good-looking—the total package. Please can we do this again soon? Maybe next Friday?"

Smitten? Cricket tried not to gape, not quite buying it. She was a suspicious soul these days. Clayton was good-looking, had a solid career, and was single. Had he just been nervous, like Honey suggested? He seemed so confident, almost cocksure of his appeal. Exhaling a shaky breath, she gazed at him. "Okay. Friday it is."

"Great!" He flashed a winning smile.

With a little wave, Cricket got in. Slipping on her seatbelt, she pulled away.

Her cell rang before Cricket was a quarter of a mile down the road. Her friend was prescient, and she may as well get used to it.

"Yes, Honey?"

Her friend wasted no time with a greeting. "Tell me every detail. Keep me on hands-free. Concentrate on driving." Honey's voice rose the way it did when she was excited. "I'm so tickled you finally went on an actual date."

Cricket gave her the highlights, including her fall. She recounted his surprising remark about being smitten. "I'm not sure what to think about Clayton. The conversation was work, plus I didn't really feel any spark. Maybe that all comes later."

"It might," Honey mused. "Or it might not. Go on a second date. Maybe even a third. You'll know. It will all come out in the wash."

"You're right." Cricket felt reassured by her friend's common sense. She was grateful that Honey wasn't pushing too hard for her to like Clayton. She hesitated, afraid to sound foolish, then blurted it out. "I did feel some zing of connection with the man I fell on. He smelled delicious in a manly way. His eyes were brown as walnuts…or coffee. Sort of melty caramel chocolate." Cricket heaved a sigh. "I'll never see him again. He's probably happily married with five kids. Maybe just divorced from his fourth wife."

"Maybe. You might see him again. Azalea is a small

town," Honey speculated. "Good to hear you're noticing men again after your awful ex's disappearing act."

"Signs of life," Cricket admitted. "Thanks for the help. I'll call you tomorrow."

Finishing the call, Cricket tooled through the small town of Azalea, admiring improvements that the Beautify Downtown! Committee had made. The freshly painted lampposts were hung with baskets of draping purple petunias and bright green sweet potato vines highlighted by deep red geraniums. American and North Carolina flags flew on the front lawn of most of the charming bungalows that lined the streets.

Cricket loved her hometown. Her heart lifted as she saw signs of its resurgence. Azalea wasn't a ghost town anymore. Thanks to high-speed internet and shows like *Fixer Upper* and *Home Town*, more bright, slightly offbeat people with lots of energy were choosing Azalea. The long-deserted dress shop, a watch repair business, and a shoe store were being bought and fixed up. Cricket felt hopeful as she cruised by the new shops that had opened in their place over the past few years—the Tempting Tea Store, a law office, Bubba's Barbecue, a hair salon, Hep Cat Graphic Design Studio, as well as Pups and Pep, a dog-friendly coffee shop. Azalea was blooming, making the comeback from deserted, run-down ghost town to charmingly alive.

Cricket spied the pink marble storefront of Girly Rae's Café, wanting to avert her eyes as the light turned red.

Braking right in front of the once-handsome building, she stared at the streaked windows, the broken neon sign that a well-known artist had created especially for the café, and the windows that were taped over with old newspaper. The place looked sad. She'd bet the Beautify Downtown! Committee was gnashing their teeth over this eyesore that she and Knox used to partially own.

The light turned green. Cricket drove on, wincing as she remembered. To build their savings, Knox invested in real estate projects with three of his buddies from dental school. Over the years, they'd flipped houses when there was still money in it. They'd owned a few modest rental properties. Finally, they were sure enough of themselves to become the backers of this upscale restaurant.

Girly Rae was a celebrity chef with a raucous laugh. Her extravagant, creative style of cooking had won her the competition on the *Primo Chef* cooking show. Her sublime Southern fare had the foodies drooling. The food critics raved, writing dazzling reviews as fast as they could type them. When Girly Rae decided to leave L.A. to move home to Azalea, Knox and the boys sprang into action. They courted her and finally convinced her to open a new restaurant with them as her backers.

Right before the soft opening, Girly Rae entered rehab for a little cocaine problem. The boys had delayed the opening for the thirty days she was away. When a newly sober, subdued Girly Rae emerged, she announced she'd bought a fifty-acre tract of land in Vermont. She was quitting her job as a chef to become a homesteader. Knox and the boys lost a boatload of cash on that sure-fire money maker.

Remembering, Cricket groaned aloud, feeling a tightness in her chest. The venture's abysmal failure plus the cash they'd all lost had probably contributed to the mother of all mid-life crises for Knox.

Before she approached her daddy's neighborhood, Cricket impulsively turned on the blinker. Visitors who weren't in the know might drive down Main Street, admire the charming town, then head home. Unless they turned on Warrick Street and headed east, they'd miss the glittering crown jewel of their little town, Azalea Lake.

Locals knew that their little town was perched on a bluff right on the edge of a twenty-seven-thousand-acre lake. Azalea Lake provided the drinking water for several surrounding towns. The state had designated it as a body of water where no motorized boats were allowed. They'd also prohibited development around the lake. Without the noise and wake from jet-skis and other boats, the lake was a draw for those who loved kayaking, canoeing, paddleboarding, and swimming. The town of Azalea had built public parks that bordered the lake, dotting the shores with small piers.

Grassy areas allowed visitors to fish, picnic, drowse in the sun, or join in a game of cornhole. The heavy-duty, all-weather Adirondack chairs—gifts from townspeople—were placed on the banks of the lake. On small brass plaques on the backs of the chairs, folks had memorialized the name of a loved one who passed or named those celebrating a birthday or anniversary. Cricket's hairstylist, Lexie Lillington, had donated a chair to celebrate her divorce. Her "Happy Days are Here Again!" message always amused Cricket.

Parking in the gravel parking area, Cricket ambled down the hill to one of the docks. She gave a wave to an older couple holding hands as they walked, then raised a hand at a pack of girls from the high school track team as they winged by. She sat, looking out at the peaceful expanse of blue water while she waited for the sunset. Tilting back her head, Cricket let a breeze caress her face. Gulls hovered and wheeled above her as she listened to the waves lap against the shore. Azalea Lake always soothed her, centered her.

Her date made her long for the security of marriage. Well, the *supposed* security. For the thousandth time, Cricket thought about her ex's disappearance. Once Knox had blindsided her by announcing he wanted a divorce, he refused to speak with her again. He never responded to calls, emails, texts, or direct messages. The lawyers handled all their divorce proceedings.

Closing her eyes, Cricket breathed a few deep, calming breaths, reminding herself she *was* moving on. As the tangerine-lit sun sank into the western shore of Azalea Lake, Cricket was awed by its quiet beauty. One thing she'd learned over the past two years was that it didn't pay to dwell on the past. Easier said than done, but still, she was trying. Cricket rose, pushed back her shoulders, and headed home.

CHAPTER 2

FRIDAY MORNING, CRICKET BLINKED OPEN her eyes and stared groggily at Angus. He had snuggled close beside her on the white down comforter, snoring softly and exhaling toxic breath on her. When she pushed him aside to find good air, her father's 110-pound rescue sighed, aggrieved, and repositioned himself on the bed, stretching out even longer. A handsome mix of yellow Lab, golden retriever, and possibly German shepherd that her father had rescued from the county dump, Cricket gave him a pat.

Yawning, Cricket scrubbed her face with her hands and closed her eyes, sending up a quick prayer for the day. *Father, help me remember to notice the beauty of the day and to be kind to people. I am so grateful for all the blessings of my life.* Cricket opened her eyes, stretched, and reminded herself of all she was grateful for, something she tried to do every morning to keep herself cheerful and positive.

Cricket's small business was growing as fast as the chickweeds, despite a few problems that she'd soon fix.

She was relatively smart and hadn't let herself go to seed completely. Her employees and her clients seemed to like her—well, except for the Bowden family—but she'd try to figure that out.

Cricket was grateful for her health, the sweet beast beside her, her friendship with Honey, and her dad's happiness with his new railroad-riding adventures. She was thankful that her little car kept chugging along despite its high mileage. She was over-the-moon appreciative that her father was allowing her to stay rent-free in the high-ceilinged, sunny apartment above his house, and that she'd found nice tenants whose rent more than covered the monthly mortgage payments on her old house. Cricket opened her eyes, kissed Angus's big head, and ruffled his fur.

"Let's get this day going, buddy."

Freshly showered and sipping a mug of black-as-tar coffee, Cricket sat at her desk—the rickety kitchen table that a former tenant had left behind—and savored every bite of the muffin from a batch she'd whipped up earlier in the week. She worried she'd experimented with too many different ingredients—blueberries, raspberries, and carrots—and that the flavors might compete with one another, but they tasted sublime. Heavenly. The buttery sweetness, satisfying crunch of the crumbled topping, and tart freshness of the fruit made for a delightful treat. This was why she went to the trouble of baking a dozen made-from-scratch muffins for herself every week. Fixing herself ambrosial muffins was a treat that helped Cricket start the day on a happy note.

Squaring her shoulders, Cricket opened her email and re-read the note from Christine Bowden, looking for clues. Did "making other arrangements" mean deciding her parents didn't need helpers? They did, clearly. Christine's mother had been serving Pop-Tarts and Vienna sausages for meals three times a day, and her father had just had his license taken away for going twenty-five miles per hour on I-40, then he'd accidentally backed into the patrol car of the officer who'd pulled him over.

Cricket tapped her pen on the table. Had they decided they couldn't afford caregivers? Forty hours a week of out-of-pocket helpers was expensive when insurance didn't cover many of the services. But neither Christine nor her parents even flinched when Cricket discussed costs. Could they have just changed their minds and chosen another service provider?

Steepling her fingers, Cricket recalled Christine's warm demeanor and exact words from two days ago when she and her assistant, Pearl, had made the home visit. "We like you and what you offer. We've heard such good things about you. Let me talk it over tonight with Mama and Daddy, and we can sign the service agreement with you tomorrow."

Their disappearance was puzzling and, given the others who'd drifted away recently, alarming. Cricket thought for a minute and, summoning gumption, tapped out an email to Christine Bowden.

> *I'm so sorry we'll not have the opportunity to work with your sweet parents. Is there anything we might do to change your mind? Would fewer hours, a different schedule, or a payment plan be something we could explore that might work better for your family? Would you mind giving me feedback about why you chose to make other arrangements? Thank you so much.*

Drawing in a breath, Cricket sent the note. She wished her right-hand woman, Pearl, was there to talk it over with. However, she and her family were gone for a week, visiting Little Switzerland, a picturesque town right off the Blue Ridge Parkway with Swiss and chalet-style architecture. The fondue, raclette, and chocolate were fabled among North Carolinians, and the welcome sign outside Little Switzerland read, "Population: 46." Thankfully, Pearl and her family were driving home from that mountain getaway today. She'd missed her assistant's calm and cool composure.

Cricket picked up the framed picture she kept on the table, one of her favorites. Gazing at it, she said softly, "Morning, Mama."

In the photo, Cricket was a scrawny five- or six-year-old girl. She leaned into her mother's side as they lounged together in the grass, underneath a sprinkler her father had set up for them one steam bath of a North

Carolina summer afternoon. In their matching plaid two-piece bathing suits, they'd partially closed their eyes and smiled as they lifted their faces toward the sun and water sprinkles. A rainbow shimmered above their heads. Rosemary's arm was draped across Cricket's shoulder, and they both looked relaxed and content.

Cricket replaced the picture, feeling equal parts happy and bereft at the memory. She wanted to remember *that* mother—the one who seemed so content, not the one whose mouth was too often turned down with disappointment and a look in her eyes that said she'd rather be somewhere else.

As she did most mornings, Cricket checked her email and, feeling a familiar pang of guilt, checked her ex-husband's Instagram. Knox had posted two new photos, one of the holes worn in the soles of his climbing shoes, and the other of the impressive calluses on his hand.

Cricket shook her head. Knox never posted a face shot.

"Still the man of mystery," she muttered.

Cricket's fake Instagram account was under the name of Alpine Girl, an outdoorsy woman in her late thirties who loved hiking and rock climbing.

After studying photos from climbing sites and *Peak Climber* magazine, Cricket had scrolled intently through the photos in her Depositphotos account and created a file of climbing pics that looked authentic for the attractive, imaginary woman climber she'd created.

Cricket had cut, pasted, and posted a longshot photo

of a slim woman climbing a rock face that looked a little like the ones Knox had recently posted from a climb at Black Canyon in Gunnison, Colorado. Knox had "liked" several of the photos that Cricket had posted as Alpine Girl.

Still too curious about her ex's new life, Cricket looked back at some of his other recent posts. There was a stunning shot of a flaming crimson sunset over the craggy peaks of Sequoia and Kings Canyon. Indignant, Cricket enlarged the shot. Since Knox left, he had visited and climbed in most of the National Parks she had longed to visit ever since her Aunt Joy bought her a subscription to *National Geographic* for her eighth birthday.

Knox had climbed at Arches and Zion in Utah, Joshua Tree in California, Grand Teton in Wyoming, and Acadia in Maine. It just wasn't fair. The national parks were on her bucket list, not his.

Cricket made herself unclench her teeth and tried to let go of her resentment. She glanced at the clock on the computer. Shortly, the calls would start coming in from the caregivers and wouldn't slow for two hours until they all got settled in with their clients. Time to get into work mode.

Pushing away a clear spot in the sea of papers, Cricket repositioned her laptop, and the whole table swayed unsteadily. Grabbing the edges, Cricket steadied it, averting disaster. She had a wry thought. Here she was, the not-so-big cheese at her kitchen table command center. But

Cricket was heartened when she of thought of how far she'd come.

Just three years ago, she'd been laid off from her customer relations job at a biotech firm, her third layoff in just six years. While she was job hunting, her grandmother got pneumonia and needed help at home until she got her strength back. Cricket had offered to help and hired a woman part-time to spell her in the evenings. Nana finally passed, and Cricket realized she loved helping others and genuinely liked older people. She took some classes, got certified and licensed, and started Cricket's Caregivers. She began with just herself and one helper, Pearl. She now had nine employees and a roster of happy clients. Well, mostly happy clients. A cold knot formed in her stomach.

Cricket clicked open the latest business statement from the bank, did a quick scan of the numbers, and gasped quietly. Something was off. Big time off. They'd had a busy year, winning work with several new clients. They were even considering hiring two more helpers, but the numbers were worse than she thought. Fingers trembling, Cricket pulled up her QuickBooks, hit refresh, and looked at the tallies for the quarter and year to date. Hunching forward, she stared at the screen. How had she not seen this?

Besides Christine Bowden's parents not signing on with them, she'd lost three other clients over the past month and a half. Worse, Cricket had no idea why. Other than clients moving in with family, going to assisted living, or passing on to the big family reunion in the sky, she rarely lost clients. Cricket rubbed the back of her neck.

Ms. Asleep at the Wheel. Why had she not looked at QuickBooks more closely every week instead of just assuming they were gaining ground? She needed to figure out why this was happening and fix it fast.

Feeling a hot flush of anger, Cricket wondered again if her clients had been snaked by that Georgina "call me Gigi" Gallagher who'd toadied up to her at Kiwanis Club, asking for advice while claiming she was planning on starting a commercial cleaning business. Instead, Gigi had launched a caregiver service that was now a direct competitor to Cricket's Caregivers. She could kick herself for being so forthright in answering the questions a wide-eyed Gigi had asked about her business.

When Cricket had first spotted Gigi tooling around town in her lime green Euro hipster car, magnetic advertising signs for her caregiver business on the doors of her car, her chest got so tight that she had to pull over to breathe out of a fast-food paper bag. On the sign, smiling and somewhat buxom women waved from hot air balloons. The logo underneath read, "Gigi's Girls: The Highest Level of Care for your Loved Ones." Cricket's blood pressure rose just thinking about it. Gigi's Girls sounded like call girls.

The phone jangled.

"Cricket, I'm turned around. Today's my first day with this client." Kiara sounded tense.

"Take a breath. Tell me where you are," Cricket said.

Kiara was directionally challenged, even with GPS on her phone.

Her helper blew out a raggedy breath. "I drove out here on Sunday just to make sure I knew the way, but now I'm seeing signs for Anson. I should be headed toward Rosewood."

After giving her directions, Cricket called the client to tell her Kiara would be late.

Now Betsy was on the line, speaking *sotto voce*. "Mrs. Hunt wants me to wash the windows plus polish the silver. How do I tell her nicely that I'm a helper, not a maid?"

After quick coaching, Betsy rang off.

When there was a lull, Cricket shot Pearl a quick text. *Welcome home, stranger! Call me when you get settled. We need to talk about missing clients, missing $.*

Cricket checked email again. In the inbox was a note with the subject line that read, "Lucky Day for Libras." It was from an astrology site she'd not signed up for called *Christelle's Cosmos*.

Impulsively, Cricket clicked open today's horoscope, which read, "You have been lonely…"

So true. She had been lonely. Cricket blew out a sigh. She thought she'd be happily married now, all the homey pieces in place. But look at her. She was a divorcee with a chip on her shoulder about men, and she also lived in the upstairs apartment of her father's house.

Rubbing her temples, Cricket felt a headache coming on. She also had a birthday barreling down on her soon, a fact that had made her say "yes" to the movie plus supper with Clayton. Cricket leaned forward. She read more.

But love is fluttering like a butterfly around your gentle aura. Let go of the past. Your future soulmate is waiting and needs encouragement. Beckon him with a note. Fan the flames of desire.

Looking back at her screen, Cricket studied the picture of the woman she assumed was Christelle. With small electric bolts shooting out of her flowing hair, she wore a purple robe. She sat on an oversized clamshell, gazing meaningfully at the stars. Cricket glanced down at her outfit, an LL Bean fleece, khaki slacks, and running shoes. She mentally harrumphed. She put psychics in the same category as seventy-five-dollar jars of magic wrinkle eliminator night cream, or workouts that promised you three-inch thigh gaps.

As Cricket closed the site, she sat back in the chair and pondered it all. Though it seemed like a long shot, maybe Clayton could be her soulmate. Perhaps the tiny flame with him could use fanning. Sighing noisily, she sipped her cooling coffee.

The thoughts about flame-fanning were not her fault. Cricket *had* been lonely. She wanted love in her life along with some version of a family. Stepchildren, grandkids, and dogs or cats were fine by her.

Maybe Clayton *was* a romantic possibility. Chin in hand, Cricket thought about it. Clayton was a tenured professor at Somerset College. Last night, he'd said that his ex-wife was an academic at a college in Georgia. "A long-distance marriage is hard," he'd told her, looking sad.

Usually a two-muffin girl at the most, Cricket reached for a third, promising herself she'd take a long walk that afternoon. Cricket imagined how lonely a long-distance marriage must have been for Clayton. Not as lonely as having a husband who went MIA, but still lonely. Poor Clayton.

Though they'd gotten off to a not-so-smooth start, the man *was* a bird in hand. Cricket rinsed her plate and put it in the dishwasher, feeling the grip of worry. She was no expert, but the professor's lines seemed a little...well, rehearsed.

Slumping in her chair, Cricket felt a rush of resolve. She sat up straighter. She'd take the lead and show the man some interest. It was high time to get love to stop fluttering. Maybe it needed to just come in for a landing.

Cricket squared her shoulders. She'd write him a note. For a touch of old-fashioned whimsy, she decided to use real paper. Handwritten was much more personal than email or text, very Jane Austen with a feather quill. Before she had time to talk herself out of it, Cricket whipped out a piece of creamy stationery. Choosing a red marker from a mug of pens, she wrote in an extravagant flourish.

Hey there!!

She blinked. Where did she get that perkiness? She wasn't an exclamation point kind of girl.

Thought about you this morning. Had a great time last night. Looking forward to next Friday. Can't wait to get to know you better!

Honestly, there went another exclamation point. Cricket shook her head at herself. Still, she signed her name with a flourish. Blowing on the ink, she neatly folded it. After the staff got settled, she'd run by the college. Finding Clayton's battered old Mercedes, she'd slide this little firecracker under the windshield wipers.

The busy morning passed in a blur. Mustering courage, Cricket drove to Clayton's workplace. She cruised under the ivy-draped arches of Somerset College with a sign that read, "Developing Minds and Character Since 1920." Sighing at the romance of it, Cricket thought about all the young men and women who'd graduated over the years. They'd gone on to build exciting new lives. Slowing, she admired the perfectly manicured quads and the elegant gray quarry stone dormitories.

Spotting the sign for faculty parking, Cricket nosed her car into the lot, scanning the cars and looking for Clayton's navy-blue sedan. Midway down the second row, she spotted it. Cruising over, Cricket hopped out with the note in hand, feeling a buzz of playful excitement. His car sported bumper stickers she'd not noticed the night before. Over a rust spot on the fender was stuck the message, "Live Simply That Others May Simply Live." That struck her funny as on the back of a Mercedes, but she liked the sentiment. On the other side, one read, "Practice Random Acts of Kindness."

Okay. Kindness was good.

As Cricket drew closer to the car, she heard what sounded like a girlish giggle. She froze, her eyes fixed on the sedan. Tiptoeing closer, she scooched down, peered into the partially fogged window. Cricket gasped. There was Clayton, leaning into the passenger seat, passionately kissing a titian-haired woman. Cricket jerked back like she'd been slapped. Her lip curled. Tacky. She stood with a hand on her hip.

Without even thinking, Cricket rapped hard on the window. Clayton sprang back so fast that he smacked his head on the glass. Wincing, he rubbed his head.

Glancing over, his eyes were wild as he saw her. Hurriedly, he fumbled to lock the door.

Cricket had never been good at snappy comebacks, but picturing his peace and love bumper stickers, she called loudly, "Acts of kindness, Clayton? Really? Telling a woman you are smitten with her then kissing another woman the next day is tacky—and not *kind*." She jabbed a finger toward the back of the car. "And that 'Live Simply' sticker on the back of your Mercedes looks stupid." Thumping the top of the car with her palm for good measure, Cricket stalked off, so hot with anger that she imagined steam rising off her head.

CHAPTER 3

IT WAS JUST AFTER SEVEN o'clock Saturday morning, but Cricket had been up since five, still feeling foolish about yesterday's accidental ambush. Channeling her restless energy, Cricket tidied the apartment. After wiping down all the counters, she took out the trash. Closing the lid with a thump, she decided to pop down to Daddy's house to check the mail that the postman always pushed through the slot in the front door. As usual, the bundle contained junk mail, along with statements from the investment companies that handled her dad's retirement accounts. With a smile, she looked at the covers of three magazines, *Train Aficionado, Historic Trains,* and *Rail Enthusiast*. Cricket had to chuckle. This from a guy who used to subscribe to *Insurance Today* and *Risk Management Monthly*. She was so proud of her father for pursuing his dreams.

Back home, Cricket baked breakfast goodies for today's road trip. Honey would be by soon to pick her up. They were headed for the Liberty Antiques Festival, an annual event that featured high-quality antiques at good prices. The festival drew vendors and shoppers from across the state and the Southeast. It took place in a small town out in the country about forty miles from home.

Cricket rubbed her eyes, which were red and irritated from her fitful sleep. The Clayton incident had unnerved her. She couldn't wait to talk with Honey about it.

Taking a long pull of strong coffee from her insulated aluminum cup, Cricket leaned back in her mesh lounge chair. She looked around at the sparse furnishings in the sunny apartment, which was oddly laid out but charming. It perched above Daddy's big Victorian house that he'd bought after Mama died. Since she'd moved in, Cricket had felt strangely reluctant to buy couches, rugs, and pictures. Leaving the stuff she'd bought with Knox at the old house was a good decision. The new tenants wanted the place furnished. Also, Cricket didn't want the memories.

Her father's last tenants had left this extra comfy, rocking recliner lawn chair that most people used for camping. Cricket fondly patted the sturdy plastic arms. She loved the chair. If Cricket leaned back, all the pressure on her back was gone.

Life after Knox had been hard and confusing. Wincing as she thought about it, Cricket felt chagrinned as she remembered one of her coping mechanisms, visiting websites for women whose husbands had left them at mid-life.

She'd felt reassured as she read about women like Jana D. from Fort Myers, Florida, whose husband had moved in with his twenty-six-year-old administrative assistant and her three small children. Jana had stayed calm. She'd gotten Botox, remodeled the house, then gone with gal pals to the Amalfi Coast with some of their retirement money. Within three months, her husband begged her to let him come home. Jana had let him—after having him sign a bulletproof post-nup. Jana claimed the marriage was stronger than ever.

Another of her favorites was Shelly T. from Mt. Pleasant, South Carolina, who'd taken her husband back after a mid-life fling. She'd let him get hair implants. She agreed to let him take up skydiving, then trade his truck for a black Chevrolet Corvette convertible. When he flung himself out of a plane on a windy day, his rough landing causing him a broken hip, she'd nursed him back to health. After he could walk again, they had a renewal of vows. They'd bought his-and-her Harleys to take a cross-country motorcycle trip.

Time and those websites had helped. Cricket felt more grounded now, thank goodness. She had stopped haunting those sites for women whose husbands had left them. Looking out the glass sunroom windows, she watched the mist rise slowly from the lawn of the pink house across the street. She loved that house. Along with its wraparound porch, it had two turrets that a modern-day

Rapunzel could use if the house had been just a story or two higher.

The house had been on the market for seven months. The railings on the sagging porch had broken spindles. The paint was peeling. The shutters hung crookedly. That house desperately needed love. She hoped whoever bought the place could revive her. Squinting at the house, Cricket could just imagine it with brightly colored flowers draping from window boxes on the front porch. With a crisp new paint job plus a bit of carpentry work, the lady would be returned to her former beauty.

Since Daddy had started traveling around the country with his new train-buff buddies, Cricket and Angus rolled around the apartment over the big house like two marbles in a tin. It suited her then, but now she was ready for more comfort.

Cricket took another sip of coffee. Reclining, she admired her green suede driving moccasins. Online shoe shopping was a guilty pleasure. With a few keystrokes, Cricket could be a girl with fabulous shoes trying on different lives. The driving moccasins made her feel adventuresome, as though she could drive cross-country in a vintage convertible with three fun-loving girlfriends, her hair blowing back in the wind. If she wore those butter-colored ballet flats she'd fallen in love with while browsing the other night, she'd be a wispy, stay-at-home-wife who was prone to fainting. Her husband would be a big guy who worried about her. In the kick-butt modified biker boots she lusted after but never put in her online cart, she might ride on the back of her boyfriend's Harley. He'd be named Chunk or Rat.

Cricket tapped her heels together Dorothy style. "There's no place like home," she said softly.

A car horn tooted. Cricket levered herself up. Giving Angus a pat and a kiss, she snagged the paper bag of goodies she'd baked. Grabbing her keys, she ran down the stairs.

With one wheel parked on the curb and the bumper dangerously close to the neighbors' new wrought iron gas lamp, her friend sat at the wheel of the gleaming black Chevy Tahoe with her window down. In the clear morning light, Honey's shoulder-length mane of highlights and lowlights shone like gold. She seemed to be multitasking, alternately examining her hair for split ends while admiring her pink nails with the black and white checked tips that looked like NASCAR starting flags.

Brightening when she saw Cricket, she called out cheerfully, "Good morning, birdy." She pointed behind her to the utility trailer hitched to the SUV. "Look what I brought in case we get lucky!"

"Good thinking! Nice ride, by the way." Cricket stepped in and noisily inhaled. "I love that new car scent."

"Smells like fresh starts. Being married to a man whose daddy owns a car dealership has its perks. I just pointed to this car, then drove it off Daddy Jay's lot. Today, we're

Chevy girls!" Honey gave her an impish grin as she expertly rolled the car gently off the curb. She slicked by the light pole with inches to spare. "How are you? What's new?"

"I've got clients bailing on us for no reason, but I've got a call into Pearl. We'll figure it out." Cricket wasn't going to let herself even think about that today. "But you won't believe what I did." Her face flushing with embarrassment, Cricket recounted yesterday's accidental parking lot ambush.

Honey threw her head back, cackling with laughter. "Goody. The mouse has roared."

Sheepishly, Cricket admitted, "It felt good. I have no idea where that car roof banging came from. I wasn't even sure I liked him very much."

Honey spoke with authority. "Transference of pent-up anger from Noxious Knox. You've had no closure with the big chicken."

"Don't sugar coat it," Cricket teased, but she wasn't hurt by Honey's candor.

Though Cricket felt she'd come to terms with her divorce, there was her Instagram stalking habit. She tuned back in as Honey summed up her assessment of the Clayton situation.

"And if I'd have found that man kissing someone passionately after saying that *smitten* boloney stuff to me, I'd have keyed his car. In my opinion, you acted mature." Honey nodded as if that was that.

"Thank you." Cricket felt vindicated. "Why do men act that way?"

Honey's lips pursed in concentration as she drummed her fingers on the steering wheel. "From what I've seen with my other divorced women friends, reasonably attractive men at mid-life who don't carry a ton of debt, have a daughter in rehab, or an ex-wife hanging around, and kids' college to pay for are catches in the dating world. They seem to fare so much better than divorced women at that age. They can have the pick of the crop." Honey raised a shoulder. "It's not fair, but I think it's true." She shot her a look. "Let's not forget Clayton turned out to be pretentious sleaze. No great loss there."

Her friend's assessment was accurate, but Cricket still felt a familiar sting of rejection.

Honey sniffed the air and looked at Cricket. "Mmmm. What loveliness do I smell?"

Cricket grinned. Reaching in the bag, she pulled out the still-warm packages. "Biscuits with white cheddar on top of soy sausage. Sounds awful, but it's tasty."

Honey held out a hand in a "gimme" gesture. "Anything you bake is tasty." Taking a bite of the flaky biscuit, she sighed rapturously. "So good," she said, swallowing. "I haven't been to an antique show in six years. I'm excited."

"I am too." Cricket unwrapped her biscuit. "What is Sanders up to?"

With no hesitation, she rattled off, "Right now, he's

FaceTiming Cole to make sure he sent out all the resumes he promised to send out. Then, he'll catch up with Josh about our latest Visa bill. He'll read him the riot act about not using the credit card like a personal ATM, then insist he get a part-time job." Shaking her head, she gave Cricket a knowing look. "Not sorry to miss the drama."

"Right. Good old-fashioned tough love." Cricket admired the fact that Honey and her husband had made it clear to both their sons that once they got their degrees, there'd be no moving back home, even for a few weeks.

"Cole and Josh will be off into the real world soon. Graduate school or a first job." Honey's mouth twisted. "They won't need me much anymore."

Cricket heard the hurt in her voice. "They'll always need you, Hon."

"Maybe." Honey gave a dismissive flip of her wrist, the corners of her mouth turned down. "Both boys stay busy with studying, friends, girls, sports. The writing is on the wall. My job as mom is coming to an end."

"How's the 'Remember Who You Are' campaign coming along?" Cricket popped the last bite of savory biscuit in her mouth.

"Oh, it's in full swing," Honey said cheerily. "Volunteering at the therapeutic riding stable is amazing. I also love my Conversational Italian class. *Bellissima*!" She kissed her bunched fingers, throwing love into the air.

Cricket grinned. Honey had a master's degree in psychology, but she married Sanders just a few days after defending her thesis. For over twenty years, she'd been a happy homemaker. Her son, Josh, was a junior in college. Her older son, Cole, was about to graduate. Now, Honey was on a mission to unearth her identity. She wanted to remember who she was before she became a wife and mother.

"How does Sanders like your campaign?" Cricket glanced at her friend.

Honey's face clouded. "Sanders is still getting used to it. He likes that I'm excited about learning new things, but he misses the stay-at-home me who focused on making life easier for him" She shook her head. "This morning, he was cool to me because I was leaving for a few hours." Honey sat up straighter. "I'm going to keep on growing, even if I shake things up a little on the home front."

"Good. He'll come around." Cricket knew what a good guy Sanders was.

Honey glanced over at her. "Anything new with Knox? Any smoke signals or little pings like they get on submarines?"

"Ancient history," Cricket said flippantly, then she came clean. "I'm following him on Instagram." She winced, embarrassed to admit it.

Honey just shrugged. "Learn anything that would make you regret the divorce?"

"No, ma'am," Cricket said firmly. "He's climbing

rocks and using jargon I don't understand. He seems to have a lot of cool new friends. He's taking adventures."

Tapping a finger on her lips, Honey looked thoughtful. "How is Knox funding this little adventure? You said he sold the practice for a fire-sale price."

Cricket rolled her eyes. "He did. I could have made a bigger deal of it in the settlement, but all I wanted was for it all to be over."

"I get that. Water under the bridge." Honey tucked a wayward curl behind her ears. "But Knox hasn't had steady, lucrative employment for a while now."

Cricket looked out the window without seeing the passing scenery. "Remember how Knox was always a MacGyver about orthodonture, the special rolling stool adjustment he designed to save orthodontists' backs? It was the fix for the dental hardware issues with braces."

"He was smart in some ways," Honey said grudgingly.

"Knox and a friend came up with a new, improved rope. It's so strong that it prevents falls, saving lives. A company bought the design. Now, he goes all over promoting it. He's kind of a hero in the climbing world." It had been another Instagram tidbit Cricket had pieced together.

"The man landed on his feet. I wish he'd suffered more," Honey mused. She looked at her friend. "Psychologically speaking, here's the problem."

Cricket braced herself. Here it came, whether she asked for it or not.

"You and Knox were casual friends in college. You ran into each other when you were past thirty, and you were both lonely. Poof, you sneak off to the justice of the peace." Polishing off her biscuit, Honey daintily wiped a crumb from the corner of her mouth with a checkered nail. "Knox had a big birthday. Looking at his life passing by, he quietly blew up the marriage. To me, you two always seemed like an unlikely match."

Cricket mulled over that observation. In confidence, she'd admitted to Honey that the deep bond was never there with Knox, even though she'd tried hard to conjure it.

"But it's hard to completely let go because you have no closure." Honey adjusted her sunglasses. "It's made you gun-shy with men. Clayton doesn't count. He was a dud."

Cricket looked out the window at the soft-edged morning. "You're right."

Carefully pulling the SUV around a tractor, Honey waved at the farmer.

"It's been a while since I was single. I thank God every day for that, but I remember how it felt to have a promising man turn out to be a toad."

Cricket snorted. "You were never dumped. Men always wanted you."

Honey's rueful laugh had an edge to it. "I love how you shine up my history."

Cricket glanced sharply at her friend, who was

slouched in the leather seat, her features perfect as a cameo. She wasn't jealous of Honey, and she never had been. Men had always flocked to Honey while Cricket was the sidekick; pretty in a certain light, quiet, and friendly. It had been that way since they met in Riverside Elementary. "What do you mean?"

"Just because I married a nice man, it doesn't mean I didn't have some good-for-nothing boyfriends. I had an awful time being single." The large diamonds on Honey's rings glittered as she adjusted the sun visor.

Cricket gave herself a mental shake. She tended to idealize her friend's life. When Honey was single, it was all a lark. When Honey married, it was easy street.

She knew better. Nobody breezed through life without hardship. Everyone struggled to find and keep love, even her gorgeous, funny, and smart best friend.

Cricket nodded slowly, remembering. "There was that real estate guy."

"Joseph. He ended up in jail for some mortgage fraud deal he cooked up with a few of his cronies," she said dryly.

Cricket winced. It was coming back now. "There was the artist who yelled at you when he drank—"

"Single Malt Scott, who called me later to apologize when he was at his 'making amends' step." Honey shook her head. "Thank God I'm married," she said fervently. Lowering the window, she yelled out, "I love you, Sanders Merritt."

Cricket felt a surge of wistfulness. "I miss being married. Not to Knox, per se, but the whole Sunday morning routine of reading the paper together, the comfort of a warm body beside me in bed, coming home to someone…"

"But you just had a date." Honey gave her an encouraging pat. "No matter how it turned out, you're getting back out there. It's going to pay off." Steering with her knees, Honey stretched her arms lazily over her head and yawned. "We should almost be there."

As the mist burned off, the early morning sun spangled down on old tobacco barns. Barbed wire fences meandered around pastures dotted with cows.

Cricket pointed to the blue, hand-lettered sign with an arrow. "That's it." She glanced nervously at Honey. "Remember my tiny budget. Let's not even look at things I can't afford."

"Okay." Honey bumped the Chevy across a plowed-under field. She pulled into the grassy parking area.

Cricket glanced at her watch. Not even eight o'clock yet, but the grounds were bustling. The two wove down aisle after aisle of booths.

A woman with a long, gray braid wished them a pleasant good morning. On her table display, she carefully arranged her wares—antique compacts, purses, women's hats adorned with cherries and feathers, and neatly pressed vintage tablecloths and aprons.

Cricket paused to admire her goods.

"This place is amazing. Quality stuff, plus great prices," Honey marveled.

Cricket pulled her friend to a stop at a table of old books. The two of them paused to admire a display of china.

When Honey stopped suddenly, Cricket crashed right into her. "Ow." She rubbed her nose. "What?"

Her friend hissed. "Look what they're sitting on."

Two men with ZZ Top beards slouched on a sumptuous purple velvet couch drinking coffee. They wore vendor name tags.

"Hope they don't get coffee on your new couch," Honey murmured. Clasping Cricket's elbow, she strode over in her long-legged tomboy gait. She twinkled at them. "Good morning, gentlemen."

"Good morning, ladies." The men scrambled to their feet, their faces lighting up.

"What's the best y'all can do on that pretty little couch for a lady on a budget?" Honey asked in a dulcet tone, pointing at it with her NASCAR fingernail.

Cricket tried not to snicker. The men didn't stand a chance.

Later, they secured the tarps on the trailer with bungee cords. Spring clamps made the load even more secure. Cricket clasped her hands together, elated at her finds. They'd carefully packed the velvet Duncan Phyfe sofa, a faded green porch glider, white wicker chairs, and had somehow finessed the handsome oak dresser in the trailer. In the score of the day, Cricket had found two matching 1950's Formica kitchen tables to replace the wobbly table that she and Pearl shared as a desk. Cricket grinned. She'd bought everything she needed yet still had money left over. These finds would transform her apartment and maybe her life from sepia tone to color.

Honey hummed as she tucked in the packing blanket around her vintage prints of dogs. She pushed the button to close the cargo door.

As they returned home, Cricket peered out the back window to make sure they weren't littering the roads with her treasures. Satisfied, she opened a paper bag of boiled peanuts. Peeling several, she placed them on a napkin on her friend's thigh. "What a perfect day."

Honey popped a few nuts in her mouth and shot her a grin. "You're feathering your nest, getting ready for your new, improved life and for looove." She drew out the word to make it three syllables.

Cricket rolled her eyes at Honey's silliness. Still, she was secretly pleased. Maybe fresh starts and do-overs were possible, even at her advanced age.

CHAPTER 4

EARLY SUNDAY, THE KITCHEN WAS still fragrant with the sweet smell of the muffins Cricket had baked earlier. With one more approving glance around her newly feathered nest, she walked over to give the velvet sofa a pat just because it felt good. Her apartment was starting to feel cozy and homey.

Stretching, she saw Angus's eyes following her every move, ready for a morning walk. Wrapping three still-warm muffins in aluminum foil, Cricket dropped them in a paper bag. "Let's hit the road, guy."

Corralling the happy dog, they clattered down the stairs. Her neighbor wasn't on his porch, so she dropped the baked goodies on a table on her porch for delivery later. Cricket and Angus set off at a fast pace for a brisk, three-mile walk.

The sunrise was still pink in the sky when they arrived at the walking path along Azalea Lake. Cricket felt a sense of quiet contentment, thinking again about how lucky they were to live in such close proximity to the water. Geese honked as they flew overhead. An owl *hoo-hoo-hooood* at them. Angus pressed his nose to the ground, making yipping noises as he picked up the scent of wildlife, maybe a deer, possum, or fox.

As they approached the lake paths that came closest to the water, Cricket pulled Angus's leash in tighter. She remembered last week when he'd seen a fish jump and marched determinedly into the still-frigid water, dragging her behind him. Her teeth had chattered all the way home.

Losing the scent, Angus slowed to a more sedate pace. As Cricket took the fork that led them toward downtown, she noticed a small brown Park Service sign with a directional arrow that read, "Boat Launch This Way." Yesterday, she was poking around in Daddy's garage looking for a bag of plant fertilizer when she'd discovered a beat-up red kayak with a wide cockpit propped against the wall. An old tenant must have left it there. Cricket had imagined how it would feel to glide quietly across the water. Intrigued, she'd stopped to google it. The extra-spacious watercraft was a tandem recreational kayak that could easily hold her and Angus.

Thinking about that red boat, Cricket detoured to check out the boat launch. She came upon a sandy beach area with a small dock.

Hmmm. Interesting.

She'd never kayaked in her life, but maybe she'd check out the seaworthiness of that old kayak.

Cricket and Angus retraced their steps, heading toward town. Like most old Southern towns, Azalea had more than its share of churches. Her route past the churches always soothed her. Today, she and Angus had beaten the early birds attending eight o'clock services. Breathing in the cool spring air, Cricket slowed to admire the richly hued stained-glass windows of Ascension Episcopal. Puffing up a hill, she was careful not to trip on the knobby roots of old oaks sticking up through the sidewalk. Chugging along, she admired the graceful spires of the new Episcopal church where her ex-mother-in-law, Bea, volunteered at the office once a week. Cricket felt a pang of loss, missing Bea.

During and after the divorce, Bea ghosted Cricket, ignoring her phone calls and emails.

A sweet-voiced, iron-willed Southern matriarch with a hairspray-shellacked silvery bob, Bea had an entire wardrobe of bright Lily Pulitzer clothes. She seemed formidable, but Cricket had discovered her big heart. She still missed her ex-mother-in-law.

Water under the bridge.

Cricket broke into a slow jog, pushing herself until she was panting.

Another church on her route was First Baptist, where Mama was buried.

Cricket sent up a quick prayer. *Hope you're doing okay up there, Mama. I still miss you.*

Swallowing hard, Cricket thought about Mama's long braid, honeyed drawl, and silvery laugh.

Pushing down memories of those dark days after Rosemary's death, Cricket ran faster. Angus bounded along beside her, his big tongue lolling out. He looked happy. Blood pumped through her heart, and the muscle in her calves worked as her stride lengthened. Cricket felt strong. After pushing it on the final straightaway on Market Street, the two of them slowed for the short walk home.

Cricket raised a hand and grinned as she spotted her across-the-street neighbor, Jackson Purefoy, whom she called *Mr. P*. A retired navy man, he sat outside most mornings come rain or shine. He'd read his *Wall Street Journal,* drink bad coffee, and listen on a portable radio to *Fox News*, *Varney & Company*, and *Cavuto*.

Cricket held up a finger, calling to him. "Be right back."

Retrieving the paper bag from her porch, she and Angus trotted back across the street.

"What's shakin', Speedy?" Mr. P held out a hand to Angus, who gave his palm a slow lick.

"Not much." Cricket sat on the porch step. The first time Mr. P saw her do her stretches before a walk, he'd started calling her "Speedy." She liked it, particularly because the pace for her walking and shambling half-runs would more realistically be described as moseying or sauntering.

Her neighbor turned down the radio.

"The liberals still ruining the country?" she asked, knowing how he'd answer.

Mr. P glowered, shaking his head. "Where's common sense, people?"

"There you go." This was Cricket's tried and true, vague comment that she used with people who tried to talk with her about politics—red, blue, or anywhere in between. "This'll sweeten you up." She held out the paper bag. "Fresh from the oven, banana-nut muffins. I tried a toasted coconut crumble topping that I'm experimenting with."

The older man's eyes lit up. "I like being your tester." Taking a bite of the muffin, he sighed with pleasure. He looked sunnier than he had a moment before.

Cricket crossed her arms, always pleased at his reaction to her cooking.

"What's your daddy up to?" Mr. P asked between bites.

"He's doing well. Meeting lots of new friends and riding trains he's wanted to ride his whole life." Cricket felt a pang of guilt that she'd not even known about this dream of his until last year.

Mr. P brushed a crumb from the side of his mouth, nodding thoughtfully. "Ah, riding the rails just like Woody Guthrie. Good for him."

Cricket dabbed at her sweaty forehead with the sleeve of her T-shirt. "How are the boys?"

It tickled her that that's what Mr. P called his cronies, the youngest of whom was in his late seventies. The group of retired men from the neighborhood met every morning at 7:00 A.M. at Biscuitville in a corner booth that a manager reserved for them with a tent card.

"Good." With wrinkled but still strong-looking hands, Mr. P unwrapped another muffin. "Petey's ticker went bad, so they hot-wired him."

"Pacemaker?" she clarified.

He nodded, chewing while patting his mouth with a napkin.

"The boys heard any news on the pink house?" Cricket pointed next door, her heart thumping faster.

"Ray and a few of the others all heard it's a group of buyers who were in the same fraternity at Somerset College. They want it as a money-making deal. Buying it as a party house to rent to alumni for home ball games." Mr. P gave a world-weary look. He threw up his hands. "There goes the neighborhood."

"I hope not." Cricket shuddered inwardly, picturing that winsome house with so much potential turned into a party pad for people trying to re-live their glory days.

"Remember the last owners, that fancy couple?" Mr. P took a too-large bite of muffin. He had to work his way through it.

Cricket did. A too-good-looking couple bought it a few years ago, gliding in and out of their driveway in a gleaming black BMW. Cricket remembered the pure green envy she'd felt about the owners. She was sure they were the perfect couple with the perfect life. But the purring sedan and the glamour couple vanished. A sheriff's deputy taped a notice to the front door. The bank took the house.

Though Cricket was on more solid footing financially now, her stomach flipped as she thought about how tight her own money was after the divorce. For stupid, prideful reasons, Cricket had ignored her lawyer's advice. She'd turned down part of the financial settlement Knox had offered her. She got their modest bungalow but had run short of cash six months after the divorce. Then, just about that time, Daddy's tenant moved out. Thank heavens he offered to let her stay in his apartment for free. About the same time, a couple showed up at her door asking to rent her house. Without looking back, Cricket gave them the keys and moved. The rent from her old home gave her a little financial security. So far, being a landlord had been easy.

Mr. P's little finger crooked out daintily as he helped himself to a third muffin. "Why don't *you* buy the pink house?"

"I can't afford it, bud." Cricket *could* afford it if she stopped letting money stroll right out of the door of her business—and if Angus dug up a rusty strongbox full of gold doubloons in the back yard while burying a bone. These days, she couldn't stomach risk. She wasn't ready to move out of her safe, rent-free cocoon in Daddy's house.

"You'd get a bargain," he persisted. "Can't hurt to throw a hook in the water."

Cricket did the math in her head. She shook her head. "My money's too tight."

Mr. P nodded his understanding. "My wife and I stretched every penny we had to buy this house when we were young, but it was the best money we ever spent. Built a life here." Swallowing hard, he looked away.

Cricket wanted to give her friend a little hug but knew not to. She just untied and retied the laces of her running shoes. Watching a mockingbird dive bomb a grackle, she gave him a moment to collect himself. The man's irascibility and irritation with the world were good covers for how profoundly lonely he was after his wife's passing.

"I need to get going." Cricket rose, her knees making a popping sound. The phones would start ringing soon. She did not want to miss Pearl's call. They needed to get cracking with damage control on the disappearing-clients situation. "Keep me posted."

"I will." Mr. P touched the brim of his hat, a courtly gesture. "See you, Speedy."

"Bye, bud." Cricket squeezed his age speckled forearm. She and Angus headed home.

Leaning against the kitchen counter, Cricket swallowed down a cool glass of water. Her phone rang.

"Cricket's Caregivers."

"Hello, Cricket dear. It's your old next-door neighbor, Eugenia Flowers. I hate to bother you, but Saturday night, the young people staying in your house had a party. The music was so loud, it rattled the Spode in my china cabinet. The racket made my cat, Mr. Kit Kat, hide under the bed."

"Oh, I'm so sorry." Cricket put a hand on her forehead, her thoughts racing. *Can this be true?*

"I know you have a lot on your plate, but I'm hoping you might have a word with them. It was impossible to sleep. The commotion went on past one thirty in the morning." Eugenia's tone was pleasant but firm.

"I surely will, and again, I apologize. Thank you for letting me know. Please call me if it ever happens again, even if it's one in the morning."

Cricket ended the call and put her hands on her hips. She paced around the apartment, trying to think. Could her old neighbor possibly be mistaken? Though Eugenia was in her late seventies, she was clear-minded. The former librarian and a member of the local Red Hat was not one to make a fuss over nothing.

If her old neighbor was right, how had Cricket misjudged her renters, the earnest-looking couple who were graduate students in the Somerset College Divinity School? They each wore large crucifixes around their necks. They'd seemed like bookworms. Cricket had felt her prayers had been answered. She'd examined their student IDs. When she asked them for names of references, they'd happily texted several names and numbers to her as they stood on her stoop.

By sundown, Cricket had offered to rent the house to them.

When they were about to sign the lease, the husband had pushed his wire-framed glasses up on his nose. His brow knitted. "Um, one thing. We just need your assurance that the neighborhood is a quiet one. Our curriculum is very demanding. We must have a noiseless environment so we can study."

Cricket had assured him it was, handing him the pen while sending up a quick prayer of gratitude that she'd found the perfect tenants.

Cricket refilled her water glass. Sipping it slowly, she considered the possibility that they *weren't* the perfect tenants.

Bristling with irritation, Cricket called the renters' cell numbers, but neither answered. Stiff fingered, she tapped out a text. *Neighbor complaining about the noise Saturday night. Said you all were having a party. Please call me.*

A text came back immediately from the wife. *We are both in class now. Saturday night, we were at the library. Exams coming up. Must have been other neighbors.*

Cricket stared at the text, not sure what to think. On the other side of their old house lived a family with small children. Middle-aged or older people lived up and down the street. Could Eugenia Flowers have been mistaken? Could it have been another neighbor making the noise?

She'd gotten references from the renters, but she'd never checked them. Why hadn't she done that? Cricket rubbed her eyes with her fingers. Maybe it was just because she needed their money.

But Cricket didn't want to lose her tenants by accusing them of something they may not have done. Their rent check helped a lot. After giving it some thought, Cricket texted back *Okay.* But Cricket's gut told her to trust her old neighbor. She sent another text to the husband and wife. *I'm glad it wasn't you all being noisy. But just to remind you, you can't have any loud get-togethers at the house. This is in the terms of the lease.*

The sweet-looking young wife who wore Peter Pan collars just texted back two words in large caps: *AT LIBRARY!*

The little snip. Add that to her list of things to worry about. Cricket would cruise by the house one weekend night soon to check on the situation. Her cell rang.

Seeing her assistant's name, she snatched up the phone with a relieved sigh. "Hey, Pearl. Hope you had an amazing getaway, but I'm so glad you're back."

"I am, too. Nothing like sleeping in your own bed," Pearl said evenly. "How are you?"

Cricket made herself resist the urge to launch into a detailed description of her worries. Drawing a breath, she made herself ask about their vacation with questions like: "How was Little Switzerland? Did you stop by Books and

Beans? How was the music and square dancing at Geneva Hall? Did you find any gems at the Emerald Village?"

Pearl described the cabin where she and her family had stayed. Chuckling, she described Dalton's—her husband—excitement when he found a huge stone he thought was a valuable gem, then the look on his face when it turned out to be a worthless mineral.

Her assistant wound down her stories. She paused. "If you're free, I'll run by your place. How about getting some coffee going? You can catch me up on work."

"I'd love it." Cricket ended the call, feeling like a huge weight had been lifted off her shoulders.

Bustling around, she brewed a fresh pot of the Costa Rican dark roast she'd found on special at Harris Teeter. She set out a small pitcher of the fancy amaretto vanilla half-and-half Pearl liked. Cricket stopped to study the two adorable Formica tables she and Honey had brought home from their Liberty trip.

She and Honey had been tired when they got back, so they'd pushed the newly acquired furniture into the hallway. Cricket used her hip to move the rickety table into the living room. Dragging the new finds into the kitchen, she set them up facing each other. She was under the table on her hands and knees, setting up the laptops, when she heard Pearl climbing the stairs.

"Come in," Cricket hollered.

Pearl stepped inside, giving her an infectious grin. "Hey there, boss."

"Hey, stranger." Cricket rose, brushing the dust bunnies off her knees. She gave Pearl a pat on her shoulder. Her right-hand woman's hair was twisted in Heidi-inspired braids. "You're looking very sharp in a Swiss way."

Pearl just patted her braids, giving her a saucy grin. "Just keeping things lively. Did you miss me?"

"More than you know." Cricket handed her a mug, gazing fondly at her assistant.

Pearl was a hard-working, no-nonsense woman in her late fifties. Before she came to work for Cricket, she'd managed a hair salon. After her successful battle with breast cancer had left her hair permanently thin and wispy, she had embraced wigs, falls, extensions, buns, and braids. Cricket never knew if Pearl would come to work as a blonde, brunette, or redhead.

Pearl stirred the creamer into her steaming mug. She gestured toward the new Formica tables. "Very cool. I like them."

"Glad you do." Blowing on her coffee to cool it, Cricket took a sip. *Ahh.*

"This is comfy." Pearl sat in the new ergonomic desk chair that Cricket had splurged on. "What's cooking?"

Cricket sat across from her. She threw up her hands. "Vanishing clients, disappearing revenues, complaints about my tenants—you name it."

"Tell me." Pearl leaned forward and sipped her coffee, her brows drawn.

"The Bowdens wrote saying they wouldn't be needing our services anymore. They won't return my email. I looked hard at the books last week and noticed that we've got three clients gone with no explanation." Grimly, Cricket told her how much the revenues were down, grateful that the helper she'd just promoted to supervisor was proving steady under pressure.

"Huh. I didn't see that problem creeping up on us either." Pearl looked thoughtful. "I've been busy training helpers trying to learn my new job. Maybe you and I haven't talked enough about what's going on with the business."

"Which is my fault." Cricket rubbed her forehead, discouraged. "We need to meet once a week to discuss every detail of what's happening. I need to pay closer attention to the numbers. But we're closing the stable door after the horses have bolted."

"We'll figure this out." Pearl hesitated, grimacing. "I got the voice mail from the Baileys when they canceled, then got the same kind of email from Ms. Nelson's family. I meant to talk to you about it," she said, sounding apologetic. "I wrote you about both cancellations, but they were puny sticky notes. Your kitchen table was kind of…"

"Messy." Cricket shook her head in disgust as she looked at the haphazard spread of papers in front of her.

Two stacks of client files leaned like the Tower of Pisa. She *had* to get organized.

"And I got the text from the Jarretts' son," Cricket continued, "but he didn't say why they were leaving. I called back, never got a hold of him, then we got so busy—"

"So neither of us followed up." Pearl finished the sentence for her.

Cricket mulled it over. "We're not the first small business to let things fall through the cracks while growing, but never again. Beating ourselves up won't do any good." Cricket should know since she'd done enough of it that weekend. "Tomorrow, let's schedule our weekly meetings for all of next year. We'll try again to call on the lost clients. We'll get to the bottom of this." She tapped a finger on her desk. "We'll make a fresh start. We'll be more businesslike."

"We can do it, boss."

"I know we can," Cricket said, sounding way more confident than she felt. She sent Pearl a questioning look. "Feel like taking a ride? I want to drive by my old house to see if there were any signs of a party last night."

"Sure thing." Pearl's mouth turned up. "After all this family togetherness, I could use the fresh air."

Cruising slowly down the street where she used to live, Cricket realized she had no sad, sentimental feelings about the neighborhood or her old home. Zip. Nada.

Good.

As they approached the house, Pearl lowered her sunglasses on her nose and looked around. "No clues.

No empty kegs on the front porch or wine bottles in the yard."

"No garbage or recycling cans overflowing with party trash." Cricket blew out a sigh of relief, but she had a niggling feeling of doubt. She still wasn't convinced that there hadn't been a party. "If they turn out to be trouble, it's my fault. I asked for references but didn't check them. I got lulled into a false sense of security because they were in divinity school. They told me that both their parents are ministers in Charlotte."

Pearl shrugged. "It happens. You're a rookie landlord."

Turning right onto the main road, Cricket glanced at Pearl. "If the tenants are bad apples, it can be hard to get rid of them. I know two women from my networking group who both have little rental houses. Both have stories about tenants who stopped paying rent. They won't move out. One had tenants that it took a year to evict. When they finally went, they stole all the appliances, leaving the house in shambles."

"Trashy people," Pearl said, sounding disgusted. "But no need to borrow trouble."

"You're right." Cricket sat up straighter, feeling a sense of resolve. "But preachers' kids or not, I'm still going to keep an eye on those two."

CHAPTER 5

Monday morning, Cricket was showered, dressed, and brewing a fresh pot of coffee by seven thirty in the morning. She was ready to get a jump on the day. Pearl was picking up office supplies and wouldn't be in until later.

Savoring a raspberry oat muffin, she cradled a cup of Kenyan Special coffee as she answered emails. Pulling up her Depositphotos account, she perused pictures of pleasant-looking caregiver types and happy-looking older people as she worked on graphics for her social media posts.

At eight thirty, the phone jangled.

Josie, a caregiver they'd only hired two months ago, sounded anxious. "I got here right on time for my new client, Ms. Roberts, but she won't come to the door even though I'm knocking and calling her. I can hear her rambling around inside."

Cricket thought for a minute. "Ms. Roberts wears hearing aids. I'll bet she hasn't put them in yet. Go around the house to the window facing the street and rap on it. I'll stay on the line."

Cricket heard a rustling as Josie bushwhacked her way through the overgrown garden, knocked loudly, and called to her client. "Yoo-hoo! Yoo-hoo, Ms. Roberts!" A moment later, the helper breathed into the phone. "She's fine. Happy as a clam to see me. She's unlocking the door now."

"Good job." Cricket felt good as she ended the call. This was a part of the job she liked best, solving problems as well as getting everybody calmed down.

Linda, another caregiver, called and sounded annoyed. "Mr. Moore only has one more heart medicine pill left. His daughter hasn't gotten the prescription refilled."

Cricket made herself a note on a scrap of paper. "I'll get ahold of her. We'll see if we can get that set up on automatic refill. Maybe the family can have it delivered."

Linda snorted. "How do you forget your daddy's medication?"

"The daughter is a single mom who works full-time," Cricket reminded her, knowing Linda had been a single mom.

"I'd forgotten. Bless her heart. The girl's running ragged," the helper said understandingly. "I'm glad my boys are grown and gone. Love them to pieces, but that was a hard row to hoe alone."

After the calls quieted down, Cricket's FaceTime tone

sounded. Clicking on the camera icon, Cricket grinned when she saw her father's face.

"Hey, pal. Greetings from Calgary," Julius, her father, boomed. He grinned like a kid on Christmas morning.

"Hey there, Daddy." Cricket's spirits rose. These days, Daddy looked so vigorous, just plain tickled with life.

"Check this out, sweetheart." Julius donned a wide-brimmed hat. Looking at her proudly, he turned to give her a shot of his profile.

Cricket spoke in the extra calm voice she used when she caught Mr. Mills driving his riding mower into town after his son took away his car keys. "My goodness! A cowboy hat!"

"Yes, ma'am. And wait till you see these." The camera panned down to a pair of snakeskin cowboy boots with toes pointy enough to stub out a cigarette in a corner.

Cricket blinked, still not quite believing the transformation. Julius, her conservative, Dockers-wearing, insurance-man daddy was stepping out. For as long as she could remember, Daddy dressed like the reserved, self-effacing actuarial he was, but he'd started wearing jeans, let his hair grow until his butter-colored curls fell below his collar, and started introducing himself as Jules instead of Julius. Bemused at the come-hither looks she'd seen women of a certain age give him in the grocery store, Cricket suspected her dad had turned into a hunk. But she had to tease him.

"Just getting in from a cattle drive?"

"The town is full of cowboys." Looking delighted with himself, Julius's eyes danced. "I always wanted a Stetson and a pair of boots like these, so I thought, why the heck not?"

"Good for you." Cricket liked the rebellious glint she saw in his eyes. "When's your next train trip?"

"Tomorrow. I met up with my buddies. We're taking the Rocky Mountaineer to see Lake Louise, Kamloops, Jasper, and Victoria. It'll be the trip of a lifetime." His eyes twinkled with excitement. "Not knocking the Napa Valley Wine Train or the Mount Hood Railroad because they were both great rides."

"I'm so glad for you, Daddy."

Cricket remembered him when he was a whey-faced sleepwalker still stunned from grief about the death of his wife, Rosemary. But when Daddy had made a startling discovery about his late wife's fidelity, he'd shaken off his sadness. He took early retirement from the large insurance company he'd worked for his whole life. Julius had found a bunch of train enthusiast buddies online. For the past several months, he'd been meeting up with them to ride on America's most scenic railroads.

Julius's brows drew down. "Can you check in on your Aunt Joy for me? She sounded down when I talked to her a few days ago. She's having a hard time being retired."

"I'll call her." Her daddy's older sister, Joy, who was nicknamed Joy for her zest for life, had recently wound down her long teaching career of forty years.

Daddy's eyes narrowed. "How are you? Business still going great guns?"

Cricket paused, not wanting him to think she couldn't handle a work problem on her own, but she needed his advice. "I've got a mystery."

"Shoot." He looked all business, even with his Stetson slightly askew on his head.

Cricket leaned forward, her words tumbling out as she told him their problem. "So, we're trying to find out why the clients left, but we're…uh…having trouble catching up with them to get answers." No need to mention it had taken her six weeks to notice their absence.

Julius thought about it, looking as serious and canny as the successful businessman he'd been. "Some attrition is normal, I would think, and older clients might not want to tell you that they or their children can't afford the services any longer, but you're wise to want to check on this." He rubbed his chin, looking thoughtful. "Carry them cookies or goodies you've baked. Leave a note saying you've been thinking about them, and that you want to make sure they're doing okay. If you run into them, tell them you're visiting to say hello. Ask them flat out how you can improve service."

Cricket shuddered inwardly. That seemed so pushy, but he was right. "I'll do it."

"Good girl." Julius nodded approvingly. "How's Angus?"

"Your dog has been sleeping on my white down comforter," she groused.

Her father chuckled. "Give that boy a scratch for me."

"I will." Cricket hesitated. "I miss you. I even miss hearing *Carolina Outdoor Journal* blaring up through my floor." How he could spend thirty minutes watching two men sit in a boat, fishing and talking about striper hybrids and rattletrap drum, was beyond her.

"I miss you too, Cricket girl. Hope you've not heard from that sorry Knox." His mouth twisted in distaste.

"No," Cricket said abruptly, not looking at him so he wouldn't see the truth in her eyes. Daddy didn't need to know she was following her ex-husband on Instagram.

"Good. You deserve so much better than that." He gave her a meaningful look.

"I know," she said softly.

Julius hesitated for a moment. "Let's make a deal. You can stay permanently in that apartment, but I know that's not really what you want. I also know you don't want to move back into your old house." Daddy rubbed his jaw. "Do you want to start house hunting? Once you've found something you like, buy it. I'll hold the mortgage. We can defer all payments for a year to give you a chance to get your money situation right."

Cricket put her hand on her mouth, eyes welling at his generosity. After a moment, she murmured, "That's so kind of you, but that's too much."

"I'd charge you interest, of course. This would be

strictly business," Julius said firmly. "You'd start a fresh new life. I'd make more money than I could in any CD or money market. Just think about it."

"I will." Cricket swallowed.

If she let Daddy help her buy a house, say that pink house across the street, would she feel okay about it, or would she seem like a pitiful charity case? This sunny apartment had been a godsend as a long-term, temporary move. It seemed safe but pitiful. The cast-off woman crawling home to Daddy. She'd mull it over.

"Tell me more about your trip," she requested.

Julius's face was animated as he talked about the Calgary Stampede and the Continental Divide, but Cricket only half-listened. Daddy was grabbing gusto, but she was stuck in neutral. As he wound down, she was careful to keep her expression bright as she compared their lives. Cricket despised self-pity, yet she was quietly throwing a big ole pity party for herself.

Julius glanced at his watch. "I need to run, pal. I'm meeting a couple of train buddies to tour the military museums. Afterward, we might head over to the Grain Museum."

Wheat? Barley? Silos? She had no idea and was afraid to ask. "Have a swell time. Take lots of pictures."

"I will. I love you." A look of concern crossed Julius's face. His voice grew serious. "Take care of yourself, sweetheart. Get on with your life."

"I will, Daddy." Cricket made herself keep smiling

as she ended the call but fought a lonesome feeling. She felt like crawling into bed and pulling the covers over her head.

The safe option of staying with Daddy forever wasn't a bad one. If Julius had stayed the grieving widower, or if he had developed a minor health problem—maybe just plantar fasciitis or acid reflux—she would have an excuse to slip into the role of dutiful daughter. Cricket would never have to deal with post-divorce trust issues, business problems, or dating again. She could stop highlighting her hair to disguise the gray. She'd only shop in the comfort shoes section on her favorite internet websites and wear those new, possibly clunky-looking shoes with socks in the winter.

Cricket shook her head at herself. Pitiful.

The next morning, Angus wove his way around her feet as Cricket yawned, pulled a muffin from the freezer, and stuck it in the oven on warm. Pausing to give him a prolonged back scratch with her fingernails, Cricket poured herself a cup of coffee. She took the first reviving sip.

Ah, heaven.

Throwing a light sweater over her cotton nightgown, Cricket slipped a leash on Angus and clambered down the stairs to let the big guy out. He lifted his nose to scan the morning air, dashing from one side of the yard to the other as he picked up the scent of squirrels or deer. After Angus took care of business, he and Cricket walked side by side upstairs. After he was fed, Cricket poured herself another cup of Joe. Feeling a twinge of shame, she sank into her chair in front of the laptop to indulge in her guilty pleasure.

Cricket quickly found Knox's account, @1MountainMan. She checked out his latest photos. The two new pics that morning were of two zero-body-fat men in outdoor gear. The raffish, handsome pair sat around a table strewn with glasses and plates. The captions underneath the pictures read, "Two rock star climbing compadres, bagged ELDO, ESTES, and RMNP!"

Cricket knew her ex had been climbing in Colorado. Fingers flying, Cricket searched for the meaning of the acronyms. ELDO was Eldorado Canyon, ESTES was Estes Park Valley, and RMNP was Rocky Mountain National Park. She shook her head. Climbers had their own language.

Cricket peered more closely at this morning's pics. Knox's two climbing buddies were abnormally good-looking men who sat close to one another, their faces animated. One had his hand on the other's forearm. Could Knox be gay? Was that why he left?

Chewing a fingernail, she pondered it. Knox had never exactly had a tiger in his tank in that part of their married life, but things had been in the normal range—well, according to a Google questionnaire she'd taken. If Knox *was* gay, wouldn't the whole disappearing act be more understandable? She leaned her chin in her hand, pondering it. Couldn't argue with biology. If it was true, Cricket would be totally off the hook in the bad wife, undesirable, and unlovable department, which she had still been worried about, despite all her positive thinking and her new life.

The second photo was almost a duplicate of the first, but the caption under this one read, "CA here we come. Elbert, Shasta, Whitney. Stoked about summer project: Denali!"

Cricket slipped on her readers, examining the second photo more closely. Behind the seated rock stars, Cricket saw the shapely leg of a woman. On her feet were the Scarlet Cloud running shoes Cricket had admired online. Enlarging the shot, she clicked over to a favorite shoe site.

Yikes.

The shoes cost $225.00. In spite of their plush air cushion technology, they were too rich for her blood.

Cricket zoomed in on the woman. She had what looked to be a fox tattooed on her calf. The two men seemed to be laughing at something hilarious she had said. Cricket put a hand over her mouth, wondering again what she'd wondered many times. Had Knox left her for another woman? That would be the biggest hurt. Scrubbing her eyes with her fingers, Cricket wondered if what Honey theorized was true. Maybe she couldn't totally move forward unless she found out why he left.

Cricket rose. Enough of these anxiety-provoking strolls down memory lane.

Downing the dregs of her coffee, she vowed she'd delete Knox's account soon. For now, Cricket needed to get spruced up for the day and look extra polished. She and Pearl had a visit with a prospective new client that morning.

After she'd showered, Cricket blew out her hair until it was sleek and shiny as a new penny. Smoothing on a beauty balm, she pinned on the diamond stud earrings that Daddy had given her for Christmas. She slipped on a pair of slim khakis, topping them with a lightweight cotton sweater. Glancing at the clock, she sat at her laptop just as the calls began.

During a lull, she thought about Aunt Joy. Picking up the phone, she dialed her number. The call went straight to voicemail. "Hey, Joy. Give me a call when you get a chance."

Cricket would check back again soon. She loved Joy, her seventy-six-year-old aunt. When Cricket was a girl, Joy took her on nature hikes and bought her birthday gifts like binoculars, a singing bird wall clock, and books about America's national parks with full-color photographs.

At ten thirty, Cricket was almost ready for their eleven o'clock appointment. After the thousands of dollars they'd let slip away with their MIA clients, they'd better land every single client who might possibly need their services. She was in the bedroom applying a berry lip stain when she heard the knock. Hurriedly, she swung open the door.

"Morning." Pearl sounded nervous but looked sharp in a bright red pantsuit, suede booties, and small gold earrings. Today, she was a sleek-haired blonde. "Do I look okay?"

"So professional. Great do. You look like Reese Witherspoon in one of her I'm-ready-for-business roles," Cricket said approvingly. As part of Pearl's supervisory training, Cricket had assigned her to take the lead on this visit.

"All set?" Cricket asked, locking the door.

"I am." Eyes twinkling with anticipation, Pearl smoothed her hair.

They got in Cricket's SUV, buckled up, and rode down Dogwood Street in one of Azalea's prettiest neighborhoods. Cricket handed her assistant a file. "Let's review."

Pearl opened the file, scanning the notes. "You talked to Mr. Hank Mayfield about his seventy-nine-year-old mother who recently broke four bones in her foot. She was released from Azalea Memorial three days ago and refused to go to rehab. The son has been staying with her." Pearl's voice faltered as she glanced over at Cricket. "Is this right? She fell off a ladder while rewiring a chandelier?"

Cricket cracked a smile as she slipped on her sunglasses. "The son said she still mows her own yard, and she even runs a chainsaw."

"A real firecracker." Pearl nodded approvingly. "That's how I want to be."

They motored through the small business section of downtown Azalea. Cricket braked gently as a couple tentatively stepped into the crosswalk, and she waved them on but gasped as she recognized the man. In a tweed overcoat with a tomato red scarf draped dashingly around his neck, Clayton had a refillable coffee cup in his hand. His arm was slung around the shoulder of a young brunette who gazed up at him adoringly.

Midway across the street, he paused to give the girl's neck a nibble. The young woman giggled. In an impulsive moment, Cricket leaned on the horn for several long, blaring seconds. Lowering the window, she gave a toothy, fake smile as she finger-waved at Clayton. The professor blanched, hustling the startled girl the rest of the way across the street. Darting into the coffee shop, he looked fearfully over his shoulder at Cricket.

Slowly accelerating, Cricket shook her head in wonder. Southern good girl to crazy lady in under three seconds—even though she didn't even care a fig about Clayton.

Lowering her sunglasses on her nose, Pearl gazed at her. "You all right?"

Cricket shot her an embarrassed look. "Sorry. The man's a player."

"Well, then." Pearl nodded at Cricket as if she'd said something very sensible.

Just as Cricket's heart rate returned to normal, Pearl said, "This is the house."

Cricket nosed the car into the driveway of a grand,

columned home. Her stomach did a backflip. Her clients usually lived in more modest digs. "Wow. Nice."

"Uh-huh," Pearl murmured, shooting her a look. "We really need this client."

"We do," Cricket replied grimly. *Have clients left because I don't know how to run a business? Maybe they don't think I'm competent.*

If she kept up this thinking, she may as well go to the door, announce that she understood why they didn't want to work with her agency, and tell them, "No hard feelings." Cricket glanced at Pearl, who looked excited. She gave herself a more positive silent pep talk.

You know what you're doing. They need you. You have a great staff. Feeling a little better, she put the car in park.

Pearl hopped out of the car as nimbly as a cat. Tossing back her shiny tresses, she waited for Cricket. With a leather binder containing the client's file tucked under her arm, Cricket smiled as she caught up with Pearl. As she rang the doorbell, Cricket heard a vacuum cleaner.

As the sound stopped, the door swung open. A tall, broad-shouldered man in jeans and work boots stood with a hand on a vacuum. In faded Levi's and a dark green T-shirt that clung to his broad shoulders and biceps, he regarded them.

"May I help you?" he asked.

Cricket drew in a sharp breath. This delicious-looking man was the one she'd fallen on top of in the booth at the Senegal Siren.

CHAPTER 6

WHAT MUST THE MAN THINK of her? He must have thought Cricket was a klutz. Of course, she had been too obvious about sniffing him. Trying to be casual about it, she fluffed her side-swept bangs over her eyes, hoping he wouldn't recognize her. Pulse racing and mouth dry, Cricket couldn't think of one word to say.

Pearl gave her a quick jab with an elbow.

Cricket stammered, "G-G-Good morning. I'm Cricket Darley. This is Pearl Lewis. We're from Cricket's Caregivers. We're here to talk about providing services for Mrs. Mayfield."

With a harried smile, the man beckoned them in. "Sorry. Forgot all about it.

I'm Hank, Gloria Mayfield's son. Please come in." He led them down the hall.

Pearl whispered, "I love a man who cleans house."

Cricket sent her a warning look, but she was feeling a zing of attraction. His dang eyes didn't help the situation.

When he looked at her, Cricket pictured pouring caramel, golden honey, and melting chocolate.

She straightened. *Business. I am here on business.*

"Mama's staying in the living room for now," Hank explained.

As they trailed him across the gleaming hardwoods, Cricket realized she was downwind of Hank Mayfield. Trying to be unobtrusive, she sniffed. Goodness. Her knees went watery at the scent of him. Today, he smelled of lemon with undertones of clean laundry, an almond soap, and maybe sawdust or fresh pine.

Mother of pearl. She needed to collect herself. Cricket made herself think about spreadsheets, plastics in the ocean, abandoned dogs, people who were unkind or who had no manners. Any of those topics usually worked to get her in a serious, concerned, possibly depressed frame of mind, but not today. No ma'am.

Pearl was no help because she was out of the man's line of sight, staring at Cricket. She kept raising her eyebrows up and down with a look that said, "Yowsa-yowsa."

Cricket stood up straighter. Pushing her fingernails into her palms, she tried to rearrange the features on her face. Maybe it was working. Catching Hank's eye, she gave a professional kind of nod at what he was saying. What *was* he saying? Her face burning and her heart beating double-time, Cricket was in hot water.

Hank was busy explaining. "Hardly ever watched television but got real tickled with it while she was in the hospital. When I got Mama home, she had me buy her a big flat screen. We got her subscribed to a streaming service."

Nearing the sunny living room, Cricket heard an enthusiastic woman's voice on the TV. "Two weeks later, my belly fat just disappeared, and my libido came back like crazy."

Perched on a hospital bed with her blue-booted foot elevated was a woman wearing a pink flannel robe and one pink slipper. With her gray hair in a pixie cut, she had a tiny build. She kept her eyes glued to the screen when they walked in.

Hank Mayfield stood between his mother and the TV, waving his arms until she looked at him, frowning.

"Mama, the ladies from the caregiver agency are here," he said.

Mrs. Mayfield scowled. "All right, but we need to be snappy. Dr. Oz is almost over. Melissa McCarthy is coming up with a four-year-old girl who can sing like Adele." The older woman pointed a device at the television, mashing buttons. Nothing happened.

"Ma'am, that may be the phone." Pearl sounded unruffled as she traded the woman her portable phone for a TV remote.

"Thank you." The older woman resumed her button-pushing, but the volume increased. Finally, she hit the power button, and the room went quiet. She turned to them.

Hank rubbed the back of his neck. "Mama likes her TV loud. And there's only one TV, so we've been watching her favorites—the *Real Housewives of Beverly Hills, 90 Day Fiancé,* the talk shows." He widened his eyes at Cricket and Pearl. *Help me,* his eyes seemed to say.

Cricket knew that look grown-up kids got when they'd been yanked from their own lives to take care of a sick relative. Yup, he was going to go crazy if they didn't get a helper in to spell him soon. Drawing closer to the older woman, she smiled. "Mrs. Mayfield, I'm Cricket Darley, and this is Pearl Lewis."

"Please call me Gloria." The older woman gave Cricket a quick, appraising look. She took in Pearl. "Pearl's a pretty name. Old-fashioned."

"Thank you. I like it." Pearl nodded. "My sister is named Agate, so I got lucky."

"You did," Gloria agreed. "Nice to meet you both, but I don't need a helper." She raised one shoulder but pointed a bony finger at a small couch. "Please have a seat."

Cricket's eyes met Pearl's, telegraphing the old "we'll take it slow" plan to her. The two of them eased into a love seat.

Hank sat in a wing chair beside the bed. Looking uncomfortable, he leaned his elbows on his thighs, clasping his hands.

Cricket began. "Your son says you may need extra help while your foot mends."

"So he says. Hank's been staying here and taking care

of me, but he's got to get back to work." An expression of hurt flickered across her face.

"Well, work is important," Cricket said in a neutral tone.

"I know." Gloria sighed resignedly. Cocking her head, she announced, "I worked at Somerset College all my life. Married young, but it didn't take. I adopted Hank when I was in my early forties." She sucked her teeth, looking thoughtful.

Cricket gazed at her admiringly. Years ago, in a conservative Southern town, it was scandal enough for a woman to divorce, much less to adopt a child on her own. The home was grand, so maybe she had family money to fall back on, but still, Gloria had single-handedly taken on the responsibility of raising a son.

Gloria went on. "Hank graduated from Somerset College in business, but he works as a carpenter."

Hank rubbed his jaw with his hand.

Cricket felt a flash of sympathy for him. Gloria sounded disappointed in his career.

"Mama, your pain medicine's kicking in." Hank looked at Cricket and Pearl, explaining in an undertone. "Makes her real…chatty."

Cricket had seen more than a few clients loopy on painkillers. "Ms. Gloria, let's talk about how we may be able to help you while you recover."

"I don't need help." The older woman's jaw was set

stubbornly. "I've lived on my own most all my life. I do just fine. Do you know I own a chainsaw?"

"We heard." Cricket broke into a smile. "We were also impressed that you were re-wiring a chandelier when you took your tumble. You sound handy."

"I am." Gloria lifted her chin. "I'm the independent type."

"We'd like to help you stay that way," Pearl offered.

Gloria lifted her chin defiantly, looking unconvinced.

"Mama?" Hank sent her a pleading look.

The older woman paused for a long moment. She finally nodded grudgingly.

Taking a folder from Cricket, Pearl took over. "Now, Ms. Gloria, I'm going to read you a list of things our helpers can do for you. They can help you bathe and dress in the morning, fix you meals, and the like. You tell me which ones you think you might need."

As the two women talked, Cricket found herself sneaking glances at Hank, melting a little as she remembered how good it felt to be in his arms.

Hank looked at her, giving her a half-smile.

Averting her eyes, Cricket noisily clicked her pen open and closed until she heard the noise. She made herself stop.

Pearl turned to Hank. "I'd like to go over the paperwork with you."

Cricket shot her a quick nod of approval. Pearl was doing well, working with the client like a seasoned pro.

While Pearl and Hank reviewed their agreement to provide services, Gloria crooked a finger at Cricket, beckoning her closer to the bed. "Let me ask you something."

Glad for the distraction, Cricket walked over, mentally reviewing answers to questions new clients typically had.

"Are you married?" the older woman whispered, gazing at her steadily.

Cricket gaped. "No, I'm divorced," she croaked. Why was she talking about her marital status with a client?

"Good. My boy's divorced." The woman raised and lowered her skinny white eyebrows.

Cricket's mouth dropped open. She made herself close it. Gazing at Pearl, she tried to send her another mental telegraph. *Get me away from this too-attractive man with his matchmaking mama.*

Pearl slipped the signed contract into the folder. "Thank you, Mr. Mayfield. Our helper will be at the house at nine tomorrow morning. Cricket will be by later this week to make sure your mama's doing well."

As they rose, Cricket glanced around the room appraisingly. She turned to Hank. "May we push the furniture back to create a clearer path between rooms?" She pointed to a few small area rugs. "Let's move some of those so your mama won't trip—" As soon as the words left her mouth, she blushed and looked at Hank.

Though he looked serious, his mouth twitched with amusement. "If you trip, no telling where you'll land."

Cricket mustered a feeble smile. He'd known who she

was the whole time. Rising, she busied herself repositioning rugs and clearing paths.

Pearl gazed at the older woman. "Ms. Gloria, how about you walk us out with that walker of yours? I hear your doctor wants you to take a spin around the house as soon as you can." Helping the woman up, Pearl walked slowly beside her to the door. "Do you think it's too early to put plants in the ground? The nighttime temperatures have been mighty cool…"

Hank stepped beside Cricket as they walked to the door. "Couldn't help overhearing your conversation with your date the other night. They put those tables so dang close." He shook his head, though his eyes twinkled with mischief. "Your boyfriend mentioned something about *existential quandaries*." Hank stuck his hands in his pockets and whistled. "Boy, there's a ten-dollar set of words."

Turning crimson, Cricket felt blood thrum between her ears. A man who'd only heard a few sentences of Clayton's conversation had nailed him as a pretentious twit. She'd spent a whole evening with Clayton but not gotten that message until the Mercedes make-out incident. Cricket needed a tune-up on her man-assessing skills. Giving him a polite smile, she hurried off. Cricket was beyond embarrassed, but at least they got the contract signed.

When they got back to the house, Pearl headed out to make the bank deposits. After that, she was meeting a new potential caregiver at Chick-fil-A for an interview.

Still rattled by meeting Hank Mayfield, Cricket was grateful when the phones started up again. Answering calls and responding to text messages made Cricket feel like her old competent self, not addled and unnerved as she'd been when she'd run into Hank Mayfield. Best to steer clear of that man.

Still, she texted Honey. *Breaking news on man front. Call me.*

When the phone rang and Honey's number came up, Cricket blew out a sigh of relief.

Instead of hello, her friend said quietly, "*Buongiorno.* Man Hotline."

In the background, Cricket heard opera music, plates clattering, and people laughing loudly. "Hon, where are you?"

"On a lunch field trip with my Italian class at La Bella Luna restaurant. Let me step outside a minute," Honey said in an undertone. "Glad you called because we're only allowed to speak Italian. I lost the thread about ten minutes ago. I just keep saying, '*Bueno, Bueno.*' "

"Good thinking." Cricket cracked a smile.

"Okay. I'm on the patio. Tell me." Honey sounded breathless with anticipation.

"First news flash. Guess who my new client's son is?" Cricket asked.

Her friend did not even pause. "It was that enticing, brown-eyed man you fell for the other night."

"It was. His name is Hank Mayfield. His mother broke

her foot, got a TV set, and he's a carpenter," Cricket said, noting her voice had slid up an octave.

"Slow down, girl. Are you worried that he's a carpenter? I know you like the buttoned-up, professional guys…" Honey began.

Cricket winced inwardly. Knox was the buttoned-up professional type, but he'd not turned out to be a blue-ribbon prizewinner.

Honey went on, oblivious. "But I always liked the manly men. So down to earth and so good with their hands." She sighed dreamily.

Cricket didn't feel the need to point out that Sanders was about as buttoned-up as they come. He was quiet, intense, and very funny, but he probably never slouched. Honey told her that he couldn't help but straighten crooked pictures. He ironed his pajamas.

Cricket thought about it. "Prior to Sanders, you dated that beefcake guy who trained Tennessee walking horses. You spent time with that stonemason who had the face of an angel."

"Neither of whom had any substance. Don't forget the Irish metal sculptor who knew a little Yeats," Honey said ruefully.

"The one who put a thousand dollars on your credit card." Cricket shook her head.

Maybe there was hope for her. Honey had accidentally married a nice man with money. When Honey ran into Sanders at a loud party, she'd thought he said he was an astrologist, not an allergist. When Honey told him she was a Pisces and asked him for an astrological reading, they'd figured out the misunderstanding, had a good laugh about it, and promptly fallen in love.

Cricket thought for a moment. "I do wonder why a guy with a college degree is doing carpentry at his age. The guys I knew who liked that work are builders now."

Honey sounded eager for a chance to make use of her master's in psychology skills. "Is he an underachiever? Does he have authority problems? Does he drink?"

"Good questions." Cricket leaned back in her chair. "I don't know anything about him except that he's divorced." She hesitated. "We also work for his mama. I can't date the relative of a client. That's crossing a professional boundary."

"Uh-huh." Honey sounded skeptical. "Maybe you're just scared. Post-traumatic Knox syndrome."

Cricket tapped a pen on the table. "Maybe. So luckily, the guy is off-limits."

"The universe is presenting you with a cute man, the first I've heard you be remotely interested in for years. You have *got* to get closure with Knox. You must move on." Honey managed to sound bossy and Zen at the same time.

"There's more news." Feeling foolish, Cricket relayed the honking incident.

Honey hooted with laughter. "You honked to let him know a car was approaching. It's a safety rule written right there in the Motor Vehicles handbook. You can get a ticket if you don't honk."

"You made that up," Cricket said, laughing. "Not too crazy a thing to do?"

"Maybe a teensy bit of transference of hostility from Knox to Clayton. No biggie," Honey assured her.

"Good." Cricket felt her shoulders drop from where they'd crept around her shoulders. "Thanks for being such a good friend, Hon. I need to go get some work done."

"Okay, but promise you'll pick strawberries with me next week before the season's over. We can meet at Becky's Berries. It'll only take thirty minutes."

Cricket's mouth watered as she imagined lush, juicy red berries on a homemade pound cake topped with whipped cream. "Let's do it. We'll set up a time soon."

"Perfect." Her friend sighed happily. "If any other man-type questions come up, call me. I'm here on the hotline."

A few minutes later, Pearl breezed in, carrying chicken wraps and two iced teas. "Hey there."

"Ah, lunch. Thank you." Cricket's stomach was rumbling.

Her brows in a V, Pearl looked troubled. "You might think I'm crazy, but I could swear I saw Gigi's ugly green car following me today."

"Hunh." Cricket chewed her lip, thinking about it.

Pearl unpacked the paper bag, handing over her lunch.

"I thought I may have seen that car behind me when I went on a new client assessment last week."

"It's a small town, so it could be a coincidence. People heading in the same direction," Pearl pointed out. "Let's both keep an eye out for it, though."

Cricket frowned. "Good. I don't trust her one bit." She took a bite of her sandwich, savoring the crisp, spicy chicken. "How did your interview go?"

Pearl took a long swallow of tea, raising her eyes to heaven. "That helper was a no-go. She accidentally told me she filed a lawsuit against her last client because she fell in his kitchen. Oh, she is also suing Food World for a slip and fall. We don't need that."

"We sure don't." Cricket was impressed. "You got all that info over a cup of coffee?"

"Yup," Pearl said proudly. A piece of lettuce fell from her wrap, and she popped it in her mouth. Chewing slowly, she looked around. "I like us working here together. It's better than me working at home and you working here."

"I have the space. Finally realized we might as well use it."

Pearl bobbed her head so vehemently that her wig slipped a little. She deftly adjusted it. "When I worked from home, Dalton was there too, and the television would blare from the next room. He likes loud shows like *Law and Order*, with lots of fighting and gunshots." She winced, remembering. "I'd have a client on the phone.

When I hissed at Dalton to cut the volume, sometimes he didn't even hear me." Pearl shook her head. "The man means well, but he's old school. It just didn't compute with him that I was in our kitchen but really at work."

"Gotcha. I'm glad we made the change too. I've got the space. If either of us has a question, we can just ask across the table." Cricket remembered a recent purchase. "I bought us something." Reaching in the desk drawer, she pulled out headsets still wrapped in plastic. She handed one to Pearl.

Grinning, Pearl adjusted it on her head. Putting a finger on the earpiece, she pretended to take a call. "Hello, Governor Roy Cooper. You say we've been nominated for North Carolina Business of the Year? Oh, we are honored!"

Laughing, Cricket tried on her own headset. "These are ergonomically better. Also, if either one of us needs to be quieter on a call, we can just walk into the living room or onto the porch."

"So cool." Pearl took off the headset. Her face grew serious. "Just so you know, I love this job. I really do. I'm using my brain, I'm helping people, and I like being so professional." Gesturing toward the laptop and new headset, Pearl looked like she was fighting tears.

The two had a practical, easy-going, and sometimes jokey way of interacting, so Cricket was both surprised and touched by her candor. "You're my right-hand woman, Pearl. I am lucky to have you." Taking the last bite of her chicken wrap, Cricket looked at her, raising a questioning brow. "You ready for more detective work Thursday? We'll go visit those clients who went missing."

"I'm ready." Pearl rubbed her hands together.

After she left, Cricket was trying to neaten her desk when she came upon an orange sticky note she'd written herself. *Call Eugenia. Flowers to follow up.* After a quick call to reassure her old neighbor that she was keeping an eye on things, Cricket hung up. She glanced over at Pearl's tidy desk. It had been so reassuring to talk to her assistant about her problem tenants.

Cricket valued Pearl so much, yet she rarely shared any personal information with her. Talking with Pearl about her renters had been a first.

Resting her chin in her hand, Cricket stared out the window. Pearl was a hard worker who genuinely cared about their clients. She'd been a big help to Cricket when she was a rookie trying to sort out staffing. With quiet comments and astute observations, Pearl had helped Cricket decide which helpers were keepers, which were fixer-uppers who might do well with more training, and which ones they should pass on.

Cricket valued the woman enough to promote her, giving her a nice pay raise, but on a personal level, Cricket really didn't know her.

From bits of conversations she'd overheard, Cricket knew Dalton, Pearl's husband, drove big rigs. On the side, he was building a business as a house mover. Their daughter, Christina, and her baby lived with Pearl and Dalton. They helped out while the young woman finished her dental hygienist coursework at the community college.

Scrubbing her face with her hands, Cricket was embarrassed. She'd never even asked about kids or grandkids. Professional boundaries *were* important. She didn't need Pearl to become her bestie, but Cricket could be a little more real with the woman.

Cricket swallowed the last of her iced tea, mulling it over. Though she came off as friendly, Cricket didn't let many people come close. Women she met at networking events had made overtures of friendship, asking if she'd like to meet for coffee, walks, or lunch. But Cricket always made excuses, usually blaming work. She subtly fended people off.

In another free, completely unsolicited psychological consult that often happened after a few glasses of Pinot Grigio, Honey had said, "Maybe you're scared you'll let people get close, but they'll leave like your mama did."

That observation had smarted enough to know that it was probably rooted in truth. Cricket sighed, thinking how much less lonely she'd feel if she had just one or two more people with whom she could be more open.

CHAPTER 7

AFTER CALLS THE NEXT MORNING, Cricket undertook a whirlwind cleaning of her apartment. How could one woman and one dog generate so much clutter and dirt in only a few days? Stripping the sheets, she got a load of wash going. Wiping down counters with a cloth rag, she sniffed the plant-based cleaner that smelled of verbena.

Ahh.

They should make a perfume out of that cleaner. After dusting all surfaces, Cricket ran the lightweight vacuum with the super suction that she'd gifted herself for Christmas. As she emptied out the second canister full of dog hair, Cricket pretended to glare at Angus.

"Stop shedding, buddy," she implored.

He just waved his plumy tail, jumping off the couch to follow her around.

With another cup of coffee in hand, Cricket began to calculate the numbers required to pay her quarterly taxes but got distracted as she thought about her upcoming home visit.

Lips pursed, Cricket thought about the dreamy Hank Mayfield. They could fall in love. Stranger things had happened. She could help him grow his carpentry business if Hank wanted her to. They'd sit side by side on her velvet couch, and Cricket would use flash cards she'd had printed to help him study for his general contractor's license. When Hank got the answer right, he would grin and squeeze her feet, which he had been expertly rubbing.

In her mind, Hank loved to give her foot rubs. She saw him opening the email that told him that he'd passed the exam. He'd pick her up, kiss her gratefully, whirling her around, her dress billowing out around her.

Cricket shook her head at her foolishness. With her track record, Hank probably was in the throes of a midlife crisis. He probably drove a low-slung, throaty-sounding car or was a gym rat who took tons of supplements. He'd wax his chest and maybe get Botox to "stay competitive," like the middle-aged businessmen she'd read about on MSN.

If she kept trying to do taxes with Hank Mayfield on the brain, she'd get on the bad side of the Department of Revenue.

Angus sidled up, his red leash in his mouth. He dropped it at her feet, looking at her beseechingly and quivering with excitement. Cricket gazed at him, giving in.

"All right, buddy. Let's go."

Finishing her last entry, she electronically filed the taxes and made a paper copy just in case. Exiting the program, Cricket stood and stretched. As she turned from her desk, she remembered Daddy's concern about Aunt Joy, so she called but just got her voice mail.

Cricket left another message. "Joy, it's Cricket. Just felt like catching up. Give me a call when you get a chance. I'd love to stop by to say hello."

Ending the call, she felt a tinge of worry. She needed to call again soon.

Changing into sweats, she put on her running shoes. Cricket performed several stretches people over forty had to do to avoid a sudden trip to the orthopedics' office followed by weeks of physical therapy.

Sheesh. Passing forty wasn't for the faint of heart.

Hooking a leash on her deliriously happy dog, Cricket and Angus whirled down the stairs. After a rusty start, the two settled into an easy stride. The wind gusted as they started their route beside the lake. As waves whipped up on the water, puffy white clouds scudded across the Carolina blue sky. Reeling Angus in, Cricket put a hand on his big head and paused to simply admire the day. The sparkling water was so inviting. Cricket made a mental note to watch YouTube videos to get a handle on kayaking.

"Let's go, buddy," Cricket called, and the two of them resumed her brisk pace.

They circled back to a small but charming neighborhood of historic homes near the heart of downtown Azalea. Cricket slowed as they walked past the well-kept old bungalows with the deep porches, baskets of hanging ferns, and inviting swings. Next, they came to a row of grand homes, the ones that had been built by founding fathers, lawyers, and businessmen. Slowing, they came to the Wayne House, a grand Italianate-style building. With graceful lines, fanciful curves, and a cool design, the house was one of Cricket's favorites. She and Angus stopped to take it in.

Stopping to re-tie the loose laces of both her shoes, Cricket noticed a shining burgundy and black box truck parked in the cobblestone driveway of the Wayne House.

She watched two men roll open the truck's rear door. Donning gloves, they unloaded gleaming panels of wood onto a cushioned dolly, wheeling them into the house. Cricket was struck by how carefully, almost reverently, they handled the wood—not at all like the door-frame-banging, slap-dash guys who'd delivered the new mattress she'd bought at the big box store. The gold lettering scrolled on the side of the truck read, "Mayfield Company—Makers of Fine Cabinetry since 1936."

Cricket thought about it. Could Hank Mayfield do his carpentry work for his family's business? Interesting.

Cricket called for Angus to pick up the pace. She'd try

the interval training she'd read about in a magazine, alternating a fast walk with a slow jog. Anything to distract herself from speculating about the too-good-looking man she didn't even know.

Cricket checked to make sure she had the green light, then she and Angus crossed Sweetgum Street. Midway across the intersection, she saw a flash of movement in her peripheral vision. Skidding to a stop, Cricket scrambled backward, jerking Angus with her just as Gigi Gallagher turned right on red without even pausing. She'd almost mowed them down with her lime green car. Her heart hammering with fear and fury, Cricket's face came within inches of the passenger window. She watched Gigi pull the phone away from her ear, glare, and blast her car horn indignantly as she sped away.

Cricket's legs were rubbery as she led Angus to the other side of the street. She leaned down to hug him, whispering, "Close call, buddy. I love you."

Once the adrenaline receded and she could walk steadily, Cricket strode back home.

The close call with rule-breaking, self-absorbed Gigi Gallagher made Cricket even more suspicious that she might somehow be involved in her clients disappearing.

Safely back home, Cricket's hot anger took a while to dissipate. Giving the dog a kiss on his head, she slipped off his collar. "Angus, if that witch Gigi is to blame for any of my clients leaving me, she'll be sorry."

Early Thursday morning, Cricket enjoyed a warm

muffin and coffee as she read online articles about kayaking. She started a mental shopping list. She'd need a paddle, water booties or sandals, and life jackets for her and Angus. Although Angus looked like he might have some water dog in his distinguished lineage, she read about dogs accidentally drowning. She would never take that chance.

Chin in hand, she read a few more articles. Calling Angus over, she held the screen to his eye level, and the two of them watched a few YouTube videos on kayaking.

"This could be fun, buddy," she murmured, stroking his ears.

The whole sport looked straightforward and possibly fun. Cricket scrolled over and started a shopping cart to order her supplies.

At eight sharp, Pearl arrived looking dressy again in black palazzo pants, a fuchsia blouse, and a high, black ponytail. She sniffed the air appreciatively. "This place smells just like a bakery in my dreams."

Cricket grinned. "I baked pies last night as bait for the missing clients. Lemon chess and a bunch of pecan pies. I made an extra pie for you and Dalton. Remember to take it home."

"Oh, you can count your chickens on that one." Pearl rubbed her hands together.

The two manned the phones on their new headsets. By nine thirty, the calls had slowed.

Cricket looked at Pearl, giving her a thumbs up. "It's go time."

"I can't wait," she replied.

Pearl helped ferry the pies outside. Carefully, they wedged them on the floor of Cricket's back seat, securing them with rolled-up bath towels.

"Those turned out *so* pretty," the other woman said.

"They did, didn't they?" Cricket got behind the wheel. "So, we're going to find out why these folks are slipping off. If there's a problem, we need to know about it."

"Can't fix it if you don't know about it." Pearl nodded, her ponytail bouncing.

The two cruised down the leafy streets of Azalea. The pink and coral blooming azaleas were putting on a show. The forsythia added sunny, cheerful color to yards.

Pearl sneezed twice. "Nasty pollen." She rummaged in her purse and pulled out a pack of tissues. A baby pacifier popped from her purse, flew into the air, and bounced off Cricket's nose.

Cricket grinned. *Okay, God. I got the message about trying to make the effort to be more personal with folks.* She turned to Pearl, who was apologizing as she searched the floor mat for the pacifier. "How old is your grandbaby now? Remind me of the name again." Flushing, she realized she didn't even know if the child was a girl or a boy.

Pearl's eyebrows flew up, but she proceeded to go into typical gushing grandmotherly detail. "Sierra just turned two. In the beginning, I thought it was a strange name, but now I like it. She's really smart and notices everything."

"Gosh." Cricket never knew exactly what she was supposed to say or how to react while asking about kids.

Looking animated, Pearl went on. "She's smart as can be, just like her mama. She can dress herself, kick a ball, and stand on tiptoes. Sierra has got Dalton just wrapped around her tiny fingers." Pearl chuckled. "She uses our basset hound as a pillow when she naps."

"Well, I'll be," Cricket murmured. Now, how hard was that to extend herself a little?

She vowed to do more of it. Flipping on the blinker, they parked in front of the Jarretts' brick ranch.

At the door, Pearl rang the bell and called out, "Hey there, Mr. and Ms. Jarrett. It's Pearl and Cricket from Cricket's Caregivers." She rang the bell again and gave a firm knock on the door in case the doorbell was broken.

No response.

Cricket rooted in her bag for her phone, found it, and sent Pearl a chagrinned look. "Sugar. I don't have their number in my phone."

"It's all right." Pearl knocked again. "I didn't think of it either."

Cricket put a finger to her lips in a shushing gesture, and the two women froze, silently straining to listen.

"I heard rustling inside," Cricket whispered.

"Me too. And look." Pearl pointed to Bill Jarett's shiny Lincoln Continental that sat parked in its usual spot under the carport. "That's one clean car for all this pollen these past few days. He washed it recently. They're obviously not out of town."

Impressed with her sleuthing, Cricket noticed the mailbox. "The flag is up."

"Mm-hmm." Pearl sent her a knowing look.

After one more knock, Cricket looked at the pie she'd been carrying and turned to Pearl. "We can't leave the pie if no one is at home. If they come home later, they could eat it after it's been out a few hours and get sick."

"Let's just leave a note," Pearl suggested.

Cricket scrawled a cheery message on a sticky note and stuck it in the storm door.

"I think they were home." Pearl pulled her seatbelt over her chest and glanced over at Cricket. "Lots of folks won't come to the door these days."

"True." Cricket put the car in gear. "But we identified ourselves, and they could look right out the peephole or the window and see it was us."

"They're avoiding us," Pearl said matter-of-factly.

"Maybe." Cricket rubbed the back of her neck, troubled.

At the Baileys' brick faux manor house, Neddy Bailey flung open the door when Cricket and Pearl rang the bell and called out their names. Looking natty in his creased khakis, he cradled an insulated coffee mug in his hand.

He beamed. "Good morning! What are you selling?

Avon? Fuller Brushes? You're both so good-lookin' that I'll take two of each." He chuckled at his own joke.

Pearl gave Cricket a wink and a glance that said, "Isn't-he-a-kick-in-the-pants?"

Neddy Bailey was a big ole flirt whose bonhomie was a cover for slowly advancing dementia. But he was harmless, never inappropriate, and he smelled like Cricket's granddaddy had smelled—Old Spice and eau de cedar closet.

"Neddy, remember us? We visited you about six months ago and sent you those nice helpers."

Neddy looked blank for a moment and then his manners kicked in. "Well, young ladies, it's sure nice to see you both again." He took a noisy sip of coffee and then gave her a suspicious look. "Didn't one of you get sent up the river?"

"No, sir," Pearl said evenly. "No river trips for either of us."

After a few more moments of disjointed conversation, they learned that Neddy's wife, the clear-headed Della, was out getting her hair done. Cricket scribbled a hasty note addressed to his wife and tucked it in the wrapped pie before Pearl handed it to Neddy.

Peeking under the tin foil, Neddy's face lit up when he saw the pecan pie. "Well, this is just our lucky day. You gals stop in and see us again real soon, won't you?"

Carefully balancing his coffee and the pie, he gave a courtly bow and closed the door.

Pearl heaved a sigh. "Sweet old sugar talker, but we're zero-for-two on our mystery-solving."

Trudging toward the car, Cricket was discouraged. They were getting nowhere.

At Arleen Nelson's tiny-framed house, the two women called out their hellos, rang the bell, and knocked, but no one came to the door. Cricket turned to Pearl, frowning. "I saw the curtain twitch. Arleen's home."

Pearl sniffed noisily and shot Cricket a shrewd detective-to-detective look. "And it smells like somebody's been cooking bacon."

After wedging another note in the door, the two headed to the car. Cricket pulled away and gave the house one more look. "I don't get it. Why would people hide from us?"

"That's the mystery." Pearl slipped on sunglasses.

Cricket hesitated. "You talked with the helpers who worked with them?"

"Right," Pearl said. "None had any hint that the clients might stop services."

Cricket drummed her fingers on the steering wheel. "Maybe this is normal. Maybe we've just been on a lucky roll when almost every client we visited signed on with us or gave us a reason why they didn't." Adjusting the sun visor, Cricket looked over at Pearl. "I ran into Gigi Gallagher yesterday morning. Literally. She almost ran over Angus and me." She relayed the story.

"Holy smokes." Pearl sent her a speculative look. "Do

you think that skinny little snake is involved in our clients going missing?"

"I don't have any evidence, but I do wonder." Cricket accelerated.

Pearl pinched her lip, thoughtful. "We'll get to the bottom of this."

"We will." Cricket accelerated around a slow-moving car.

Pearl turned to her. "You've got your follow-up visit with Ms. Mayfield today?"

"Right," Cricket said, trying to sound nonchalant.

"That son of hers, Hank, was easy on the eyes. He seemed like a good man. If you see him, try to act more friendly and less rabbity." Pearl busied herself re-pinning her ponytail.

Cricket just shot her a look, shaking her head while trying not to smile.

At home, Cricket put on more makeup and fiddled with her hair as she prepared for her visit with Gloria. Realizing she was primping in case she ran into Hank, she made herself stop.

Outside of Gloria Mayfield's front door, Cricket knocked. Waiting patiently, she listened for the rolling sound of a walker on a wood floor. Purposely, she'd planned her visit in the half hour between helper shifts so she could get unfiltered feedback from Mrs. Mayfield about her helpers. Hearing a rumbling engine, she turned as the distinctive burgundy and black Mayfield and Company truck pulled into the driveway.

Cricket tried not to stare as Hank Mayfield swung down from the driver's seat. He wore a blue Oxford cloth shirt and jeans that she thought fit him particularly well.

When he spotted her, Hank looked surprised, but his face lit up as he strode toward her. "Hey there, Cricket."

"Hey yourself." Cricket drew in her breath as she noticed his eyes. In this light, they were an even more dazzling caramel brown, fringed with luxuriant, black lashes.

Hank's brows furrowed, and a worried look flitted across his face. "I didn't know you were coming by. Everything okay with Mama?" he asked hurriedly. "She didn't fall, did she?"

"I don't think so. I've rung the bell twice. She hasn't come yet, but I don't have any reason to think she fell." She sighed inwardly, knowing she sounded rabbity.

Hank rubbed a spot between his eyebrows, looking confused.

Cricket composed her features. "I'm here for the follow-up visit we scheduled to see how your Mama's doing. We want to make sure she's happy with her helpers."

"Right. Good." Looking relieved, Hank took keys and unlocked the door.

Gracious. The man was personable, adorable, and quite a hunk. Working to keep her face impassive, Cricket tried to look like she was thinking professional thoughts.

Hank pushed the door open. "Mama? Mama."

"Hold your horses, child." Gloria Mayfield wheeled her walker toward them. As she got closer, she called out, "And, oh my goodness, Cricket is here too."

"Hey there, Ms. Gloria." Cricket pointed at the walker. "You're using that like a pro."

With a twinkly look, Gloria gave a little half curtsy as she motioned them inside. "Come in." She was as gracious as a hostess welcoming guests to a dinner party.

"Mama, you told me to come quickly because the power was out." Hank peered inside at the lit lamps and glowing chandelier.

Maury Povich's voice wafted out the open door from the TV. "Jason, you are not the father!"

"Seems like you've got power to me."

Gloria's eyes darted about. "My goodness. It just now came back on. Right the very minute before I opened the door."

Puzzled, Cricket glanced at Hank for cues.

Hank gave Gloria a speculative look. "Really, Mama?"

"Really." Gloria's eyes were wide, the picture of innocence, then she looked guilty. "Well, the power did flicker off twice this morning. It never stayed off, so I really was telling the truth."

Hank raised a brow. "Mama, when did you take your last pain pill?"

"About a half hour ago." Looking exasperated at a question she clearly deemed irrelevant, Gloria went on with her convoluted explanation. "So I thought to myself,

'Gloria, that nice girl Cricket is coming over. Your only son is working on a job just down the street. Why not have a little impromptu get-together?' It's so much fun to have company." She dimpled, throwing up her hands gaily.

Not sure if Gloria was confused or just being whimsical, Cricket shot a glance at Hank. He looked amused.

"It's such a superb spring day. Let's just sit on the back porch. We can visit for a few minutes, shall we?" Without waiting for an answer, Gloria speed-rolled away.

"They're weaning her off the pain pills. She's too bright as it is, and she's bored. Add pain pills, and you've got a party in the middle of a workday." But Hank gave an indulgent shrug, steadying Gloria as she walked down a step to the porch.

Noticing she was downwind of Hank, Cricket surreptitiously sniffed him again.

Yep. Just as potent as he was last time.

Cricket feigned interest in a mediocre oil painting on the wall, pausing to collect her wits. From the corner of her eye, she watched Hank hold the door for his mother. Gentlemanly behavior was so appealing.

Gloria sank into the cushions of an antique wicker sofa. She folded her hands in her lap, looking ready to settle in for a good long chat.

Cricket perched on the edge of an antique wooden rocker, trying to steer the conversation to normal. "How are things going with your new helpers?"

"Marvelous." The older woman beamed. "I like them both. Precious girls."

Cricket's mouth twitched. Both "girls" were pushing sixty. She turned to Hank. "Do you mind if I just spend a few minutes alone with your mother to make sure we're helping in all the way she needs us to?"

"Sure." Hank rose before glancing at his phone and stepping outside.

After Cricket found out how she was progressing, Gloria leaned forward and spoke in a confidential tone. "So, dear, Cricket's Caregivers is your own business. Very industrious of you. Hank's ex-wife was a dancer." She heaved a dramatic sigh.

CHAPTER 8

PICTURING STRATEGICALLY PLACED BOA FEATHERS and firemen's poles, Cricket choked out the only response she could think of. "Well...I'm sure... she was physically fit."

Hank stepped back onto the porch, easing into a wicker rocker. Apparently, he'd overheard the last snippet of their conversation. "Mama, no need to trot all that out."

"Well, you're single again. Cricket is single. I just wanted you two young people to have a chance to talk more to each other." His mother ignored Hank's imploring look. "What do you like to do besides work, Cricket? Any hobbies?"

Cricket blinked, realizing she was being interviewed for a wife position. She glanced at Hank for help, but he was busy scrubbing his face with his hands. In a thin voice, she just spoke the truth. "Cooking. Walking. I take care of my father's dog." Good gravy, she sounded like a sad spinster.

"You're independent and domestic." Gloria sent Hank a meaningful look.

"Mama, let's not grill Cricket. Her personal life is not our business."

Beaming, Gloria's helper, Carmen, poked her head out of the door of the porch. "How are you all? Good to see you outside on this gorgeous day. I need to fix Ms. Gloria a little lunch, then try to get her to take a nap."

Relieved, Cricket made a show of glancing in the direction of her watch. "My goodness. Look at the time."

Hank shot her an apologetic look and stood. "Let's let Cricket go, Mama."

"I'm sorry our visit is over." Gloria Mayfield held up a finger. "Remember, the course of true love never did run straight." Stifling a yawn, she wobbled to her feet with Carmen's help. She rolled slowly away. "Bye, my dears," she called over her shoulder.

"Goodbye, Ms. Gloria." Cricket rose as Hank kissed his mama's cheek.

"You've been a good sport." Hank sent her a grateful look as he walked her out the screen door. "Sorry you got pounced on. Mama is ready for me to get hitched."

"It's all right," Cricket said. "She just wants you to be happy."

As he opened her car door for her, Cricket pointed at his truck. "I saw a truck like that at the Wayne house this morning. So, you work for your family's company?"

He nodded slowly. "That's right."

Flustered by his closeness, she wasn't sure what to say next. "What kind of cabinets do you make?"

"All kinds." He ran a hand through his close-cropped hair. "We build cabinets to hide electronics and security systems. At the Wayne House, we're replacing hand-carved panels in the library that got water damaged. We have a niche in working with historic homes, high-end boat builders, and avionics companies that build private jets."

"Wow. So interesting."

Cricket liked that his face grew animated as he talked about his work. It was clear Hank enjoyed his job, but he spoke with more authority than she'd expect from a carpenter. Cricket shot a quick look at his hands to check for calluses just as he stuck them in his pockets. Her face suffused with heat, hoping he hadn't caught her accidentally staring at his pocket and crotch area.

Hank must have noticed her glance because the corners of his mouth twitched. "Bye for now, Cricket. I hope to see you again soon."

"Same here," she muttered gracelessly as she slid into her seat. *Same here?* Just a titch more gracious than "ten-four" or "back atcha." Still rattled, Cricket carefully pulled away.

Both hands gripping the wheel, Cricket's heart thudded like she'd just sprinted her usual walking route. In the mirror, she sneaked another peek at Hank Mayfield. He leaned languidly against the column of the white brick house, watching her. Safely back on Main Street, Cricket rolled her shoulders, relieved.

Yikes. The man was scarily attractive, kind to his mama, and happy with his work. Seemed too good to be true.

The doubts crept in. Everyone thought Cricket's ex-husband was such a nice guy. After the champagne toasts at their engagement party at one of Azalea's fanciest restaurants, Cricket had run into Knox's mother, Bea, in the ladies' room as she freshened up her lipstick. Smiling affectionately, Bea put her hand on Cricket's cheeks.

"Cricket, honey," she'd said in the honeyed voice that still caused her grown sons to quake in their tasseled loafers. "Knox will make an excellent husband."

But he hadn't. Honey's theory was that the men who never rebelled in high school or college had the biggest whoppers of mid-life crises. Maybe that's what had happened to Knox. Men who seemed like nice guys weren't always nice.

But despite this memory and the nerve-jangling visit with Gloria and her son, Cricket couldn't stop smiling as she headed home.

As she drove along, Pearl called. Traffic was light, so Cricket took the call.

"Hey, there."

"You won't believe it," Pearl burbled. "I just got commitments from two new clients. They're both the nicest couples. The families are as sweet as pie, too."

"Fantastic. You are doing great, Pearl." Her spirits rising, Cricket felt fizzy with excitement.

Along with the new inquiry she'd gotten from a family this morning, plus the interview she had tomorrow with the daughter of another woman who might need their help, things were looking promising. Business *was* coming along.

"Don't forget your meeting tomorrow with Lila Merriweather about her mama, Cora Granville," Pearl said.

"I remember." Cricket wasn't looking forward to it. "When she called for information, she was snappy. Like a queen, only a mean one."

"That's the one. You can handle her," Pearl assured her.

"If we take on her mama as a client, we need to match her with a helper who won't get intimidated by the daughter." Cricket braked at the stop sign. She was working on delegating, which was not the easiest thing for her, but she needed to do it. "I'll let you decide who would be the best fit."

"I will," Pearl said, excitement in her voice about a new challenge. "I'll catch up with you tomorrow."

That evening, Cricket poured herself a celebratory glass of buttery Chardonnay. Sitting at the kitchen table, she sipped, nibbling at red grapes and wheat crackers topped with a creamy Gouda. Glancing out the window, her eyes rested on the pink house she daydreamed about. It was just so appealing.

Cricket took a swallow of wine, looking at the For Sale sign that tilted to one side. Purple wisteria draped gracefully over a rickety-looking arbor while pink and white azaleas were starting to dot the yard with color. The broad back porch sloped a bit but still looked inviting.

Cricket pictured herself barefoot, draped languidly in an Adirondack chair as she read a book. She'd be wearing a delicate cotton summer dress she did not yet own, looking more glowingly lovely than she was in real life. Angus would be curled up in a ball at her feet. A man in jeans would push open the screen door with two glasses of iced tea in his hands and walk toward her. Though she knew he was gorgeous and kind, Cricket couldn't quite picture his face.

Cricket mulled over what Mr. P had said. Her money wasn't as secure as she'd like, but maybe she *should* make an offer on the house.

Her breathing shallow, Cricket pulled up a local real estate website and studied the details on the house. Her pulse went raucous when she looked at the price. It was a steal.

> *Charming Victorian in one of Azalea's most desirable neighborhoods. Fixer-upper but has great bones. Rocking chair porches. Built in 1904. 1600 SF with a downstairs master. Two BR, two baths. Stained glass windows. High ceilings, original hardwoods. Bring your checkbook bc home priced to sell!*

Cricket found the calculator on her phone. Her personal finances were okay. She paid the mortgage on the old house every month, and she steadfastly contributed to her retirement account. Pulling up her online banking, she looked at her modest savings.

Tapping in numbers, Cricket held her breath as she got to the bottom line. This could be doable.

If she asked for a ninety-day close, she could accept her father's offer to be her bank and set up the loan with him.

Cricket felt giddy with excitement. Now, she needed a realtor. She'd call Tinsley Hoke. She'd known her from high school and knew she was now a big-time agent. In a full-page spread in every Sunday's *Charlotte Observer,* Tinsley leaned on a gleaming Audi parked in front of a Tudor mansion, crossed her arms like a boss, and held what the newspaper boasted were "the keys to your new castle!"

With trembling fingers, she texted her father about what she was suddenly burning to do.

Julius's text response came quickly. *Go for it, darling girl!*

Her heart beating double time, Cricket found Tinsley's number and called. There was no answer.

In a coolly confident voice that she hoped sounded like she made offers on homes all the time, Cricket left a message. "Tinsley, it's Cricket Darley from high school.

I want to make an offer on a house at 146 Mimosa. Will you please call me?"

Cricket had trouble falling asleep that night, abuzz with anticipation. Though she counted sheep, conjured fields of lavender in Provence, and sipped a fruity drink from a coconut in Bermuda, she flipped around, bouncing on the mattress and earning affronted looks from Angus.

After finally falling into a restless sleep, Cricket heard the ping of an arriving text.

It was eleven thirty. Fearing bad news from her dad or Joy, she snatched up the phone. She stared blearily at the screen.

Tinsley Hoke had texted back. *Booked solid 2morrow but can show u house early. 6:30 AM. R U game? Let's make an offer!!!*

Cricket shook her head. Grinning, she texted her reply. *OK!!!*

No wonder Tinsley was a top producer. No grass grew under her feet.

When she fell back asleep, Cricket dreamed about Angus and her ensconced in the pink house. In her dream, the dog was hers, not Daddy's. They were snuggled under a faux fur throw on the velvety couch in front of a blazing fire. Cricket was reading one of the classics while the same yet-to-be-identified adoring man was in the kitchen pouring her a cold beer and fixing her extra-spicy homemade guacamole with chips.

Early the next morning, Cricket hurriedly dressed,

keeping an eye out for Tinsley. At a quarter after six, she heard the blare of a radio playing Bruno Mar's "24 Karat Magic." Her realtor had arrived. Smirking, Cricket watched as the red Audi convertible screeched to a stop at the curb in front of her daddy's house. Good thing Mr. P's bedroom was in the back of the house, or he'd have the police on the horn. Grinning as she pulled on her sweater, she watched Tinsley back-comb her black hairdo with a hairbrush, take a slug of coffee, and stride to the door in four-inch heels.

Tinsley took Cricket on a whirlwind tour of the pink house. "The possibilities are endless," she trilled, pointing vaguely at features with a manicured hand. Tinsley used the phrase "diamond in the rough" three times, called the ten-foot ceilings "soaring," and repeatedly talked about "old-world charm and graciousness."

Cricket let her prattle, taking in the house. The large floral wallpaper was brown, which made the house seem dark. The bedrooms were small, but the high ceilings made them look bigger. The hardwood floors were scarred but could be re-done. The living room had stained beige Berber carpeting she could pull up. Hopefully, she'd find wood underneath. The kitchen appliances were circa 1960, but there were small fireplaces in the living room and bedroom.

Bubbling with excitement, Cricket turned around slowly to take one last look. "This is the place I want."

Fifteen minutes later, Tinsley gave her a gay little

wave as she peeled out, leaving a patch of rubber on the road and a small poof of smoke in the air. Cricket was trying to decide if she was more nervous about the offer getting accepted or not getting accepted. The check she had just written was huge.

Blasé, Tinsley had snatched it, paper clipping it to the offer before the ink was dry. Good gracious. Putting hands on either side of her head, Cricket sent up a prayer that she wasn't making a colossal mistake. But when she thought about the possibility of the house being hers, she could not stop grinning.

Back home, Cricket tapped out a text to Honey. *Put in an offer on the pink house!*

Honey shot back. *Mercy! You're kickin' butt and taking names! Keep it up. XOXOXO*

Between elation that made her feel like she could float and stomach-grabbing nerves that made her worry she'd lose her breakfast, Cricket was all over the place. She needed a long, brisk walk.

Lacing her running shoes, she then stretched and clipped the collar on Angus. Passing First Baptist, she breezed down the quiet streets and slowed to admire the beauty of a Carolina spring, the fan of fuchsia redbuds, and the cheerful green buds on almost every tree she saw.

Cricket sent up a prayer. *"Thank You, God, for all this loveliness. Help remind me not to race past it because I have things to do. Hope this house is a good idea, and help me get it if that's what You want for me. Thank You for my friends.*

Thank You for guiding me. I'm going to try to listen to You more, so I won't be so nervous."

By the time Cricket and Angus swung back onto Mimosa, Mr. P was sitting sentry in the glider on his front porch, sipping coffee. He looked so reassuringly calm and normal. Panting, Cricket slowed her pace and picked up his Wall Street Journal that had been flung higgledy-piggledy underneath his Nellie Stevens Holly bushes. She drew to a stop in front of his porch, watching as Angus greeted his old friend.

"Morning, Mr. P." Leaning over, she put her hands on her knees, beginning to breathe more normally. The hitch in her side subsided.

"Morning, Speedy. Cup of Joe?" Raising his mug, he gave her a questioning look.

"No, thanks." Cricket had accepted a cup before, taken a swallow of the sludge-like instant brew and regretted it. "How are you?" she burbled, feeling elated.

"I'm well." Mr. P pulled a pipe from his shirt pocket and put it between his teeth, looking as jaunty as Eisenhower. His late wife had convinced him to stop smoking, but some days, he clenched the unlit pipe between his teeth just for old time's sake. "Called the gang prevention squad yesterday morning because I saw what I reckoned were gang signs painted on the road down near the corner. Watched that WBTV's special about gangs taking over North Carolina. They call graffiti *tagging,* you know." Mr. P gave her a canny look. "Anyhow, they came out to investigate. Turns out it was a paint spill. The city workers marking the sewer grates were being sloppy."

"Best to be on the safe side," Cricket said mildly. The man needed a hobby or a lady friend.

Mr. P gave a curt nod.

Cricket pointed next door. "I made an offer on the pink house this morning."

There was the giant stomach clutch again. Cricket couldn't catch her breath for a long moment. Making herself breathe again, she glanced up at him for his reaction.

Mr. P beamed. "Good for you, Legs."

Cricket broke into a grin. "Thanks. The offer's not been accepted yet."

"I'll keep an eye on things for you." He tapped a finger to the side of his nose, giving her a wily look. "If the realtor shows it to anyone else, I'll tell them about the black mold problem."

Cricket gasped and stood up straight, her eyes widening. "There's a black mold problem?"

"No." He waved a hand dismissively. "But it's possible. These homes are old. Why just last year, I had a mold problem."

"Oh, no." She felt a tidal wave of buyer's remorse. Could she rescind the offer?

Her neighbor smirked. "Well, it was in my shower, and as it turns out, I just needed a new shower liner. But still, it could have been a very toxic situation."

Out of relief, Cricket laughed hard. Suddenly aware of the newspaper in her hands, she glanced at the headline. Something dire about China. Handing it to Mr. P, she tried to decide if the idea she'd just had was brilliant or foolhardy.

"You all right, Speedy?" Mr. P asked.

"Just woolgathering." She smiled. "I'll catch up with you later. Remember, if anybody looks at the house, tell that mold story."

"I'll mention the gang problem, too." Her friend hid a devilish grin as he waved her off.

Back home, Cricket showered and got ready for her meeting with Ms. Granville-Merriweather. Wearing navy slacks and a cream-colored blouse, she hooked on her good gold earrings and applied lipstick.

She and Pearl usually met with prospects in the clients' own homes, but when new clients wanted to see Cricket at her "office," she met with them in Daddy's library in the main house. It was better than having them traipse up her stairs and walk right into her small living space with a dog on the couch, the smell of last night's supper lingering in the air, and her personal pictures on the walls.

Cricket glanced at her watch. A quarter after eleven with time to spare. Hurrying down the stairs, she entered the combo for Daddy's keyed door. It was a damp, overcast morning. In the library, she turned on the heavy brass table lamps, fluffed the pillows on the downy couch, and flipped on the gas logs in the fireplace to knock off the chill. The room lent a certain gravitas to her business that her Formica kitchen table did not. When the doorbell rang, Cricket swung open the door with a smile.

Lila Merriweather did not smile. With unnaturally black hair, Lila wore an expensive-looking black pantsuit and short gladiator-inspired spiked boots. She had the whippet-thin build of a marathon runner or a woman who stuck her finger down her throat after meals. There was not a soft edge to her.

Cricket extended a hand, introducing herself. "Good morning. I'm Cricket of Cricket's Caregivers."

"I'm Ms. Granville-Merriweather." The woman offered just her fingers in a cold handshake.

Cricket thought about frozen fish sticks and tried not to giggle. Nerves. She led the woman to the library.

The woman's eyes swept over Cricket, and she glanced around the room appraisingly, taking in the wall of hardbound books, the Remington bronze of a proud-looking buffalo, and the antique prints of fly fishermen.

"Nice house. Is it yours?" Lila the Queen cocked a perfectly groomed brow.

Cricket bristled. In all the first meetings she'd held in this office, she had never had anyone ask if she owned the house. Flashing on to an old Miss Manners column she'd read, she drew in a breath and ignored the intrusive question. "Please, have a seat and tell me all about your mom." She gestured to the armchair and took a seat behind Daddy's imposing desk.

Lila Merriweather's face registered a flash of surprise and possibly respect as she sat, crossing her long legs. "My mother, Cora, is getting on in age and getting forgetful. We probably should have put her in a home years ago, but she did not want to go. Now she's having some…issues…getting around on her own. She won't use the expensive new walker we just bought her." With an exasperated sigh, she went on to describe the care her mother would need. Clearly, her mother's mobility issues were an inconvenience.

Every time Cricket drew in her breath to ask a question, Lila beat her to it, firing off queries about Cricket's Caregivers. "What are your hourly fees? Do we have to pay mileage too? What if Mama doesn't like a helper? Do you do background checks? Do you check their driving records?"

All were questions Cricket had answered for concerned family members a hundred times before, but when she answered, usually there was a sigh of relief, a quick joke, or a funny story about how Mama or Daddy liked things. They were things like "Daddy likes his martini every evening at precisely 5:00," or "Mama hasn't cooked a thing since the Obama administration," or "I'm so glad the helper will take her for a walk. I ask and ask her to exercise, but she flat out won't." Lila offered no fond stories.

Cricket scarcely had time to respond to a question when the woman moved on to the next, tip-tapping answers into her tiny tablet. Funny. Though it had never bothered her before, today that tappity-tap of the woman's acrylic nails on the tiny keyboard was as irritating a sound as the open-mouthed smacking of chewing gum.

"The going rate is significantly lower back in Georgia." Lila the Queen glanced at her heavy gold wristwatch and gave a harried-sounding sigh. "Well, I guess we'll just have to go with you after all. I've got a flight back to Atlanta for a five o'clock meeting. Email me the specifics and the contract, and we'll get this deal done."

Cricket paused, a voice inside her head loudly telling her this client would be trouble. Lila might be one that she wished she'd never agreed to work with, but she flashed back to the offer she'd just made on the pink house and the sketchy numbers that came from the missing clients. If they didn't win every piece of new business they could drum up, she'd struggle to afford the payments on her possible pink house.

Feeling a cold wave of dread at that thought, Cricket made herself smile. "We look forward to helping care for your mama." As she saw the woman out, Cricket watched as she strode over the blacktop, the *click-click-click* of her boots as irritating a sound as her acrylic nails tapping. Lila waved her key fob at the shiny cream-colored Lexus she must have rented and climbed in.

Closing the door to Daddy's house, Cricket leaned against it, shutting her eyes and wondering if she had just made a big mistake.

That afternoon, Cricket was restless. Frowning, she

studied the to-do list she'd scribbled on the back of a receipt from Piggly Wiggly. She considered renaming it her slacker list.

Cricket had not swung by the MIA clients' homes one more time, nor had she worked on social media. She hadn't called Honey back about strawberry picking, nor had she scheduled Angus's overdue shots and wellness check at the vet.

Although Cricket finally heard back from Aunt Joy the previous night and had arranged to visit the next afternoon, she hadn't put it on her list, so Cricket carefully wrote "catch up with Joy" on her Piggly Wiggly list and felt a hit of satisfaction when she crossed it off.

Cricket paced a circle around her apartment. She held her phone and willed it to ring. Waiting for the callback from Tinsley was driving her crazy. She had to get out of the house.

As she grabbed her keys and purse, Cricket noticed a car pulling in front of the pink house. Stationing herself at the window, Cricket gaped as she saw a woman in a pink and green swirly print sundress jump out of the driver's seat and slide a red starburst rider on top of the For Sale sign that read, "Under Contract." Dusting off her hands, she jumped in the car and whizzed away.

CHAPTER 9

HER HEART BANGING AGAINST THE walls of her chest, Cricket raced downstairs, hurrying to the street. Shielding her eyes from the sun with her hand, she gazed after the car, but the street was empty. Realizing how tense she was, Cricket drew a shuddering breath.

Could the Under Contract rider mean that Cricket's own offer had been accepted? Her thoughts whirled fast. Wouldn't she have heard back from Tinsley if that was so? Somehow, in her gut, she knew the sign was not good news.

Hurrying inside, Cricket looked out the window at *her* pink house. Feeling grim, she called the realtor. Expecting voice mail, she was startled when Tinsley picked up.

"Hey, Cricket." The real estate agent had to holler to compete with the thumping rap on her blaring car radio.

"Tinsley, a woman just put an Under Contract sign over the For Sale sign at the pink house. What's going on?" Cricket asked, her voice cracking.

"Not sure. Hold tight. I'll get the other agent on the other line." The phone went quiet. A moment later, Tinsley clicked back on the call, sounding sympathetic. "I'm so sorry, Cricket. The owners just accepted another offer."

Cricket felt like she'd been punched in the gut. A buyer had snatched the house out from under her. Taking a slow and deep breath, she tried to compose herself. "So, we got outbid?" Her offer was the absolute best she could do, even with Daddy's backing.

Tinsley paused. "Maybe not. The other offer may have been all but signed when they got ours this morning. Deals can come together fast, but also go south just as fast."

"Who bought it?" Cricket asked in a wobbly voice, brooding about the aging fraternity boy investors with their stupid alumni party house.

"They won't tell me that. Confidentiality, ethics, blah-blah-blah." In a bright voice, Tinsley added, "If it falls through, we can try again. I also know of another precious little house. It needs to be shined up, but it's in a hot neighborhood—"

Rubbing her eyes with her fingers, Cricket interrupted, "Sorry, Tinsley. I can't even think about that now. I just wanted that pink house."

"Gotcha," the woman said. "I'll keep an eye on things and will ring you right away if the deal falls through."

"Do that." Cricket ended the call. She sat at the table

feeling bleak, staring out the window at someone else's fairytale house.

Pulling a pillow over her face, Cricket yelled, "Aaaahhhh!"

Angus barked and dashed around the room, looking for any threats. Calling him over in a soothing voice, she hugged him. Pushing his cold nose to her face, Angus started licking her chin and cheeks. Cricket kissed his nose, comforted by his concern.

Drawing in a deep breath, Cricket let it out slowly, trying to sort her runaway emotions. Realistically, she knew deals fell through. Cricket covered her face with her hands, noticing her fingers had gone icy cold.

Grabbing her phone, Cricket called Honey. No answer. With shaking fingers, she texted her. *Looks like somebody bought the pink house right out from under me.*

As she hit the Send button, Cricket realized her hands were shaking.

Honey texted back. *On way home from Italian class. Be by in a jiffy.*

Hot tea might steady her nerves. On rubbery legs, Cricket stuck a mug of water in the microwave. The box of tea had a poem on the side that read, "Our tea will make your worries float away, like dandelion wisps in a spring breeze."

Cricket's worries weren't floaters. They were the heavy-duty, rugged kind that seemed to weigh a ton.

Ten minutes later, Honey thumped up the stairs to

Cricket's apartment, gave a perfunctory knock, and let herself in. Giving Cricket a hug, she swung into the kitchen chair and looked searchingly into her eyes. "Doin' okay, puddin'?"

Cricket realized she was crying. She grabbed a paper towel to dab at the tears that trickled down her cheeks. "I'm just so disappointed."

"I understand." Honey gently smoothed the hair back from Cricket's face. "Cry, sweetness. It's about time."

Touched by her friend's caring, Cricket suddenly felt overwhelmed with grief and began to sob pitifully. Every time she drew a breath to try and regain her equilibrium, she got caught in another tidal wave of sadness.

Honey just gently patted her back, scrabbled in her purse for tissues, and handed them to her.

After a while, the tears seemed to subside. Cricket choked out, "I'm done."

She drew in deep breaths but glanced out the window at the pink house and broke into a fresh round of tears. Thankfully, they seemed to be the grand finale.

Honey glanced at the mug of weak tea that Cricket had been nursing and gave a dismissive snort. Jumping up, she opened Cricket's liquor cabinet, a grand name for a cabinet that contained a dusty bottle of melon liquor, tequila someone had brought her from the duty-free shop, and a single green fifth of Tanqueray gin that had been her father's favorite when he came up for his nightly martini.

Honey dumped out Cricket's tea, rinsed the mug, put in a few ice cubes, and added a healthy glug or two of gin. She thrust the drink into Cricket's hands. "Drink. Gin is so good for you. Full of antioxidants that fight free radicals."

Cricket smiled weakly, knowing Honey had just made that up, but she took a few swallows of the piney, citrusy drink. She *could* feel those free-radical fighters kicking in. A warmth spread over her.

Pouring herself two fingers of the gin in a juice glass, Honey took a healthy swallow. Staring intently at Cricket, she held up a finger. "If you didn't get that house, the house wasn't meant for you. There's a karma element with houses. Your perfect house finds you. Remember all those scary stories your investor gal pals told you, and you told me?"

Rubbing her forehead, Cricket remembered. Jill had gotten into a bidding war on a sweet little ranch she and her husband wanted to buy for her mama. She'd cried when they got outbid. Turned out, the house had foundation problems that would have been stunningly expensive to repair. Sophie and her husband had missed out on a house and now the new owners swore it was haunted. Knox and his pals had tried and avoided getting a house that turned out to have easement issues and later heard that the folks who bought it were still in a court battle with neighbors.

"So, you need to release that little pink house into the

universe." Honey raised her hands, fluttering her fingers as if they were floating away. Tilting her head, she gave Cricket a speculative look. "Why do I get the feeling that all those tears are about more than losing that house?"

For a few seconds, Cricket just looked at her blankly. But then her eyes welled with tears again, realizing she had other losses she may or may not have fully dealt with. She patted her dripping eyes with a sodden Kleenex. "That pink house would have been more than a cozy home for me. It would have been my perfect haven, and it would have been *mine*. Not a house I used to live in with Knox." Cricket made a whirling gesture with her finger. "Not this sweet, stop-gap apartment of Daddy's. Buying that house meant I was coming into my own again, making a fresh start, and finally moving on from my ex."

"Gotcha." Looking like she was mulling it over, Honey tipped back her glass to swallow the last little sip. "The thing is, I see you as having already moved on. Your business is coming along. You're making good money renting your old house. You have nine employees and a great reputation in the community."

"But I don't have any idea why Knox left," Cricket said plaintively.

Honey nodded gravely. "He was too yellow-bellied to ever tell you why."

Cricket bobbed her head as she hiccuped from her tears—or the gin.

Honey held up a finger. "Wait there."

Hopping up, her friend rummaged in Cricket's freezer, triumphantly pulling out a fresh half-gallon of Chocolate Peppermint Stick ice cream. Scanning the refrigerator, Honey plucked out the caramel topping and closed the fridge with her hip. Finding the pecans in the tin Cricket kept in the cabinet above the stove, Honey busily began assembling a sweet treat.

While she waited, Cricket rested her chin on her fist, remembering the day Knox took off.

It had been a normal Monday morning. After a quick run to the grocery store, Cricket had pulled back into the driveway, anxious to get back to the computer to work on Facebook posts for her fledgling caregiver business.

The UPS truck had pulled up, and Maurice, her kind and friendly UPS driver, had wheeled a loaded dolly to her front porch, unloaded it, and hustled back to his truck for another stack of packages. Cricket turned off the ignition and gaped. Fifteen or twenty boxes were stacked outside the front door. Despite her occasional overindulgence in online shoe shopping, she couldn't remember ordering a thing.

With a jaunty wave, Maurice had pulled away. Leaving the groceries in the car, Cricket had trotted over to the porch and examined the packages. The return addresses were from companies she'd never heard of: Hawk's Peak Gear, Cray-Cray Climbers, and Vertical Heaven. She had hefted them inside the front door, trying to remember the return policy for packages delivered to the wrong address.

Hurrying to the kitchen, Cricket had found scissors in the junk drawer and began to slice open the boxes. Bewildered, she held up what looked like men's ballet shoes, then read the attached label. Climbing shoes. These were rock-climbing shoes.

Mystified, Cricket sliced open other boxes and pulled unrecognizable objects from white tissue paper. Again, she needed the label to help her identify what she held—climbing helmets, ascenders, ascender slings, crimping tools, crampons, lever hoists, and carabiners. Gear. It was all rock-climbing gear.

Had the packages been delivered to the wrong address? But Knox's name and their address were on every label. Hands shaking, Cricket had struggled to rise to her knees that had gone numb and hurried to the laptop to pull up their recent orders.

Her husband had just purchased nine-thousand-dollars' worth of climbing gear.

Cricket put her hands on each side of her head, trying to make sense of it. Knox had not done any climbing since college.

Knox had told her of his glory days in college when he was a hiker, rock climber, and skier. Four years at Appalachian State in the mountains had given him plenty of opportunities to practice and excel at those sports. But once Knox had been accepted into dental school at

Carolina, he'd given it all up, knowing his time would be consumed with studying. He had worried, too, about the possibility of injuring his hands.

If Knox was taking up climbing again, why hadn't he mentioned it to her? What happened to his concerns about his "hands as instruments?"

Cricket had held up the shoebox, studying the graphic of a yellow-helmeted young man dangling from an immense rock face, casually adjusting the strings around his hips that kept him from plummeting to his death. Cricket's thoughts had sped around her head as she tried to make sense of it.

On a hunch, she had quickly pulled up their credit card statement and gasped. Knox had also signed up for a three-month-long program at Great Heights, a mountaineering, rock, and ice climbing school in Colorado.

This had to be a mistake. Hands trembling, Cricket reached for her phone to call Knox, but outside the window, she'd watched him pull up. It was the middle of his work morning.

Knox strode inside. "Hey there."

Cricket had pointed at the packages, staring at him. "Why?"

"I'll need it for the mountains." He had nodded as if reassuring himself. Giving her a vague smile, Knox had gathered boxes from the floor and gone outside to toss them into the SUV.

"What are you doing?" Cricket had tried to grab his

arm, but he gently shook her off. From the guest room, he had gathered duffels he'd apparently already packed and unplugged the laptop. Tucking it under his arm like a football, he'd loaded them all into the cargo area of the SUV.

Knox had given her a quick hug like you'd give to a frail grandparent and had driven away, leaving her to pick up the pieces of her life.

Cricket shook her head as if to clear it. That was the last time she had ever spoken to Knox. Through her lawyer, she learned that he had sold his orthodontics practice to an associate at a fire-sale price. The divorce proceedings got underway. A year and a half later, she was officially a divorcee.

Cricket blinked, giving herself a little shake as Honey slid a man-sized bowl of doctored-up ice cream onto the table in front of her, then handed her a spoon.

Nabbing her own bowl, Honey sat beside her and dug in. "Yum. Gin and Chocolate Peppermint are tasty together."

"So good." Cricket savored the crunchy, nutty sweetness of the ice cream and swallowed, pointing at Honey with her spoon. "So, this has stirred up some feelings. Was he bored? Did he fall in love with someone else? Has he got a rock-climbing addiction?" Dubious, she gazed at Honey. "Is that a real thing?"

"Possibly." Honey shrugged. "People have addictions to eating drywall. They have plastic surgery to look like

Madonna. I'm guessing that Knox probably just had a garden-variety, mid-life crisis." She studied Cricket. "You're sure you'd never consider reconciling with him?"

Cricket flinched at the thought. "One-hundred-percent sure. Not in a million years."

"Good." Honey pushed back her fringy bangs, giving Cricket a steely look. "I've said it before, but I think one honest conversation with the man would help you stop blaming yourself, put this all behind you, and get on with your life."

Cricket felt her chin wobble. She sipped her gin. "That's tricky when he won't talk, plus he's so secretive about his location."

Finishing her ice cream, Honey patted her mouth with a paper towel. "I never *got* you and Knox. I just acted nice to him because you married him. He *was* good-looking." Tapping her lip with a finger, she looked thoughtful. "Underneath all those Southern good manners, Knox had a lot of repressed anger, maybe from being so bossed around by his strong-willed mama."

Cricket gave her friend a crooked smile. "I've thought that too."

"Good." Leaning back in her chair, Honey gracefully crossed one long leg over the other. Her friend gave her a cool smile. "Girl, we've got a road trip to plan."

Cricket blinked. "We do?"

"We do indeed," Honey said with quiet intensity. "We will track Knox down. You will confront him and make him talk to you, or else this weak little man will keep you stopped up emotionally for the rest of your life."

Cricket's chest tightened at the thought of seeing Knox again. Deep down, she knew Honey was right. She *had* to talk to him. Taking another swallow of gin, Cricket coughed, pushing the glass aside. She needed a clear head.

Honey spun Cricket's laptop around, commandeering it. "Tell me every mountain Knox has climbed or place he's mentioned in the last year."

"He was climbing in California and Colorado." Cricket sat up straighter, feeling a flurry of excitement. She grabbed her phone and read the mountain names in the most recent posts. "I'll go back through every text, Snapchat, TikTok, and Instagram photo he's sent or posted." Cricket's fingers flew, and she read aloud clues about his whereabouts.

"Good." Honey was quick, web pages zooming by on the screen as she searched.

"I can't believe I missed this one. It's practically local." Cricket enlarged the screen, holding up the phone to Honey.

The Instagram photo showed a close-up of a poster that read, "Climbing Stars to offer Clinic at Big Sky Rock Climbing Clinic at the Expo Center in Asheville, North Carolina, May 27-28, 2019. Climbing towers, indoor and outdoor coaching, expeditions to Linville Gorge and

Looking Glass, latest on technique and gear. Bluegrass music, craft beer, food trucks, and pig pickin'."

"This is just two weeks away," Honey breathed, wide-eyed, and held up a hand for a high-five.

On the poster was a photo of a now hard-bodied Knox and two other men dangling from ropes on the steep rock face of a mountain, giving a thumbs up to the photographer.

"The highest mountains in North Carolina aren't that high, are they? Some of those other mountains he mentioned in his posts were twelve to fourteen thousand feet," Cricket offered, still slightly ashamed of her stalking behavior.

Honey tapped away, stopped at a site, and stared at the screen. "This site says that North Carolina is a destination for climbers and mountain types. Mount Mitchell and Clingman's Dome are about 7,000 feet high, challenging for moderately experienced climbers. Plus, Asheville is picturesque, has great restaurants, and is close enough for all the east coast climbers to attend." Honey gave a decisive nod. "Perfect."

Cricket was almost afraid to ask. "So, what exactly is our plan?"

Honey clicked around to one or two other sites, looking determined or possibly dangerous. "We're going to that expo in Asheville two weekends from now. We'll blend in with the crowd. Probably need to dress the part of wannabe climbers. Goody. New clothes." She beamed and enlarged the climbing clinic website again. "Looks like most people are camping. Let's do that. I've never ever slept in a tent. It'll be so rustic and fun."

Cricket widened her eyes at Honey, who now looked extra-animated and clearly full bore in her "try new things" mode. Sleeping on the ground, even on a luxury air mattress, was not for gals over forty. Still, if Honey wanted to camp, Cricket would camp with her.

Honey went on. "We can borrow a car from Daddy Jay for the trip, one that would help us blend in with the mountain crowd. Maybe a 4-wheel drive vehicle for when we go off-roading." She made a rolling motion with her hand.

Cricket eyed her. They had never gone off-road unless she counted the time she had Honey in the car. She'd run over two curbs trying to escape from a tight parallel parking situation at the Pups and Pep Coffee Shop. That was after she'd unwisely downed three cups of a caffeinated drink called Rocket Fuel.

"No off-roading, Honey," Cricket advised. "We don't know how to do that."

Her friend looked crestfallen but quickly recovered. "We can cook on a Coleman stove and sing around the campfire with all the other campers."

"Not sure campers sing like that," Cricket said diplomatically.

"We'll go, you'll get the truth, and you can finally let

go of the 180 pounds of dead weight you've been carrying around," Honey said firmly.

But there were other practicalities to consider. Cricket cocked her head, the flutter in her chest a mix of hope and dread. "How are we going to approach Knox?"

"We're going to sign up for one of his sessions, silly billy." Honey's eyes danced. "We'll wear disguises and sit in the back. He'll give his talk. During the Q & A session afterward, you'll have a question or two for him."

Cricket broke into a smile. "I'm in."

The plan seemed half-baked, but with Honey's steely will plus her own readiness to get answers, their little ambush might just work.

"Yay!" Honey clasped her hands together, her eyes sparkling.

CHAPTER 10

SATURDAY MORNING, CRICKET WOKE AT 4:36 a.m. and could not get back to sleep. Thoughts about the pink house and dread about seeing her ex had made for a restless night. Cricket felt like lounging in bed all day, wallowing around, and feeling sorry for herself, but she needed to shake off this mood.

Pouring herself a cup of coffee before it even finished brewing and holding her mug in two hands, Cricket leaned against the counter, ruminating. As the caffeine kicked in, Cricket began her planning for the day.

Angus needed a long walk to blow off steam. She'd promised Joy she'd stop by that afternoon. Cricket ran her fingers through her uncombed, tangled mop of hair, pondering what she'd do this early morning to shake her blues.

It came to her. She'd bake. Baking always lifted her spirits. Cricket would whip up some extra special treats for her employees to nibble on at this week's staff meeting.

Pulling her mama's recipe box from the shelf, Cricket tapped a finger on her chin as she tried to decide what goodies the staff would enjoy the most. She could bake today, freeze what goodies froze well, and get the others ready to mix and pop in the oven the morning of the meeting.

Riffling through the recipe box, Cricket found the note cards she needed. There were lemon bars, brownies she made from an American Diabetic Association recipe, oatmeal chocolate chip cookies that she made with whole wheat flour and applesauce instead of butter in a nod to healthy eating, and an out-of-this-world Hummingbird Cake, a moist spice cake that her mama said was so named because each bite you took made you want to hum with pleasure. She would make muffins for the week, maybe those mouthwatering Morning Glory muffins with orange zest—her secret ingredient for their unusual delectability.

Cricket buzzed around, pulling cookie sheets and baking dishes from under the cabinets. Assembling ingredients, she began feeling better. Remembering a pie her mama was famous for at church and ladies' club functions, Cricket flipped through the open box, finding the recipe card that was soft-edged and faded from use.

Feeling a pang of loneliness, Cricket examined her mother's hand-written, neatly printed instructions for pecan pie. Her elbows on the counter, Cricket came to the end of the recipe and felt a wave of fondness as she read the note Rosemary had written in an elegant, loopy script,

> *This pie is divine for breakfast too. Top with a big 'ole scoop of vanilla ice cream. Have it with your coffee for a lovely way to start the day. Don't we all deserve it?*

Cricket sighed. Though she loved the idea of pecan pie for breakfast, she had never tried it. It seemed too decadent. Today, Cricket needed a mood-enhancing treat, and pecan pie for breakfast seemed like a brilliant idea. While she was baking, she'd make five or six extra pies, wrap them airtight, and freeze them. Why not? One never knew when a pie would come in handy.

Smoothing the curled edge of the recipe card, Cricket glanced up at the photo of Mama and her in the sprinkler. "Love you, Mama," she said softly.

By eight, the kitchen smelled like paradise. The air was redolent with the aroma of caramelized brown sugar, rich butter, melted chocolate, and browned pastry crust. Cricket turned off the oven, put her hands on her hips, and looked with pride at the baked goods cooling on racks on the kitchen counter.

Atop the chopped pecans in the golden filling of the pecan pies, Cricket placed rows of toasted pecans inside the perimeter of the flaky brown crust.

Cricket admired that little touch. It gave the pies an elegant appearance. Pouring herself a fresh cup of coffee, Cricket sliced herself a generous piece of pecan pie, topping it with a scoop of vanilla ice cream. The bite literally melted in her mouth. Groaning with pleasure, she sipped her coffee. The day was looking better and better.

Savoring the last bite, Cricket glanced up at the sprinkler picture. "Your pies are still the best, Mama."

As Cricket finished washing the last of the pans and mixing bowls, the doorbell rang. Peeking out the window, Cricket spied the big brown truck. Grinning, she knocked hard on the glass pane. Maurice, her UPS driver, looked up. Breaking into a big smile, he pointed to the bulky, oddly shaped packages he'd just pulled from the truck and pointed a finger at her.

Cricket gave him a thumbs up and a wave, trotting downstairs to retrieve them. Back in her apartment, she shook her head, bemused, as she pulled open the boxes containing double-sided paddles and life vests—one for her and one for Angus. Slipping the orange coat on Angus, she adjusted the Velcro closure tabs. Afraid he might try to shake the whole thing off, she watched him stroll around, take a long slurping drink from the water bowl, and languorously stretch. Angus seemed to hardly notice his new orange coat. Cricket took a quick snapshot to send to her father.

Cricket made a decision. Today was mild and not breezy. They'd take that faded red kayak to the lake for a shakedown cruise.

At the sandy and sloping boat launch area, Cricket was relieved that she and Angus were the only ones there. She heaved the kayak into the water with a splash, scratched her head, and paused for a moment to think about her game plan.

The lake was flat as glass. The kayak was a sit-on-top number, so there was no chance of their kayak twirling underwater in a roaring, washing machine like eddy with Angus and her gasping for breath and requiring rescue. Cricket shuddered. She should have never watched that video.

Slipping on her life vest, Cricket called to Angus, who sat on the shore looking so handsome in his matching orange vest. Wading out into the cold water, she kept up a stream of calming chatter with Angus, who now looked like he wasn't sure about the idea.

Cricket pulled a plastic bag of her dog's favorite treats, carrots, out of her pocket.

With the treats and more sugar talk, Cricket steadied the kayak, coaxing Angus to wade into the shallow water and step into the kayak.

Instead of immediately launching the watercraft, she sat facing him, chatting for a while. "Let's just sit here, big guy. They say this isn't hard once you get your sea legs."

Angus turned his head away, pointedly ignoring her, but several carrots later, he began to relax.

Cricket took hold of the two-sided paddle. She tried to remember the video clip on how to move smoothly and propel the kayak forward, backward, and make turns.

Staying close to shore in case they tipped, Angus readjusted his rear end, heaved a contented sigh, and settled in for the ride. Cricket was thrilled about his composure. Angus held his head erect, calmly taking in the sights. A family of ducks swam by. Cricket tensed, ready for the dog to spring into the water and chase them. However, Angus just looked mildly interested. He raised his head to watch the Canada geese honk by in their V-formation. If Cricket got Angus a vest with pockets, a funny hat, and hung a pair of binoculars around his neck, he'd look like a bona fide birdwatcher.

Cricket just shook her head in wonder. Instead of an anxious, boat-tipping, wiggle-worm of a companion, Angus had turned out to be a boaty dog who seemed to enjoy the ride.

They glided off, heading toward deeper water.

When they got back home, Cricket was feeling proud of them both. She was thrilled with their adventure. As she unloaded the kayak, she saw Mr. P at his usual spot on the porch. He raised his hand in greeting, but Cricket just waved back instead of going over to chat. She wasn't ready to talk about the pink house and averted her eyes when she walked past it. As she headed upstairs, she felt a pang of sadness for her neighbor. Mr. P was lonely.

After she'd showered and spruced up, Cricket nosed her car up in front of the mill house that her Aunt Joy had lived in forever. Property prices had been soaring the past few years as young professional couples moved there—ones who wanted a leafy, quiet old neighborhood to raise their families and who didn't mind a commute to work. As she pulled in, two dewy-faced women with glossy, high ponytails strode by, chatting as they pushed high-tech-looking strollers.

Stopping to scoop up her aunt's *Wall Street Journal* from the sidewalk, Cricket saw the budding Clematis on the trellises that flanked each side of the wide front porch. She remembered summertime visits to her aunt when they'd sat on this porch eating homemade butter pecan ice cream, their privacy shielded by drapes of indigo blue blooms—an enchanting flower fort. Cricket rang the bell, and Joy swung open the door.

Looking wan, she quickly pinned a cheerful expression on her face. "Come in, sweetheart."

Cricket gave her a brisk half-hug. Joy wasn't big on overt displays of affection.

Her aunt handed Cricket a glass of iced tea, and they sat in her living room. "Your daddy sounds like he's having the time of his life."

"He *is*." Cricket bobbed her head. "I think it's the first time in my life that I've ever seen him genuinely happy. I mean, he never seemed unhappy, but..."

"Your mama turned him into Casper Milquetoast," Joy said bluntly. "She got to be the vivacious, fun one and made him into the bill-paying, serious guy. Growing up, he was a late-life surprise to Mama and Daddy. We all adored him. He was an avid reader, curious about the world. Did you remember he was an Eagle Scout? Julius was a fine, bold young man." Joy took a long swallow of tea. "Sometimes good things come after tragedy."

Cricket wanted to defend her mother, but she knew it was true. Joy was right. Daddy was finally paying attention to interests he'd neglected for years, and that was wondrous.

Cricket studied her aunt. "How are you? How is it being a lady of leisure?"

"You mean being an old workhorse who's been put out to pasture?" Joy sighed.

"How are you dealing with it?" Cricket asked, tilting her head.

"I'm bumping along. Going to my Senior Center classes. Tuesdays and Thursdays are Golden Oldie Yoga-licious. Wednesday is Line Dancing for Swinging Seniors. Mondays and Fridays are Sexy Senior Abs and Butts." Joy rolled her eyes, looking disgusted. "I pointed out to that gal who schedules classes that the titles were just plain silly. She just giggled and told me, 'They're fun names.' "

Hiding her smile, Cricket tried to find some silver lining in her aunt's mostly cloudy mood. "Are the classes good?" She eyed her Aunt, noting that she looked as enviably trim and fit in her navy-blue tracksuit as she always did.

"They are." Joy sipped her tea but then gazed at Cricket frankly. "It's me. That's the problem, child. Everybody's getting on my nerves."

Cricket shifted in her chair uncomfortably as she thought about her own windshield rapping and pedestrian honking. "I get like that sometimes."

"No. I mean all the time," Joy clarified.

"Okay." Cricket understood now. "What else?"

"I hate the television these days. Bad news, more bad news. Then, the inane. The drama housewives. People marrying people they have never met. Naked people in the jungle." Brows drawn, she looked baffled.

"Anything else?" Cricket asked. Although she agreed with her aunt's assessment, Joy had to be crabby about something other than bad television.

"At the post office yesterday, a lady my age was holding up the line because she couldn't decide whether to buy the stamps with the roses or the peonies." Joy threw up her hands. "What if I get like that, with too much time on my hands and no inkling that other people need to get in and out of the post office quickly so they can get back to work."

"Never," said Cricket. Her aunt was briskly efficient about everything, from weeding a garden to making a bed and frying okra.

"I could," Joy insisted, her jaw set.

Cricket thought about it. "So, I'll bet it's hard to not be teaching."

Joy scrubbed her face with her hands, blinking back tears. "It's hard."

Cricket had never seen her no-nonsense aunt show emotion, and it scared her. "I'm sorry," she said softly.

"I can't seem to make friends at the Senior Center. This neighborhood has gotten wealthy. A lot of the women my age never worked outside the home. I have trouble finding things to talk with them about."

"What do they talk about?" Cricket asked, genuinely curious.

"They talk about their families. I can't exactly jump in there." Joy said dryly. "Some talk about recipes or their ailments. I try to steer clear of those women."

Cricket raised a brow. "That's all they talk about?"

"Not all of them," Joy admitted. "And they're basically a good bunch, but they all seem to stay busy. Most of them still have live husbands."

"As opposed to dead ones." Cricket tried to tease her, but her aunt was on a roll.

Joy reached for the newspaper on the sofa beside her, stabbing at the front page with a forefinger. "I'd like to talk with someone about the threats from China and what in the world bitcoin is."

Cricket swallowed, knowing only a snippet about both topics. She got her news online, although she still subscribed to the *Sunday Observer* because she liked the lifestyle section, the comics, and the sale ads. Reading headlines and scary political news could jangle Cricket for the whole day.

"Can you find friends who like current events?" Cricket asked.

"Where?" Joy asked, sounding plaintive. She pushed back her hair, composing her face. "I'll just have to make the best of it."

Cricket leaned forward. "Do you miss helping people or using your brain? Do you want to volunteer somewhere? Do you want to adopt a dog or cat?"

"I just don't know what I need to make me happy right now." Joy gave her a rueful look. "Looking back, I wish I'd found a husband and had kids. Teaching was my life. Now, it would be a comfort to have a man to piddle around the garden. One to travel with on weekend trips. Grandbabies to spoil might have been nice, too." She gave Cricket a pointed look.

Cricket held both of her hands up. "Glad you didn't hang your hopes on grandbabies from me."

Joy gave her a knowing look. "A husband and kids aren't every woman's cup of tea."

"True," Cricket agreed, glancing at her watch. "I need to get going. Promise me you'll try to find something to make you happier."

"I'll try." Joy rose and walked with her toward the door, her New Balance sneakers squeaking on the wood floors. She held up a finger. "Just remembered two other things that steam my grits. I saw a man spit on the sidewalk this week. Another used one of those portable plastic flossers then dropped it right there in the parking lot. Nasty."

Cricket put an arm around her shoulder and gave her a squeeze. "If you ever decide to look for a husband, we'll screen them for manners and hygiene."

For the first time that morning, Joy broke into a smile.

On the drive home, Cricket felt forlorn. She wasn't used to her strong, smart aunt seeming so vulnerable. Besides missing her work, Aunt Joy was plain lonely. Cricket shuddered, knowing she could be in the same exact boat later if she didn't find love.

As she cruised slowly through the small downtown, Cricket lowered the window to let in the fresh air. She returned the waves of a few pairs of walkers and the husband-and-wife team who were setting up more tables outside their Pups and Pep Coffee shop. Cricket started thinking about how she could help her aunt.

Aunt Joy was lonely. Mr. P was lonely. The two of them came from similar backgrounds. Both had lived in Azalea for most of their lives. Each were bright as pennies and kept up with current events. Could she possibly be a matchmaker for the pair? Wouldn't it be amazing if they fell in love?

Cricket got caught up in a happy thought, imagining Mr. P and Joy laughing gaily as they rode a bicycle built for two, blew kisses to friends and family as their small ship left port for a leaf-peeping tour of New England and Maritime Canada, and breezed through the crossword puzzle as they finished breakfast together while on their honeymoon. It could happen.

Frowning, Cricket tapped her hand on the steering wheel. She knew them both well enough to know they'd be appalled at the idea of a blind date.

Back home, Cricket pondered how to be crafty about matchmaking as she gave Angus a good all-over scratch. The big dog wandered off. She'd start the setup while she still had the nerve.

Glancing out the window, Cricket saw Mr. P adjusting his radio, probably trying to get better reception for his next news program. Yup, time to help Cupid shoot a few arrows at folks in Azalea. The whole plan could blow up, but something compelled her to try to add sweetness and zest to the lives of two people she cared about.

Cricket would make the call while her newly hatched scheme was fresh in her head. Hurriedly, she entered Joy's number. "Hey, Joy. It was sure good seeing you."

"Same here, sweetheart," her aunt said, sounding flat.

"I'm going up to the mountains two weekends from now. Would you please do me a big favor and take care of Angus?"

Joy gave a happy sigh. "I'd love to. He's a baby doll. I'd enjoy the company."

Cricket was flying by the seat of her pants now. "Instead of just coming by to check on him, do you think I could get you to stay here at the house with him? He's been more timid than usual with Daddy gone. His appetite's been off."

Angus galloped back into the room. In his mouth was a road-flattened, sun-dried squirrel with a still plumy tail. Cricket gasped quietly, revolted. Where had the dog found it, and how had he sneaked it into the apartment?

"Oh, it's a sure sign they're grieving when they can't eat." Joy sounded touched. "I'm so sorry that boy is missing his daddy. He is such a sensitive dog."

"He is very sensitive." The phone pressed between her ear and shoulder, Cricket grabbed a paper towel and tried to snatch the squirrel jerky from Angus's mouth, but he danced away, dropped the remains on her favorite fluffy white faux fur rug. He began to roll on it.

"I had students like that at school," Joy reminisced, wistful. "Some had the delicate souls of poets."

Yup. Angus was a poet. Cricket shot him the evil eye as he delicately picked the squirrel back up and chomped away.

Pressing the phone to her chest, she pointed at him, hissing quietly, "Drop it. Drop it." And he did, but he gave a blissful groan, stretched luxuriantly, and rolled on it again.

"I'd be glad to come take care of him. Just tell me when you're leaving and give me my instructions," Joy said briskly.

"Great. You'd be helping me out big time. Do you

have time to stop by next week sometime so I can walk you through the ins and outs of everything?"

"Surely," Joy replied. "I'm free Thursday morning after my exercise class."

"How about around ten?" Cricket plowed on. "One other thing, Joy. My neighbor across the street is recently widowed. He has become practically a shut-in. Since his wife died, he's just mooning around, lost as a lamb." She sighed sadly. "The poor sweetie. I thought you might check in on him. If you cook anything for yourself, you might save some for him. Just walk it over. All he eats is TV dinners."

Lying was easy once you got going with it. Mr. P loved to cook. His specialties were many, including a risotto shrimp casserole, slow-cooked pork tenderloin, and grilled Caesar salad.

"Of course, I would. That poor man. Men just don't do at all well when their wives go before them." Joy tsked. "Sounds like you really need me over there." She sounded positively perky. "I might bake some peanut butter cookies for Angus and that poor man. Separate batches, of course. One for dogs, one for people," she clarified.

Ending the call, Cricket tilted her head back, exultant. Hands on her hips, she stalked toward the sensitive soul, who was lolling on the roadkill squirrel.

Steeling herself, Cricket donned a pair of Daddy's garden gloves and managed to snatch the squirrel away from the smiling dog. Gingerly wrapping it in newspapers, she marched downstairs to drop in the outside garbage can.

Closing the green lid, Cricket removed the gloves, holding them pinched between a thumb and forefinger, promising herself she'd wash them or at least spray them off with the garden hose. She was headed back upstairs when she saw a beat-up white truck idling in front of the pink house. The body was partly covered with big patches of gray primer.

A red flare of anger burned in her chest. Was that an inspector or a workman? Could it possibly be the new owner stopping by to check on the pink house, which should have been *hers*? She thought her friends involved in real estate had told her that most closings usually took at least thirty days.

Black smoke belched from the exhaust, and the back bumper was held on with duct tape and bungee cords. Three successive backfires sounded, loud as gunshots. Cricket's heart thundered as the truck pulled away. She craned her neck to catch a glimpse of who was at the wheel, but the truck was too far away to see much more than the driver's ball cap.

Mother of pearl. She wasn't sure which was worse, the alumni ball game partiers or the Beverly Hillbillies.

CHAPTER 11

Upstairs, Cricket brooded about the next-door neighbor as she poured kibble in Angus's bowl when a call rang on FaceTime. It had to be her father.

Cricket eagerly clicked on the green camera. "Hey there, Daddy. How are you?"

"Grand. Fantastic. Couldn't be better." Julius gave her a toothy grin. Ruddy and bright-eyed, he wore a red scarf draped rakishly around the neck of his Anorak with wraparound sunglasses perched on the top of his red-brimmed cap.

Cricket looked more closely at the screen. Daddy looked like Indiana Jones or a rugged geologist, exploring an archeological dig on a History Channel show.

Julius's face grew serious. "Got your text about not getting the house across the street. I know you were disappointed, but there'll be others."

"I know. The right house will come to me." Cricket tried to sound mature, though she didn't want another house. She wanted the pink one. "What rails have you ridden?" She longed for his calm, reassuring presence and his unwavering belief in her.

"We rode the Alaska Railroad from Anchorage to Seward and saw glaciers, bears, and eagles. It's God's country, but cold as the dickens. I'll never complain about North Carolina winters again." He paused, leveling a gaze at her. "Did you get to the bottom of your work mystery? Little things can snowball, sweetheart."

"No, but I will." Cricket tried to look like a steely-eyed businesswoman, not a woman whose only plan was to hope for the best. "We're getting new clients, though."

"Good girl, but you've worked too hard to let what you care about just slip away from you," Julius persisted, giving her a concerned fatherly look.

"You're right. I'll get to the bottom of it." Cricket sat up straighter in her chair, even more determined to get answers.

"Heard anything more from Knox?" Daddy's mouth twisted when he said his former son-in-law's name.

"Not a peep." Cricket had already decided not to mention her mountain ambush plan. Julius just wouldn't understand the need for it. "I've got to run, but let me get Angus over here so he can say hello."

Grinning, she held up the phone to Angus's big ear, listening as her father told Angus what a fine, good-looking, brave dog he was. After the lovefest wound down, Cricket blew a kiss to Julius.

"I love you, Daddy." Blinking back tears, she felt lonesome for him.

"Love you back, darlin'," he said gruffly. He blew her a kiss, ending the call.

Seconds later, Cricket heard the ding of a new text.

Her father wrote, *Afterthought re. your missing clients. Could your caregivers be causing business to leave you? from your lovin' Dad.*

Cricket sat down hard in the kitchen chair, staring off into the distance. Could that be? She always followed up with clients to make sure the helper who was assigned was a good fit, but maybe a client didn't want to get a helper in trouble or was scared to create animosity with a helper who might still end up taking care of him or her? But after several bum steer bad hires, Cricket thought she had a stellar group of helpers. She rubbed the spot between her brows. She needed to be realistic and at least consider the possibility that she had an unkind, inattentive, or not a very skilled helper.

Cricket's once-a-month staff meeting was scheduled for Tuesday afternoon. She'd talk with Pearl. With fresh eyes, the two of them could size up the helpers who'd worked with the missing clients to see if they'd overlooked any signs of bad eggs.

Staff training had improved their caregiving skills, plus Cricket had worked individually with the ones who needed the rough edges smoothed off. The Bowdens had quit without even meeting a helper, so that made her think something else was at play. However, if a helper was creating problems, she needed to know.

Tara, Marla, and Florence were the only three helpers who'd worked with the missing clients. She'd ask Pearl to talk again with each of them. Cricket couldn't afford to keep letting business walk out the door.

After the calls died down on Tuesday morning, Cricket pulled lemon bars, brownies, cookies, and layers of the Hummingbird cake from the freezer and left them on the counter to defrost for their staff meeting. She'd top the Hummingbird Cake with a low-calorie, low-sugar, low-fat whipped cream topping that she suspected tasted like whipped air, but she was trying.

Cricket offered other healthier snacks too. She'd texted Pearl last night, asking her to swing by the grocery store and pick up a veggie platter that featured a ranch dip made with nonfat Greek yogurt instead of sour cream.

Eyeballing the messy pile of papers on her desk, Cricket decided to make another start at tidying it. Just as she sat down, Carmen called.

Her helper spoke quickly and softly. "Cricket, I'm at Mr. Bell's, and I'm out in the hallway. Mr. John just fell again. I called 911 and his daughter, and they're on the way." She paused for a breath. "I didn't move him in case he broke something and just put a blanket on him. I don't think he's hurt too bad."

"Good." Cricket made herself sound measured and calm. "He's had a few falls lately, hasn't he?"

"Three," she said grimly. "I told you he's just eating like a bird, wants to sleep all day, and keeps saying that he wants to go to heaven and be with Mary." Carmen's voice cracked.

Cricket slumped in her chair, knowing the signs. "It may be time to call in hospice. I'll talk with the daughter, and she can discuss it with John's doctor."

"Okay." Sniffing back tears, Carmen drew a shuddery breath. "I'll sit beside him on the floor until the EMTs get here."

"You're doing everything right, Carmen," Cricket said with quiet intensity.

"Thanks." Sounding stronger, the helper signed off.

Cricket put her head on the desk for a moment, sending up a prayer for John Bell.

This was one of the hardest parts of the job for her and her helpers. It never got easier.

After lunch, Cricket plated the baked goods, arranging them neatly on dishes she'd found at thrift stores or flea markets. Cricket admired her handiwork. Rich chocolate brownies sat on a red and white striped serving plate, lemon bars lay fanned out on a royal blue delft platter, cookies rested on an amber depression glass serving dish, and the tall, ambrosial-looking Hummingbird Cake took center stage on a milk glass cake plate.

Meetings were held on the three-season sunporch of Daddy's big house, the only room big enough to accommodate all of Cricket's staff. Though the meeting officially started at 5:15, staff members usually arrived early to eat and socialize. At a little after 5:00, Cricket and Pearl stood side by side, calling out greetings to helpers as they arrived.

"We are all set to go." With beringed fingers, Pearl patted her hair, which today was brunette with gold highlights and slicked back into a French knot that trailed ringlets.

As she heard helpers' cars pulling up outside, Cricket felt a sense of satisfaction. All of her employees were planning to attend, except for Linda, who was throwing a surprise party for her husband.

"We're going to have a nice crowd," she murmured to Pearl.

Pearl nodded approvingly. "You *do* feed 'em good."

But they both knew that it was more than just the food she served. Cricket paid her helpers more than the going rate, which helped morale, but one of the main reasons her brief monthly staff meetings were always well-attended was because the helpers enjoyed the opportunity to socialize with their peers. Caregiving could be a lonely business, especially for helpers who worked with clients with memory problems.

Carmen arrived, looking subdued and red-eyed.

Cricket approached her and gave her a hug, "I hear Mr. John's holding his own. You did great today, Carmen. I'm really proud of you."

With a shaky finger, Carmen wiped away brimming tears. "Thanks. He's a sweet ole fellow."

Giving her shoulder a brief squeeze, Cricket pointed her toward the food table. "Go get you some goodies."

All the others arrived. Cricket was pleased as she saw a helper sigh rapturously after she took a bite of the Hummingbird Cake. The section of the table with the platter of the raw vegetables and dip was as lonely as a ghost town.

Josie stood hesitantly at the door, shifting her weight from one foot to the other as she glanced nervously around at the other chatting helpers.

Pearl slipped over to her. "Afternoon, Josie. Come on over here and get you some refreshments. Tell me how you're liking things so far." Patting the woman on her shoulder, Pearl steered her toward the food table.

Surreptitiously, Cricket stood on the outskirts of the conversation groups, trying to listen and see if she might pick up any discontent about her agency or gripes about clients. All she heard was cheerful banter and gentle teasing.

Next, Cricket focused on the three helpers who'd worked with the missing clients, Tara, Marla, and Florence. All seemed like such straight arrows but knowing who to trust was hard.

Pearl went over to greet Tara, a Jersey transplant, who wore a studded leather biker jacket and a one-inch buzz cut of red-orange hair. She was gentle and adept at sweet-talking the balkiest clients into bathing or taking their medicine. Cricket did have to ask her to button her shirt one button higher, so cleavage and her scorpion tattoo didn't show so much, but once clients got past her tough-girl veneer, usually they didn't want to work with anyone but Tara.

Still, Cricket eyed her. Maybe her clients' children were put off by her appearance, or maybe she wasn't as sweet and gentle as Cricket and Pearl thought.

Cricket welcomed Marla, a good-natured woman who was an experienced caregiver. She clomped around in her comfortable clogs, voluntarily wore scrubs, and kept a large print Sudoku book in her purse for when things got quiet. She was kind, steady, and calm in handling dicey situations—like when Mrs. Vickers had a stroke or Mr. Ames started answering the door without wearing britches. Cricket never had one complaint about Marla, though she was deeply religious and tended to talk about it. Could she have been too churchy with people or tried to convince them they needed to be saved? Cricket rubbed the back of her neck.

Florence was a curvy gal in her mid-sixties who talked a lot, mostly about the latest diet she was on, such as the baby food diet, the Shangri-La diet, or the apple cider vinegar diet. She was standing beside a wide-eyed Josie, shoveling in Hummingbird Cake and talking rapidly between bites. "I'm the same age as Christie Brinkley, who is one of my all-time celebrity favorites, and she uses the watercress soup diet—the same one I'm on—and..."

Sipping ice water, Cricket watched as Pearl glided over to rescue the increasingly desperate-looking Josie. Though she genuinely liked the helper, if Cricket spent four or eight hours a day with Florence getting diet tips, she would have to strangle the woman or strangle herself, although she wasn't exactly sure of the logistics for the latter. Yet Florence was sweet and meant well. Clients praised her liveliness and cheerful energy, but could her chattiness have driven people away?

Their youngest helper, Randy, slipped in one minute before the meeting was to start. He wore skinny jeans, a bored expression, and hipster sunglasses so black you couldn't see his eyes. When he took off his shades, he gave the others a warm sunbeam of a smile that lit up the room. The women grinned and waved at him, several patting the empty chairs beside them. The caregivers loved to mother and cluck over Randy, and they were all so proud of their college man.

"Good afternoon." Cricket waved both her arms to get everyone's attention.

With some good-natured grumbling, the helpers shuffled to their seats.

She and Pearl co-led the meeting, keeping it brief and fast-moving.

Cricket started by sharing some industry news about slowing dementia in seniors. "So, those of you who are doing jigsaw puzzles, crosswords, and playing Scrabble with clients, keep it up."

Marla proudly held her Sudoku book aloft. "I buy these for my clients too. They love them. Two for a buck at the dollar store."

"Good initiative," Cricket said. "If they don't like that kind of thing, talk to them about current events. If you have clients who tend to watch TV too much, work on ways to get their minds active." She pointed out the window and the sunny late afternoon. "Let's get our folks outside more. Can we start taking more walks with them, take them to the lake, and bring lunches outside for picnics now that the weather's getting nicer?"

Many helpers bobbed their heads at her suggestions.

"A reminder. Please give us as much advance notice as you can about needing time off. In the last month, a few of you, whose names I will not mention, have asked for time off for a non-emergency with not much notice." Cricket swept her eyes over the group. "Also, please don't come to work if you don't feel good. Our clients don't have the strongest immune systems. We want to keep them healthy." Many of the helpers bobbed their heads in agreement. "I'm turning the meeting over to Pearl." Cricket held out a hand and pointed to her assistant. "As you know, Pearl is taking on a supervisory role and will be handling more of the day-to-day business here."

"Thanks, Cricket." Pearl flushed pink with pride as she rose. "I've got shifts that need to be covered. Call or text me if you want to pick up some extra money by helping out with any of these hours." She read aloud available days and hours. Pausing, Pearl looked up at the group. "We had an occupational therapist come to talk with us last week about the best way to help a client out of bed while protecting your own back. Can one of y'all come help demonstrate?"

With an impish grin, Tara's hand shot up.

"Come up here, young lady." Pearl had a twinkle in her eye as she patted the table that she and Cricket had dragged in from the yard just for the demonstration.

Toeing off motorcycle boots, Tara nimbly jumped onto the table. She reclined, hamming it up with a tragic expression and a wrist over her forehead.

Pearl tried to hide her grin as Tara clutched at her chest, rolled her eyes, and did a bucking, writhing movement, clearly in the throes of death.

"You're reclining, not dying," Pearl said dryly. Planting her feet, she bent her knees, sucked in her abdomen, squared her shoulders, and held out a sturdy forearm.

Tara grasped Pearl's arm and easily pulled herself up.

Grinning, the helpers hooted, clapping as Tara hopped down and did several elaborate curtsies.

Pearl gave her a fist bump. "Thank you, Ms. Tara." Now solemn, she met the eyes of several helpers. "We want you to take care of your backs. Please transfer clients the way we showed you. If you have a tricky back, you know how easy it is to throw it out of whack. This is one simple way to make sure you don't." She turned to Cricket. "You ready to close this show up?"

"Yes, ma'am. But I've got good news to pass on." At the end of each meeting, Cricket had started having a good news segment where she shared praise she'd gotten about a helper. "I want to remind you of just how important your work is. Every day, you all change lives for the better." Cricket glanced meaningfully at the group and held up a flowered card. "I received this note from the son of one of our favorite clients, Mr. Barefoot, who passed away recently. Mr. Barefoot was Randy's client."

Randy, a redhead, had a face that flamed whenever he felt strongly about something. Now, his cheeks were pink as steamed shrimp. Randy was finishing up his degree at Somerset College, and in the fall, he was bound for graduate school in education at the University of North Carolina at Wilmington.

"Mr. Barefoot's daughter wrote, 'I can't begin to tell you what an excellent helper and companion Randy McNeil was to my father in the final year of his life. Mr. McNeil was professional and pleasant, but he also was so kind to my daddy. They played chess together and watched the DVDs on the history of the presidents. He asked my father about his experiences flying bombers in World War II. There was a mutual respect between the two of them, and Mr. McNeil added meaning and love to my daddy's life. Please thank him for us and know that you have a fine young man in your employ. We wish him all the best in his future, which promises to be bright. We believe he was a godsend. Thank you from every member of our family. Best Regards, Jane Barefoot Randolph.' "

Cricket blinked, moved by the note. Her helpers were similarly touched. Tears trickled down Marla's face, and she blotted them with a paper napkin. Others dabbed at their eyes. Several helpers slowly began to clap. Soon, the whole group was applauding.

The helpers seated beside Randy clapped him on the back.

Feeling a swell of pride for her group, Cricket used her fingers to brush back her own tears. "Meeting adjourned."

After more visiting and munching, the last helpers left the room.

"You did really well at the meeting, Pearl." Cricket slipped chairs back underneath the table.

"Thank you." The corners of Pearl's mouth turned up as she gathered up paper plates and napkins.

Picking up empty drink cups and tossing them, Cricket turned to Pearl. "I'm having trouble seeing any of the helpers who worked with the MIA clients causing problems. What's your take?"

"I still can't see it, but I could be wrong." Pearl covered the brownies in plastic wrap.

"Still, we need to talk with them again, more in-depth. Can you do that over the next few days?" Cricket packed the last of the food in storage dishes.

"I will." Pearl's eyes sparkled, looking excited about the responsibility she was being given.

"Let's visit those missing clients next week." Cricket realized the truth of her father's words about small problems snowballing. "We'll bring them pies again. We'll get to the bottom of this mess."

"Right." Pearl grinned, looking eager at the prospect. "We'll be just like lady detectives on television."

After Pearl left, Cricket locked up the house, still buzzing with good feelings about the meeting and their plan to fix the work problem. As she trudged up the stairs to the apartment, Honey rang.

"Hello, girly. I'm downtown, waiting for my Italian class to start. We still on for picking strawberries this Friday?"

"Yes, ma'am." Cricket huffed as she got to the top few stairs.

"*Favoloso.* We can talk about our camping trip slash manhunt," Honey said, sounding girlish.

"We sure can," Cricket said, thinking how crazy the whole idea was.

"I need to skedaddle. My stylishly dressed and *molto bello* Italian instructor, Giorgio, just walked in," she said in a stage whisper. "Ciao, sugar."

Kicking off her shoes, Cricket poured herself a glass of wine, foraged in the fridge, and put a hunk of leftover lasagna into the oven to warm. Slipping into a t-shirt, her fuzziest fleece top, and fleece sweatpants, Cricket stretched out on the velvet sofa. She covered herself with an afghan. The day had been busy, and she was ready to just chill.

Angus sprang gracefully up beside her, curling up in what he considered to be a snug ball, though he was partially on top of her and partially in a space on the couch. Reaching for the stack of mail, Cricket glanced through it. Flipping through the bundle, she pulled out the letters and bills. She set aside the junk mail to put in recycling.

With a sigh of pleasure, Cricket pulled out the catalogs. Lately, she couldn't concentrate enough to read a good book. Catalogs calmed her frayed nerves. Adjusting the pillow that propped up her head, Cricket draped her legs over Angus and peeked into a sunlit, dappled world of women in *Soft Surroundings, Sundance, Garnet Hill,* and *J Jill.* Those women knew how to live life, floating around in earth tone-colored linens with sexy over-blouses that hid any age-related gravitational problems.

Flipping through the pages, Cricket felt a flash of envy. After finishing a watercolor painting, the next chapter in their novel, or selling their small business for a fortune, these serene gals looked out the window of their villas in Santa Fe or waterfront homes in Newport Beach, waiting for their wealthy but attentive husbands or man friends to come home from work.

Putting down the glossy catalogs, Cricket glanced at the small corkboard beside her Formica desk. As she saw the handwritten thank you notes from clients and their families, she felt better about her life. Whether written on pink floral cards or expensively monogrammed letterhead, in the shaky script of an eighty-year-old or the bold script of a busy son or daughter, the message was the same: What her little business did changed people's lives for the better.

Cricket wouldn't trade her hectic—sometimes frustrating—but always meaningful life for the lovely, airbrushed world of the catalog women. Well, except she'd like the attentive, loving man coming home to *her*. Again, Cricket thought about that hunky Hank Mayfield. Grabbing a dayglow green sticky pad, she wrote herself a note with a red sharpie.

Figure out a way to run into Hank again soon!

CHAPTER 12

THURSDAY MORNING WAS DRIZZLY AND gray. After Cricket and Pearl manned the phones and got everyone settled down, Pearl left for a continuing education course. Cricket was enjoying her coffee and combing giant puffs of hair from Angus's winter coat when she heard the distinctive pulsing rattle of her aunt's blue 1964 Volkswagen Beetle. A rap sounded at her door. The dog gave a quick bark, ran to the door, and began sniffing and whining with excitement.

Cricket briskly hugged her Aunt Joy, who looked slim and sporty in her white velour zip-up jacket and khakis. "Good morning. It's soggy out."

"April showers bring May flowers." Joy gave her umbrella a shake, leaving it outside the door.

"Come sit. Can I get you some coffee?" Cricket asked.

"No, dear. I know you're busy." Joy scratched Angus behind his ears, smiling adoringly at him. "You can show me the ropes about what I need to do as dog sitter for this noble fellow, and I'll be on my way."

Cricket felt a flash of guilt. Dog-sitting Angus wasn't that complicated. Joy could easily have just stopped by the apartment a few times a day instead of staying over, but

Cricket needed her to stay there to maximize the possibility that her matchmaking went as planned.

Cricket handed her aunt a two-page list, a fluff-filled, overly detailed set of instructions she'd come up with to justify the need for Joy to stay. "Here's Angus's feeding schedule. Remember not to go overboard on the kibble even if he tries to look hungry. He's scared of thunderstorms, so if one comes up, you can just put him in the bedroom and turn the white noise machine on high. That keeps him calm."

Joy nodded earnestly.

Cricket described which collar he should wear for walking versus which he should wear in the yard and reviewed the map she'd drawn of the most scenic and least-trafficked walking routes. As she wound down, she stroked the big dog, knit her brows, and tried to look concerned. "I'm so glad you'll be here because Angus gets so nervous when I leave." Groaning, Angus sprawled on the floor, stuck out a long tongue, and gave the old college try to drink from his water bowl while reclining. "So nervous," Cricket reiterated.

"You sweet little thing." Joy crouched to pat Angus.

Next, Cricket showed her how to jiggle the handle on the toilet so it wouldn't run, how the washer-dryer combo worked, and she demonstrated how a right-hip bump to the door helped the spare key work properly.

Joy's eyes started to dart about, signaling the end of her patience. She looked down at her list and back at Cricket. "You're only going to be gone for three days, right?"

"Yes." Cricket flushed.

"Right. Well, I think that about covers it," Joy said hastily. "If I have any problems, I'll just call you."

"Just one more thing," Cricket said, taking Joy's arm and leading her over to the front window. She pointed to Mr. P on his glider. "That's the neighbor I mentioned to you, Jackson Purefoy, the one who was so recently widowed…" Well, ten years ago, but widowed was widowed.

"That poor man. That poor, poor man." Joy peered out the window. "He's the one who only eats frozen dinners?"

Cricket tried telling herself she was not really lying. Last night, Mr. P had grilled baby back ribs he'd made with a special rub and braised brussels sprouts with a recipe he'd gotten from *Southern Living*, but those ingredients may have been frozen at one point.

Joy shook her head, tsking in sympathy. "When I drove up, he was just sitting there on his porch in the rain."

Cricket knew Mr. P was probably listening to Hannity on the radio, and in his head, he was writing an indignant letter to the editor of the *Charlotte Observer*, blasting them for perpetuating the myth about rising sea levels. He was probably also mentally chiding readers for traveling to Cuba because "Castro is still in charge and it's still Communist, people." Cricket nodded solemnly. "Yes, it's so sad. So if you get a chance to just say hello, or even bring him a meal, you'd just brighten his day."

"Well, of course I will," Joy said staunchly. "The good Lord put us on the earth to bring sunshine into other peoples' lives. He wouldn't want any one of his flock to be lonely or forgotten."

"I agree," Cricket murmured, wondering if she was in hot water with the big guy for lying.

Patting her aunt's shoulder to say goodbye, Cricket saw her out and closed the door. *Whew.* The tap dancing and scene-setting involved in playing Cupid were exhausting.

Friday morning was drizzly, too, but the showers passed. The day grew sunny, and the sky was blue. A little before noon, Cricket's car tires crunched into the gravel lot of Becky's Berries. Honey was waving madly out the window of a sporty-looking red car, whose back end was raised up higher than its front.

Cricket grinned, pulled into the empty parking spot beside her friend, and stepped out. "Hey, sweets."

"*Buongiorno, bella.*" Honey locked her doors and extravagantly kissed her on both cheeks in the way she sometimes did since she started the Italian lessons.

"New ride?" Cricket hooked a thumb toward the jacked-up car.

Honey beamed. "Daddy Jay again. This little baby was sitting on the lot. I always wanted to drive a car like this." Looking pleased with herself, she patted the car.

"It's a looker," Cricket said.

"Thanks." Honey preened at the compliment for her car. "Can we eat lunch after we pick? I want to try that new place, Sissy's Sandwiches. We can get our lunch to go, maybe eat by the lake. We can talk about our mountain trip."

Cricket paused, thinking about the paperwork piling up on her desk and the payroll that was due tomorrow. But it was a glorious spring day, and she was with her best friend. How could she turn down the offer? "Sure."

"Yay!" Honey hugged Cricket. Keeping an arm across her shoulder, she walked Cricket toward the weighing and paying station for the berries. "Let's get to pickin', girly."

Honey skipped, pulling a reluctant Cricket along with her. Laughing, Cricket let herself be pulled and gave skipping a whirl. An older couple walking by watched them, enjoying their foolishness.

While Honey walked ahead in the mounded-up rows to look for the most untouched patches of berries, Cricket stood with her hands on her hips and breathed deeply, catching a scent of wood smoke and damp earth. She took in the perfect blue sky with a puff or two of white clouds rolling by and the expanse of green fields rolling out all around them. It was a perfect Carolina spring day.

Remembering her gratitude list, Cricket sent up a quick prayer. *I'm grateful for this glorious day and for You making plants as wonderful as strawberries. I'm grateful for loyal, funny friends. I thank You for the loveliness of this place and for spring.* She paused, deciding whether she'd throw in the not-very-Christian kicker. *I'd be grateful if Knox ate bad mayonnaise and had gastrointestinal problems while on a climb with his new flame.* There. All done.

"Girl, up here." Honey beckoned her to a spot halfway down the line two rows over. "No one's been here, and the berries are beauties."

Plastic bucket in hand, Cricket crouched and searched for the plumpest, brightest fruit. The two worked quietly, plucking ripe, red berries and placing them gently in their buckets. The prettiest fruits were tucked beneath bright green leaves, brilliant as rubies against the golden straw used for mulch. Feeling a twinge of guilt, Cricket popped a berry in her mouth. Closing her eyes, she savored its sweet juiciness. She glanced over at Honey, who was also sampling the fruit with an impish grin on her face.

"The sign at the pay station said we were welcome to sample a few," Honey reminded her. "You were having good-girl worries about stealing. Am I right?"

"You're right." Cricket should be used to Honey's mindreading skills by now.

After finding a good haul of plump, perfect berries,

the two paid up and headed to the parking lot. Their buckets of berries safely wedged in the trunks of their respective cars, they agreed to drive together and talked about which car to take.

"I feel like being driven," Honey announced grandly, lifting her nose in the air.

Cricket snickered. "Get in, princess."

Honey hopped in, and Cricket drove them downtown. At Sissy's takeout window, they studied the menus.

Honey murmured quietly, "I've heard their pimiento cheese is scrumptious—fresh as can be, with a little bite to it."

"Then that's what I'm having." Cricket closed her menu.

"On to the lake."

As Cricket nosed her car from her parking spot, a couple stepped out in the street in front of her, and she waved them on. The man patted the woman's rear end, and she giggled. Bottom-patting in public was just plain tacky.

Slipping on her sunglasses, Cricket got a better look at the man and scowled. It was Clayton. Without pausing to think about it, she slammed her palm down on the horn, holding it there. Sticking her hand out the open window, she gave a manic wave. Clayton did a double take and panicked. He lunged toward the blue Mercedes with the "Random Acts of Kindness" bumper sticker, dragging yet another startled coed along by the arm.

Feeling oddly calm, Cricket slowly pulled onto Main Street.

Honey examined a nail. “Clayton, I presume.”

Cricket nodded, hearing blood rushing in her ears. She turned to her friend. “Why am I acting like a stalker?”

Honey waved a hand. “Garden variety transference, or is it displacement? You project emotions meant for one person to another. You bared your teeth like Jack Nicholson did in that scary movie.” She chuckled. “You need to put things to rest with Knox before you scare that poor professor to death.”

Cricket felt better. If Honey, an almost-practicing psychologist, thought she wasn’t crazy, that was good enough for her. And instead of transferring anger to other men, she’d make a special delivery to Knox.

At Azalea Lake, they settled in on two Adirondack chairs, Lexie Lillington’s gay divorcee chair and a new one that Ivy Pratt had bought in memory of her husband of thirty years, Emory. The plaque read, “A fine husband and father, love of my life, once bowled a 300.” Cricket chose that chair and gave the arms a friendly pat, saying hello to Emory.

Quiet for a few moments, the two savored their sandwiches and enjoyed the view of the lake that was blue-green today. A young woman in a long skirt sat leaning against a tree reading, a group of seniors went through their stances in a tai chi class, and several mothers chatted a mile a minute as they watched their toddlers play.

An elegant heron winged by, almost skimming the water. An osprey dove feetfirst into the water and came up with a fish. The soft breeze ruffled their hair.

With regret, Cricket swallowed her last bite of tastiness and took a swallow of tea. "Stellar sandwich, and what a dazzler of a day."

"I so agree on both," Honey enthused.

Two kayaks glided by. Cricket pointed at them with her cup of iced tea. "Did I tell you that Angus and I are big kayakers now?"

Honey looked enthralled. "Is that right? So exciting."

She cracked a smile. "Well, we've only been once, but we've got big plans to go again. We both did okay and didn't tip over."

Honey shook her head admiringly. She'd always been a big fan of Angus's. "I'm not surprised y'all were so good. You two can do whatever you set your minds to." Pausing, she pulled a small notebook and pen from her purse. "May I go over my packing lists, and can we talk about our Asheville plans? We leave in just seven days."

"Sure." Cricket wondered if it was excitement or dread thrumming in her stomach. *Fifty-fifty,* she decided.

"Here's what I'm bringing." Noisily sipping the last of her drink, Honey rattled off her list. Finally, she finished and chewed the end of her pen. "Did I miss anything?"

"Sounds…thorough. You're ready for anything," Cricket said tactfully.

"Thanks." Honey looked proud. "Any updates from Knox?"

"Knox and his rock stars are still on for the climbing clinic. They've been hyping it on social media. Workshops and demonstrations all day Saturday and Sunday."

"Good." Honey glanced again at her notebook. "I made reservations for us at the Thunderbird Resort, a nice campground with a lake, bocce, and shuffleboard courts."

Cricket groaned. "You still want to camp. I was hoping that was a whim."

"No, ma'am. We want the whole back-to-nature experience." Honey took her pen, making a little checkmark beside an item on her list.

Cricket grimaced. "The last time I camped, it rained buckets. Bears ate our food. I was afraid to go to the bathroom because I thought wildlife might eat me." She could not quite believe she'd agreed to sleep in a tent again.

Honey lifted her chin. "You need to camp. It's just like getting back on the horse that threw you. You need a corrective emotional experience."

Cricket rolled her eyes, but she thought again how lucky she was to have a friend willing to drop everything and go to Asheville to help her go a round or two with her ex-husband. "For you, I'll camp. I said I would, and I will."

"Good," Honey said firmly. "You don't even have to lift a pinky finger. I've found the quickest routes and put them in Waze. I researched the best restaurants on TripAdvisor. No eating freeze-dried hamburger casserole for us." She shuddered prettily. "I'm bringing sleeping bags, a tent, and gear the boys got when they were still in Boy Scouts. Oh, and the Keurig." Check, check, check went her pen on the pad.

Cricket wondered where Honey thought she'd plug in the coffee maker but didn't say anything. The realization that she'd be seeing her ex-husband for the first time in almost two years, however, was sinking in, and Cricket suddenly felt a heavy, bleak sense of dread.

Staring at the lake unseeingly, Cricket turned to Honey. "What am I going to say when I see Knox?"

Honey just arched a brow at her. "Seems like you only want to know one thing."

Cricket nodded glumly. "Why? I just want to know why?"

Honey squeezed her arm. "You can do this, girl. You need to do this."

"I know." Cricket heaved a sigh.

Sunday morning, Cricket was in a funk.

Weekends can be hard for single gals, Cricket thought glumly as she brushed her teeth and pulled her hair into a ponytail.

All that unplanned time could lead to rumination and dwelling on missteps she'd made in her life, not a thought process that made for a happy day. Making herself another cup of coffee, Cricket slipped on sweats and went to collect Daddy's mail. While she was downstairs, she walked around a sunny little plot of grass she was considering rototilling and planting with cheerful flowers—maybe zinnias, poppies, or lavender if the soil allowed. That would give her something bright and colorful to see every time she went outside and into the yard.

After answering emails that had come in Friday evening, Cricket looked up the growing zones for Azalea. They were in zone 7A, so zinnias and poppies should do fine, but lavender had trouble with humidity, so they might not thrive. She'd give it a whirl anyhow, Cricket stubbornly decided. Now, she needed to figure out how to get Daddy's rototiller running.

Bringing her phone with her into the yard, Cricket swatted away mosquitos as she watched a quick YouTube tutorial shot by a guy drinking beer, cracking bad jokes, and wearing flip-flops. If he could do it, she could do it.

Rolling the beast of a rototiller out of the garage, Cricket checked the oil and gas levels. After giving the starter cord a few strong pulls, the engine sputtered and roared to life. Cricket had never driven a rototiller, so she just pointed it in the right direction, leaned into it, and put it in gear. Cricket couldn't stop grinning as it roared off, and she held on for dear life.

When she finished, the small square she'd pictured had become a 16x20 bed of dirt with raggedy edges. Still, Cricket stood back admiring the plot. The garden would be eye-catching and brighten the yard. She was sure Daddy wouldn't mind.

Upstairs, Cricket drank two full glasses of cold water, cleaned up, and took a break for lunch. While working her way through a tuna salad, she checked Facebook and saw posts from two women she knew from college. On the beach at sunset, Cheryl, a former mean girl, stood with her wholesome-looking family, who were all dressed in matching blue shirts. Lisa and her husband beamed in the photo taken from a gondola in Venice, or Vegas. Lisa had unusually plump lips now, and her husband—Cricket had heard he was her third—looked at her adoringly. The caption read, "That's amore!" Cricket groaned aloud. Why did she look at these doctored-up versions of peoples' lives?

Before Cricket knew it, she was on Knox's Instagram. Today, there were two shots, one of him perched on the side of a huge cliff, his hands and feet dug into tiny gaps in the rock. The other was a sunset shot of a young woman climbing. Though the shot was taken from far away, Cricket thought she might be the gal with the fox tattoo.

Disgusted with herself, Cricket closed out the screen. She *had* to stop doing this. It was ridiculous to be checking Knox's posts. She'd see him soon and put this mess to rest.

Clicking around, Cricket distracted herself by watching a few enlightening slide shows on her home page, including "10 Ways to Whittle Your Waistline While

Watching Television" and "5 Things That Make Men Go Ga-Ga for Older Women." On to the shoe sites. She scrolled through the latest five-star strappy sandals at ShoesToGo but kept thinking about the foxy lady in Knox's post. Her finger hovered over the mouse. With a click, she was examining those Scarlet Cloud running shoes.

Twice, Cricket read the details of the "air cushion ride" and "spring coil stability sole" that one buyer said gave her "a dreamlike ride through the universe." Who was the mystery woman in the photo? She thought about all the pics she'd been in. There was something about the way the rock gods looked at her that made Cricket think they were at ease with her. Who was she to Knox, and how did she fit in so cozily with that group of alpha males? How old was she? Her leg looked prettily muscled and young.

Cricket touched her own leg, trim from walking but slightly stringy and festooned with skin that was getting crepey. Add the clunky black brace with the Velcro straps that she had to wear when her knee bothered her, and Cricket shook her head, wondering yet again how she had gotten so old. The clock was ticking. She'd been dawdling. Time to get on with her life.

CHAPTER 13

PRACTICALLY CRACKLING WITH RESTLESS ENERGY, Cricket threw on a light jacket, rounded up Angus, and took off at a fast clip. The sun was still shining as she got her second wind. She and Angus did an interval walk, trot, and walk around the neighborhood.

Angus trotted along but looked back at her, watchful, seeming to sense her restlessness. The big dog was a perfect gentleman on the first leg of the walk. He did not try to drag her into Azalea Lake and refrained from launching himself at a few ducks paddling by. He did not make his usual screeching stops to indignantly sniff the pee other dogs had left on signs, then huffily raise his own leg on those spots. Leaving the lake behind, they strode toward town. At the Wayne House, Cricket was disappointed when she didn't see the shiny burgundy Mayfield and Company van.

Heading home, Cricket felt calmer. After thirty minutes of moving fast and puffing up hills, her equilibrium had returned. Her edginess dissipated, Cricket felt flexible and stronger. On the last leg of the walk, Cricket saw the raggedy white truck parked outside the pink house again. Her palms went clammy. Craning her neck, she was trying to get a glimpse of the driver when a squirrel darted this way and that, bounding across their path. Angus lunged forward. Cricket tripped on the oak tree root protruding from the old sidewalk and flew forward, slamming hard into the ground.

Oomph. Cricket saw stars but kept a death grip on the leash. Angus dragged her forward across the dirt, headed toward the street, but Cricket held on. A Mercedes approached, zooming too fast. Angus was less than a foot from the blacktop and still straining at his leash to follow the squirrel across the street.

"Stop, Angus. Stop," Cricket called, but her voice was reedy and weak.

The black car was bearing down on him. Holding the leash with every ounce of strength she had left, Cricket's heart slammed in her chest and her breathing stopped.

Please, God. Please, God. Please, God, she thought. Seconds later, Cricket saw a man's boot on the leash and felt a hand on her shoulder. Dazed and terrified, she looked up.

There was Hank. Calm, capable Hank with his kind eyes. Cricket burst into tears.

"It's okay, Cricket. I'm here." His brown eyes lit with worry. He pulled Angus toward him and stood firmly on his leash. Hank took the tail of his blue chambray shirt and gently brushed dirt from Cricket's face, wiping away her tears. "You're okay, and your buddy is too."

Cricket closed her eyes, the flood gates opening on all the sorrow she'd held inside for too long. Her tears turned to racking sobs. What if Angus had been killed? She could never forgive herself. Why did bad things keep happening to her? Why was everyone else finding love except her? Why did everyone keep leaving her?

Hank tried to take the leash from her, but Cricket held on, crying too hard to think.

"You're safe now, Cricket. Let it go. I've got it." Hank pried her fingers one at a time off Angus's leash, sat her up, and lowered himself beside her in the dirt. Patting her on the arm, he waited out her tears.

Angus hovered over Cricket, whining and licking her face. After a few minutes, Cricket's tears slowed. She circled her arms around the dog and hugged him.

His strong hands on her shoulders, Hank helped her up. He gave her a level gaze. "What's hurt?"

She held up her hands that were bleeding from her drag across the sidewalk. "I think it's just scrapes."

Hank took them in his big, work-calloused hands and gently examined her palms, her fingers, her wrists, and the back of her hands. Cricket gave an involuntary sigh. Hearing herself, she flushed bright red.

"Think you're all right. We can clean these up and bandage them." He gave a wry grin. "I keep a first-aid kit in the truck. Hands get banged up in my work."

She nodded, feeling tears welling again at his concern.

"Anything else hurt?" Hank looked at her gravely. "Did you hit your head?"

"Not hard. Caught most of the fall with my hands and knees." She wiped her still-wet face with the sleeve of her t-shirt, breathing normally now. "Whew."

He watched her, his brows drawn in concern. "Let's get you standing. See how those strong legs of yours fared."

"Ow." Cricket winced as she put her weight on her right ankle and felt a sharp pain.

When he put an arm around her shoulder to steady her, she blushed furiously.

Cautiously trying again, Cricket found she could stand. "I don't think anything's broken."

"Good." When Hank let go of her shoulder, Cricket felt a pang of longing. She missed his steadying hand already.

Leaning over with his hands on his knees, Hank touched the side of her abraded knee to examine it, and though it hurt, Cricket was struck by a lightning bolt of pure attraction.

Good Lord. Even crying, banged up, and stumbling, she felt the charge of electricity at his touch. "I'm okay," Cricket muttered.

Hank raised a brow, unconvinced. "You sure?"

She nodded. "I'll just ice everything and take a few Aleve."

"Let me at least give you a lift home," Hank said. "Where do you live?"

She pointed to her house, not twenty feet away. "I live in an apartment there."

Hank shook his head, grinning. "You'll never guess where I just bought a house. Right there." Looking proud, he pointed to the pink house. "The owners let me come by to size up repairs before the closing."

Shocked, Cricket just stared at him. "But I wanted that house," she cried, petulant as a four-year-old. Snatching the leash away from him, Cricket pulled Angus in close, glaring at Hank.

Holding his hands with palms up, Hank tilted his head to one side. "I wanted it too."

Was he the money man for the frat pack? She threw up her hands, glaring at him. "I thought you were such a nice guy, but you're not. You're only in it for yourself."

Hank rocked on his heels, stuck his hands in his pockets, and glanced away as though looking for answers.

Cricket tried to calm down, but she couldn't. "And why a rental party house for alumni? Aren't there better ways to make money? AirLodgings like that can ruin stable, historic neighborhoods."

"Possibly." Hank scratched his chin, looking thoughtful. "I'm not quite tracking with you."

"Of course, you're not," Cricket snapped, disgusted.

"You sure you didn't hit your head?" Hank's eyes flicked over her, looking concerned.

"I didn't." Guessing she was overreacting, Cricket thought of Honey's transference theory and flushed. "Sorry. I'm mad at everybody. I love your pink house and put in an offer on it, but you got it." Swallowing hard, Cricket tried not to cry again.

"Plus, you had a tough fall," he said quietly.

His kindness made the tears start again. "I'm going to the mountains next weekend to try to find my ex-husband and learn why he deserted me." *Why* was she over-sharing?

"Gotcha." Hank gave a matter-of-fact nod like he heard stories like this all the time.

Cricket felt herself softening toward him but remembered what he was planning for the pink house.

She'd just had her fill of men who couldn't take responsibility for what they did. Why was it so hard for men to just step up? Couldn't he just say, "I'm in to make a buck, and tough turnips about the house or the neighbors?" She started to hobble toward the house, turned, and shot daggers at him. "Is that your truck?"

"It is." Hank rubbed his head, looking chagrinned. "Haven't had a chance to spruce her up. Sold it to my nephew on the payment plan, he stopped paying, and I took her back."

Cricket pointed at it. "Well, *she* backfires and spews black smoke."

She stalked toward the house. If Cricket concentrated on the pain in her knees, she didn't feel her ankle so much. Angus walked beside her, now as perfectly behaved as a champion in the Westminster Dog Show.

"Oh, Cricket," Hank called in a gravelly drawl.

She turned and shot him a hard look, hand on hip.

"Better ice that eye. You're going to have a shiner tomorrow," he said softly, his eyes holding hers.

Cricket wanted to look away and huff off, but she couldn't. Her eyes locked on his, and she felt a wave of attraction so powerful that she trembled.

Raising his hand, Hank gave a crooked smile and ambled toward his truck.

Monday morning, Cricket was feeling the fall from the day before. Although she'd iced and elevated her ankle, she limped along. Her hands and knees were sore too, despite the doses of Aleve she'd taken. Shuffling into the bathroom, she caught a glimpse of herself in the mirror and breathed in sharply. Pulling her auburn curls back from her face, Cricket studied her bruised right cheek and eye that had turned a soft violet color, despite the bag of frozen peas she'd pressed on them the night before. Gingerly, she washed her face with a cool facecloth.

Cricket texted Honey. *Had a fall while walking Angus. Am okay, just banged up.*

Honey's response came back almost immediately. *Oh, you poor little thing. Are you really okay???? Send pics.*

Grinning, Cricket took photos of her shiner and other injuries and sent them to her friend. *DELETE immediately,* she texted. *Guess who rescued me and is the almost new owner of the pink house?*

Honey responded, *Re rescuer/new neighbor, must be that hottie, Hank.*

Almost immediately after came another text from her. *Yowsa! Re injuries: You poor little thing! Go to doctor if you need to. Are you well enough to travel?*

Yes. Let's get this done, Cricket tapped into her phone.

Honey responded by sending an emoji of a woman black belt giving baddies karate chops and leaping into the air to give them roundhouse kicks.

Cricket burst out laughing as she put her phone up. Stepping gingerly on her sore ankle, she got ready for work. In the bathroom mirror, she winced when she caught a glimpse of her face. Cricket's black eye was impressive, her eyeball was bloodshot, and the area around her shiner was blossoming into a purple and green splotch. She grimaced.

Holy smokes. Cricket hoped it was gone or almost gone for their mountain trip.

That afternoon, between answering phones and responding to email and texts, Cricket started to pack for the trip. Mountain mornings and evenings in late April would be chilly. In the closet, she stared at her teal-colored fleece, the lightweight peach cashmere sweater she'd found at a thrift store, and the dark purple performance-rated shell she'd bought on sale at the outlets. Cricket had so few clothes. Besides her fondness for shoe sites, she viewed shopping as a necessary evil.

Honey had raised the idea of wearing disguises, but at the time, Cricket thought the idea silly. Why not just walk up to Knox, bold as a monkey, and confront him? Pinching her lip, Cricket thought about it. Maybe she *should* surprise him. She could get a good look at him and his new life and maybe understand it more. Cricket could watch him with all his rock groupies, the foxy girl with the expensive red shoes, and his possible boyfriend, one of the young and buff rock-climbing buddies with gold-streaked hair. Spying on him would probably help get to the truth faster than asking him to explain himself. Knox was, after all, an artful dodger.

Firmly closing the closet, she texted Honey. *Let's wear disguises.*

That evening, Cricket was feeling virtuous because she'd decided to cook an extra healthy supper instead of having pizza delivered. Spatula in hand, she was leaning on her good foot as she pushed around broccoli, peppers, snow peas, and carrots in a big frying pan. She heard the ping of an incoming text. Wiping her hands on a dish towel, she pushed back a lock of hair, put a lid on the pan, and moved it to the cool back burner.

Sinking down on the sofa, Cricket grinned as she read an extra-long text from Honey. *Re disguises: I'm on it. Looking at climbing magazine for wardrobe tips. Will also check with Josh re the look we should be going for. Lots of mountain women up in Blacksburg where he's at school. Look I'm going for: Brainy but sexy, free spirit who quits her corporate job and moves to mountains to reinvent herself. Works as barista to pay for rent and climbing habit. Favorite author of all time is Pam Houston. Loves blogs about hiking, rocks, and life.*

Texting Honey a thumbs up, Cricket shook her head, smiling at her thorough character analysis.

Tuesday passed quickly as Cricket and Pearl stayed on the go. When a helper's car broke down while she was driving a client home from a visit to the doctor, Pearl ran to pick up the two grateful women and arrange a tow. Cricket had to figure out the problem with the new accounting software and fix a software glitch in their website that caused the site to keep disappearing. With only two days left before the manhunt, Cricket moved as quickly as she could to fix problems, but she had trouble concentrating. If she hadn't stayed busy with work, she would have gotten even more anxious about seeing Knox and stewed even harder about Hank Mayfield's plans for the pink house.

After Pearl left for the day, Cricket stared balefully out the window at the house she should have had and sent up a quick prayer of gratitude. *God, I'm grateful if You keep Daddy safe and let him keep being happy. I'd appreciate if this trip to see Knox is successful and if the mortgage company finds that Hank Mayfield has a credit score of 300.*

Glancing at her to-do list, Cricket saw that she and Pearl were slated to do their drive-by reconnaissance on the missing clients later in the week, but she had time now. No reason she couldn't do a quick swing-by on her own. Cricket grabbed her purse and headed out the door, still limping from her recent tumble.

At Arleen Nelson's house, the yard was newly mowed and edged, and the smell of freshly cut grass still hung in the air. On the front porch, Cricket rang the doorbell and glanced at the small white wrought iron table on the porch that was filled with colorful pots, Arleen's herbs, and plant cuttings. An avocado seed was suspended by toothpicks over a green aluminum travel mug.

Just like at Cricket's last visit, no one came to the door.

Wilting, Cricket remembered her father's words about little problems snowballing and motored on to the other two clients' houses. She experienced the same disappointing results.

Cricket drummed her fingers on the steering wheel. She wasn't getting anywhere. She and Pearl would cruise by again.

Frustrated, Cricket decided to treat herself to an iced coffee at Pups and Pep. The barista with the painful-looking brow piercing surprised her with a dazzling smile as he handed her the drink. Cricket smiled back. Though she'd like to think it was because she looked friendly and nice, it was probably because he felt sorry for her about the shiner and the limp. Still, a sweet smile was a sweet smile. Cricket walked slowly to her little SUV, feeling expansive as she sipped the cool, reviving sweetness.

As she opened her door, Cricket heard a distinctive "Yoo-hoo!" She froze when she saw the European car with the sloping windows.

Gigi Gallagher's skinny arm snaked out of the window of her car in a big, friendly wave as she whipped into the parking space beside her.

Quickly, Cricket gave herself a pep talk. Even if Gigi was grating and competitive, Cricket could be Zen-like and magnanimous. At least she could act that way for a few minutes. Warily, she watched the woman step out of her car.

"Heeeey, there!" Gigi trilled as she minced over in her pencil skirt and chunky suede wedge booties. Coming closer, she put a hand to her mouth, leaning in to look more closely at Cricket's shiner. "Oh, your face looks ghastly, like you've been in a horrible, horrible car accident. Or had a facelift."

"Good to see you too, Gigi." Cricket reluctantly opened her car door.

Looking chic, Gigi's tailored jacket had a colorful scarf draped around her neck. A huge orange bag was slung over her shoulder. "We saw you at Senegal Siren a few weeks ago. Goodness, that was a fall. Not everyone can handle boots."

Cricket made herself unclench her teeth and said blandly, "Good food there."

"Yes." Gigi blinked, realizing her dig hadn't had its

intended consequence. She made a Vanna White hand gesture toward her purse. "Notice anything different?"

"New bag?" Cricket guessed.

"It's an Abbott," she purred, patting it reverently and doing a half-turn back and forth to make the fringe swish. "There's a year's waiting list for this one. It's called 'The Helene.' "

"Huh." Expensive bags weren't even on Cricket's radar. She didn't know what else to say, so she said it again. "Huh."

Placing the orange bag on the trunk of her car for maximum visibility, Gigi's eyes flicked over Cricket appraisingly, and she oozed sympathy. "How are you? You still living with your daddy? So good of him to take you in after..." Trailing off, she gave a delicate cough.

Cricket bristled. "I pay rent for an apartment he owns." Why was she explaining herself to this woman? Glancing at the green car, Cricket remembered her recent morning run-in with Gigi and felt her hackles rise. "You almost ran over me and my dog the other day."

Her kohl-lined eyes widened. "What? What are you talking about?"

Cricket fixed her gaze on her. "My dog and I were in the crosswalk on Sweetgum Street around nine on Wednesday morning. Remember?"

Gigi's face clouded, then cleared. "Oh, you were the woman who walked out in front of me. You need to be more careful, Cricket." She wagged a finger at her playfully.

Cricket spluttered, "Gigi, I had a walk light. A right-turn-on-red law doesn't mean you don't have to stop or that you can just mow down pedestrians."

"Well." The woman furrowed her brow, seemingly struggling to understand why Cricket was so upset, then gave up. "How's business?" Gigi asked, her eyes bright.

Why was she still talking to this woman? "Steady." Cricket was careful to keep her face as blank as a Vegas card shark.

"We're just busy, busy, busy. More business than I know what to do with." Gigi fanned her face with her hand, seemingly tired just thinking about it. "We've got clients on Bluebird, just around the corner from your daddy's place. The husband and wife are both doctors and *very* prominent," she added in a confidential tone. "The poor lambs had no kids and are alone in the world, so they need us to take care of *everything*."

Good grief. The woman was infiltrating Cricket's own neighborhood. She and Pearl needed to ratchet up their marketing.

Gigi's phone shrilled, and she scrabbled in her "Helene" for it. Cricket saw her chance and edged away.

"Gigi's Girls." She held up a finger at Cricket, but after a moment, she put a hand over the mouthpiece, raised her eyes to heaven, and whispered loudly, "More business. Coffee will have to wait. So good to see you!" Phone pressed to her ear, Gigi clomped back to the driver's side in her boots. With just a cursory glance behind her as she backed her lime green car, Gigi zipped off in the direction of downtown.

Cricket didn't mind. She just waved. The orange Abbott bag looked so festive, perched precariously on the back of the ugly slumping car.

CHAPTER 14

Wednesday, Honey called her at 6:10 a.m. "What's up, sugar pie?" she asked brightly, as if it were a normal time to call. She had Cricket on speaker.

Tying her terrycloth robe closed, Cricket was fixing coffee and groaned inwardly at her friend's cheerfulness. "Morning. What are you doing up so early?"

"I'm on my way to the barn. We have a clinic for volunteers at the therapeutic riding program this morning with a fellow who is a horse whisperer. He's in town from Wyoming to give us tips on keeping horses calm and building rider confidence. I can't wait!" Honey burbled.

"Cool." Cricket loved those television shows about the dog whisperers who gentled troubled dogs. "I'm waiting for the coffee to drip through. Give me a minute." Phone pressed to her ear, Cricket poured a cup. Taking a greedy gulp, she felt the hit of the reviving caffeine almost as soon as it slid down her throat. "Ah."

"First, how are all your injuries?"

"Better," Cricket said firmly, though she was still favoring the ankle that had rolled over when she fell. Her face was still a sight.

"Good. I'm so excited about our mountain trip. I stopped by Daddy Jay's, and I have the perfect vehicle picked out. I can't tell you what it is because I want to surprise you," Honey confided. "Sanders says he's counting on you to keep me out of trouble. He reminded me about not being too nice or bringing home stray people."

"Tell him I'll keep an eye out." Honey had one of those kind faces that made people come up to her and say things like, "I'm just recently widowed, and I don't quite know what to do with myself" or "I need a place to stay, and I don't have any money."

"What's going on with you?" Honey called over the road noise.

Thinking about tomorrow, her mouth suddenly went dry. "I'm a little nervous about seeing Knox."

Honey took a noisy sip of her own coffee. "Tracking him will help you get on with your life. I'm proud of you."

"Thanks." Though warmed by the praise, Cricket rubbed the back of her neck to ease knots. She was starting to think this whole trip was a bad idea. "We'll see how it goes. I'll give you all the details on my news when we drive to Asheville."

They ended the call. At the thought of seeing Mr. Perfectly Physically Fit and Too Handsome Knox, Cricket groaned aloud. If she'd planned better, she'd not be bruised, would have lost ten pounds, would have had fresh highlights put in her hair, and gotten Botox shots, something she'd always wanted to do if she hadn't been too cheap and too much of a scaredy-cat to do. Though she didn't want him back, Cricket wanted to look so good that Knox would be filled with regret about losing her.

Touching her tender cheek, Cricket shook her head. Grumpy, she got a stick of concealer and went to work trying to see how it did at covering up.

Though she'd mentioned her weekend trip to Pearl earlier, Cricket needed to be confident that Pearl knew how to handle every potential problem or emergency that could come up while she was gone. After lunch, the two of them sat on the front porch and talked. Cricket reviewed every contingency, from no-show helpers to clients who needed to be hospitalized, and Pearl took copious notes on a yellow legal pad.

"All set," Pearl announced as she clicked her pen closed. She gazed over at Cricket. "I hope you have a happy getaway."

Cricket decided to spill the beans. "I'm going to Asheville to try to trap my ex-husband and make him tell me why he left. We might even wear disguises to surprise him."

Pearl just nodded. "Good for you. That's one sorry man who'd leave you."

Blinking back unexpected tears, Cricket felt a wave of

gratitude for her assistant's support. "Thanks, Pearl. That means a lot."

Pearl waved a hand dismissively. "Drive safe, boss. We've got it covered here, so don't worry about a thing."

By mid-morning Thursday, Cricket had finished packing. Her clothes were neatly stacked and rolled in her only piece of luggage, a Kate Spade pink paisley rolling suitcase that she'd been so thrilled with when she'd spun it 360 degrees so easily in TJ Maxx. As she eyed the bag, Cricket had a feeling that it would be a standout with the tent campers at the Thunderbird Resort—and not in a good way.

By Friday morning at ten thirty, the morning calls had subsided. Pearl buzzed with excitement as she left to go to Sierra's "Bring Your Grandmother to Lunch" Day. Cricket was drinking too much coffee, running through her mental checklist of last-minute things to do before leaving, and double-checking what she'd put in her suitcase.

Instead of her usual choice of outfits based on whatever was clean and in the front of her closet, Cricket was determined to wear her most flattering clothes. Though the climbing clinic didn't officially start until the next morning, for the first time in a long time, she and Knox would be in the same zip code, so she wanted to look her best. Cricket slipped on a deep-red Henley that looked good with her hair, along with her favorite jeans that fit her curves but didn't bag in the bottom after a few hours.

Reluctantly, she pushed aside her Frye boots for a pair of running shoes. Her ankle was still swollen, and she was erring on the side of comfort all around.

Feeling a buzz of anticipation, Cricket placed bottles of water, cut-up cheeses, a few cups of yogurt, whole wheat crackers, apples, and a bunch of plump green grapes in the insulated cooler bag. Carefully, she wedged in the cold packs and zipped it up. In a matching bag, she slipped in a wine opener, a Washington State Sauvignon Blanc, and a bottle of Rodney Strong Chardonnay. If the mission was a bust, they'd have enough wine to soothe their pain. In terrycloth tea towels, she wrapped two wine glasses and gently placed them on top of the bottles and the cold pack. Hopefully, she and Honey would be able to celebrate a firmly closed door on an unhappy part of her past.

Cricket glanced at her watch. Honey would be here soon, but she had more to do before they left. She'd better get a move on.

She ran the sprinkler on the seeds she'd planted in her plowed-up area out back. The tender new petunias she'd just planted in the flower boxes on the porch needed to be babied, so Cricket carried her big green watering can downstairs to give them one more drink. Under the welcome mat, Cricket spotted a bright turquoise paper bag with a note taped on it. The handwriting was Pearl's. Cricket's mouth turned up.

Her right-hand woman had baked them chocolate chip cookies for the road trip. What a sweetheart.

Under the foil-wrapped cookies, Cricket felt something light and soft. Puzzled, she reached in and pulled out two wigs. One had long golden plaits like a Rastafarian flower child, and the other was a long, gleaming tangle of russet tresses. Cricket shook her head at Pearl's thoughtfulness. She'd loaned them wigs for their expedition. A sticky note was on the wigs. Cricket pulled it off, grinning as she read it.

The note was one line. *Go get him, tiger.*

Just one more errand. Cricket tried not to limp as she made her way across the street. Mr. P was getting set up for the morning, unfolding his newspaper and fiddling with the radio.

"Hey, Speedy. What's happening?"

"I wanted to tell you that someone bought the pink house." Saying this, Cricket's lip started to tremble. She tried hard not to cry.

Mr. P gave her a sympathetic glance. "Sorry, Speedy."

Working to keep her composure, Cricket went on. "I'll get over it, but I also came to tell you that I'm going to the mountains for a few days. My Aunt Joy will be staying at the apartment to dog sit Angus."

Mr. P's face fell. "I would have done that for you. That big guy and I are buddies. Last time he stayed here, he watched *The Woodwright's Shop* and *This Old House* with me."

Cricket felt a pang of guilt. Mr. P loved taking care of Angus.

"I know you would have watched him. Angus adores you, but Joy really needs to get out." She lowered her voice and spoke in a confidential tone. "Joy recently retired from a lifetime of teaching. She is having trouble adjusting and could use cheering up. I was hoping that you could..." With a concerned look, Cricket trailed off, hoping he'd take the bait.

Mr. P held up a hand. "Say no more. Certainly, I'll check in on her." He paused. "Maybe I'll just invite her over for a cup of coffee."

Cricket tried not to wince. Good heavens, not that awful swill. Maybe Joy would take a sip of that instant store brand, bought-on-sale brew, and in her agony, see just how much help Mr. P *did* need. She planted a quick kiss on the top of his Go Navy cap and gingerly walked home to finish getting ready.

After Cricket made one final sweep of the apartment, she reread the instructions she'd left for Joy to make sure she'd left nothing out. Calling Angus to her, Cricket gazed into his expressive eyes and kissed his glossy head several times. "Baby Boy, your Aunt Joy will be here soon. You be good for her. Love you."

Feeling bereft, Cricket had to turn away and leave quickly or she'd start crying.

Bumping her pink bag down the stairs of her apartment, Cricket began to buzz with excitement. They were going to the mountains! Her eyes widened as she watched Honey wheel up in a gleaming Cadillac Escalade SUV with a full camouflage print paint job.

Honey eased down the window, grinning at the surprise on Cricket's face. Gracefully swinging down from the driver's seat, she gave Cricket an appraising once-over. "Your eye looks better, and it looks like your knees are healing. Let's get you loaded up."

"I'm good as new," Cricket said firmly, wheeling her shiny pink bag to the back of the Caddy.

Honey popped open the cargo area with the key fob.

"Remarkable SUV," Cricket said diplomatically.

"It's an almost-new model trade-in with a custom paint job, and we're lucky we got it. Hardly any SUVs on the lot because of some big recall. Brakes or steering column or something." Honey waved a hand dismissively. "Anyhow, Daddy Jay has three buyers all trying to outbid each other for it, but he'd already promised he'd let me drive it this weekend." Honey neatly stowed Cricket's suitcase beside her three oversized, red patent leather rolling bags.

"That many people wanting a camo Caddy," Cricket said wonderingly as she opened the passenger door. "Think we'll look, well…a little conspicuous?"

Brows furrowing, Honey strapped on her seatbelt. "I thought about that, but we needed four-wheel drive." Doubt flickering across her face, she glanced over at Cricket. "But I see what you mean. It does stand out."

"A bit." Cricket tried to keep a straight face as she thought about the two of them rolling into the Thunderbird Resort in their Escalade, passing beat-up Toyota trucks, Subarus, Jeeps, and scruffy Ford Rangers with camper shells. Then, they'd bump toward their campsites with their oversized girly rolling bags. Cricket burst out laughing. "We *are* going to look conspicuous. Like two city girls. If you see any mud puddles on the way up, just drive on through them. We need to cover up some of this shine."

Honey chuckled and then began to laugh so hard that she snorted a little. "Wait 'til you see our outfits. They're so good. They'll think we are the real deal when they see our climber girl clothes."

"Doubtful," Cricket said, and they started laughing again.

As Honey glided away from the curb, Cricket glanced in her rearview mirror.

Outside the pink house, Hank Mayfield's truck was parked, and he stood leaning against it, a bemused expression on his face as he watched them drive away. Not sure why she was doing it, Cricket lowered her window, stuck out an arm, and gave a backward kind of wave to him. Peering hard in the side mirror, she watched him break into a grin and give her a thumbs up.

Cricket grinned as she raised the window, blushing but feeling somehow pleased with herself.

Honey turned to her, brow raised. "I'm assuming that

yummy-looking man was Hank. So why were you waving at him? I thought you thought he was a rat."

Cricket adjusted the comfy leather seat. "I've got a lot to fill you in on."

"Tell me everything." Honey gunned the big engine, and they eased into traffic on I-40, heading west.

Both women were swilling coffee as they chatted, so shortly after they got on the road, they stopped at one of the neatly landscaped brick buildings of the rest area, stretched, and hit the restroom.

"Let's do a tour of downtown Asheville while we're there," Honey suggested as they strolled back to the Caddy. "Sanders and I went to the Biltmore House one Christmas when it was all decorated, and it was the most festive—"

Pausing mid-sentence, Honey elbowed Cricket and pointed at the cars pulling into the rest area. Men in beige minivans and SUV crossovers slowed as they drove by the Camo Caddy and gazed longingly at it. Two fellows snapped photos of it.

Honey shot her an impish grin. "Told you. Men love that Caddy."

Cricket laughed and shook her head as they clambered back into the car.

"I've got a surprise for you," Honey announced as they pulled away, and she shot Cricket a mischievous grin.

"What is it?" Cricket looked at her friend.

"When I heard about your fall, I made an executive decision. No roughing it for you." She gave an airy wave of her hand. "I canceled at the campground. We're staying at the Whispering Aspens B & B. It's got five stars, they had a cancellation, and it's an eight-minute drive from the Expo Center."

"But you really wanted to camp. I would have done fine," Cricket insisted, feeling guilty that her friend wouldn't get the adventure she'd been so excited about.

"It's a done deal," Honey said firmly. "This trip is going to be tough enough without you stumbling around in the middle of the night on a bum leg trying to find the washhouse so you can pee."

Cricket started to protest, but she thought about sleeping on an air mattress on hard ground versus an elegant mattress made of organically grown bamboo and a luxurious linen-topped puffy comforter. She pictured traipsing to a communal bathhouse with possibly icky floors versus lounging in a jetted claw-foot tub and reaching languorously for a fluffy white towel hung on the towel warmers.

"Okay," Cricket said as if she were making a great sacrifice, but then she looked at her friend in alarm. "How much is it? Even the name makes it sound like the rate would be high."

Honey shrugged. "Consider it an early birthday gift from me and Sanders."

Her birthday was months away. Cricket knew Honey

would throw some over-the-top celebration for her then, but with all she had to deal with on this trip, for once, she'd let herself be taken care of. "Thank you, Honey. You're the best."

Honey gave a quick nod, fiddled with the GPS, and once again, they were flying along in the quiet and powerful luxury ride. After stops at the Christmas Store and the outlets, shopping both women deemed necessary, they got back on the road. The miles flew by, and Cricket saw a sign that read, "Asheville—14 miles."

Cricket blew out a shuddery sigh. In less than twenty-four hours, she'd have answers to the questions she'd had every day for way too long, questions that had eaten at her confidence and fed her self-doubt. She shivered.

Honey shot her a look. "All right, sweets?"

"I am." Cricket gave a firm nod, trying to sound more confident than she felt.

Soon Cricket spied the sign for Whispering Aspens B &B, and Honey eased the Caddy into the winding cedar and rhododendron-lined driveway. When they glimpsed the grand Arts and Crafts-inspired home with the sloping roofs, big open porches, and ornamental details, they both drew in their breaths.

"What a beauty," Cricket breathed.

A petite, curvy woman with tousled brown curls stepped outside and raised her hand in a friendly wave.

As the two stepped from the Camo Caddy, the woman approached. "Hey, there. You must be Honey and

Cricket. I'm Gillian, and my sister and I are the innkeepers here."

Cricket liked her firm handshake and open face. After they registered, Gillian insisted on carrying Cricket's bag and one of Honey's as they walked to their room.

"Whispering Aspens is a fifteen-room B & B that was built in 1901 as an inn for weary travelers. My sister, Annalee, and I bought it ten years ago when it was in disrepair." Gillian's mouth twisted wryly. "That's a prettied-up way of saying it was a falling-down heap. We've done a lot of fixing up."

"You must have if you got all those stars on the travel sites," Honey said admiringly.

Gillian looked tickled that Honey knew about the rating. "Last year, *Gracious Southern Travel* magazine named us one of North Carolina's best B & Bs."

"Congratulations." Cricket felt a connection with the fellow small business owner. "That's a big deal."

"Thank you." Gillian ducked her head, coloring. "Now, a little more about the property. We have eight acres of land here, with hiking trails, scenic overlooks, a small private lake for canoeing, and a butterfly garden. Of all our rooms, the one you'll be staying in has one of the prettiest long-range views of the Great Smoky Mountains. Are you two here for some sightseeing?"

"We're here for the Big Sky Climbing Clinic," Honey offered, stepping down the hall in wedge high-heeled boots. Her long French-tipped nails gripped the handles of her shiny red suitcases that rumbled along the wood floors behind her.

"Ah." Gillian's face betrayed not a hint of surprise, in the same way that she'd not blinked at what was left of Cricket's shiner or at the Camo Caddy. She helped them unload their bags. "You'll want to get an early start to-morrow. We start serving breakfast at seven o'clock. Each night, we have a happy hour from five thirty to six thirty in the great room, and on gorgeous nights like this one's going to be, on the front porch too. My sister is an excel-lent chef and puts out a nice spread of farm-to-table hors d'oeuvres. Join us if you're feeling social. If you're not, we totally get that too." Slipping a key card in the lock, Gillian pushed open the door, stepping back to allow Cricket and Honey to enter. "Have a lovely stay."

With a friendly little wave, the innkeeper left.

CHAPTER 15

"TRIP ADVISOR RATERS SAY THE food is fabulous!" Honey got like a hunting dog on point around well-prepared, healthy food.

Stepping into the room, they dropped their bags.

Honey put a hand over her heart and slowly spun around, looking reverent. "My stars. This place is spectacular."

Breathing in the good smell of new pine, Cricket took in the room's spacious feel and simple furnishings. A feeling of hopefulness swelled in her chest. This place would be a pleasant and calm mission control center for their little caper.

With wide-planked pine walls, high ceilings, and expansive windows in front, the room was gold-lit in the afterglow of the sunset and felt airy and spacious. The two queen beds were dressed in snowy white linen coverlets with fluffy down duvets folded neatly at the foot of each. On the walls hung richly hued vintage paintings of majestic elk and wild turkeys.

Cricket hurried to the windows, drinking in the view laid out in front of her. The hills looked like dark blue ocean waves that rolled on forever. The sun was just beginning to sink down behind the mountains, and the sky looked like ribbons of coral, pink, and yellow.

Honey joined her in admiring the grand panorama. "Wow. Just wow."

Cricket gave her friend a sideways look. "Better than tent camping, right?"

"So much better." Honey bubbled. She gave Cricket a searching look. "You ready for this, shug?"

"As ready as I'll ever be," Cricket croaked out, her mouth suddenly cottony. "But can we *not* go out to a restaurant for supper? Sorry for being a wimp, but I'm tired. We've got a big day ahead of us tomorrow."

"We'll make happy hour hors d'oeuvres our supper." Honey rubbed her hands together. "I'd love to sip wine and taste fabulous local specialties."

"As long as we don't have to talk to other guests." Tonight especially, Cricket couldn't force herself to make small talk with people she'd never see again.

"Promise." Honey gave her a four-fingered version of the Girl Scout sign.

Downstairs, guests with good haircuts who were within ten pounds of their ideal weight wore casually chic outdoor clothing, a look that was Brooks Brothers meets Orvis Outfitters. Cricket looked surreptitiously at guests' feet, admiring hand-tooled leather boots and lace-up brogans. They looked like pleasant people, Cricket thought, but she still didn't want to talk with them. She eavesdropped as guests sipped wine and talked almost reverently about Annalee's offerings, using words like "piquant," "unexpected," "bright," and "succulent." Groups were scattered around the sitting areas in the great room, and there was a gleaming grand piano in the corner.

Honey had peeled off immediately, chatting with a woman who'd complimented her sweater. Cricket poked her head outside to the broad front porch.

Ah. Million-dollar views.

Guests sat in double Adirondack chairs with handy wooden drink-and-food trays built in between the two chairs. Whew. Thank goodness. She and Honey could sit together by themselves.

Spotting a pair of open chairs, Cricket draped her fleece over the back of one to claim it and headed back to the food table. Suddenly starving, Cricket admired the inviting spread. She read the handwritten card propped in front of each dish. She saw fresh caught smoked mountain trout pate, mozzarella with basil and cherry tomatoes, roasted pork sliders on sweet potato buns, braised root vegetables in small white ramekins, boiled peanut hummus with crusty herbed crackers, roasted peppers wrapped in bacon, marinated mushrooms, and a plate of cheese straws.

Honey, the social butterfly, drifted away from her chat

with a silver-haired couple wearing matching motorcycle jackets. Discretely, she took a picture of the food table to post on Instagram, then loaded up a plate. Cricket picked up a plate, joining her.

"Those two are honeymooners and were just fascinating. They fell in love at a house fire. He's an EMT, she's a firefighter, and they have eight kids between them," Honey whispered, looking enthralled.

Cricket leaned in and spoke softly. "Remember Sanders says no strays. No inviting people back to Azalea."

"Oopsie. Already did." Honey looked unrepentant as she forked roasted asparagus onto her plate. "They'll probably never come see us, but they were just the nicest folks."

With a fond look, Cricket just patted her arm. After this trip, Sanders needed to get ready for visitors.

A few moments later, the two sat on the green and white striped cushions of the tandem chairs. They looked out over the mountains as dusk fell.

After a few more photos of her plate and some gushing about the succulence of the pork and the delicate melding of flavors in the beets and the carrots, Honey turned to Cricket. She raised her glass in a toast. "Here's to fresh starts, brave women, and finding your happily-ever-after at any age."

Her friend had said it perfectly. Cricket raised her

glass. "And to lovely, loyal friends who stand by you through good times and bad."

Honey clinked her glass and sipped. "We're going to have so much fun trapping this little rat," she said with a gleam of excitement in her eyes.

The woman honeymooner in her Born to Ride leather motorcycle jacket slipped onto the piano bench and softly started to play "The Tennessee Waltz." A few moments later, Gillian padded up, fiddle in hand, and stood behind her as she put the instrument under her chin. Drawing a bow across it, she joined in, playing a heartbreakingly sweet accompaniment. The woman tilted her head at Gillian, smiled, and played another verse.

Cricket and Honey shifted their chairs around so they could better see the impromptu performance.

Her hands clasped together, Honey looked charmed. Cricket watched the woman at the piano who looked dreamy as she and Gillian moved seamlessly into "Wagon Wheel" and "Carolina in My Mind." Guests' conversations trailed off, and several gathered at the piano to sing along softly. She and Honey quietly sang along.

When the musicians segued into "Amazing Grace," Cricket felt a wave of poignant connection and blinked back tears. "Amazing Grace" had been one of her mother's favorites. Rosemary hummed the hymn on Sunday afternoons after church. Cricket had the strong sense that she was hearing this song because it was a heaven-to-earth message—a sign that her mother was sending on the airwaves. A sign that she was doing the right thing.

Cricket closed her eyes a moment. *Hey, Mama. I'm thinking of you. You'd be proud of me. I'm about to get on with my life.*

After the last note faded, the room burst into applause, and the two musicians twinkled at each other and nodded thanks to the guests.

"That was phenomenal," Honey breathed, her eyes sparkling. "Just like singing around the campfire but with better food and comfy chairs." She sipped her wine.

"Exactly," Cricket agreed, even though a five-star B&B wasn't remotely like camping.

Gillian drifted up to them. "How are you ladies this evening?"

"Lovely—and even lovelier since that little concert," Honey enthused, her eyes sparkling.

"Y'all were amazing." Cricket gazed admiringly at the woman and had a hunch. "Are you playing at the climbing clinic tomorrow?"

"We are," Gillian said. "I play in a group called the Stony Gap Ramblers."

"We'll look for you," Honey said delightedly.

"Me and the boys will be there bright and early to set up, and we'll be there all day. It's a fun event," the woman said.

"Can you visit with us a minute?" Pulling over a rocker, Honey patted the seat.

Gillian gave a crooked grin and sat. "Y'all big climbers?"

"No, ma'am. We're here to trap a man." The word "man" came out as "may-an." Honey's drawl always got more pronounced at the end of her first glass of wine.

Gillian crossed her legs and looked intrigued. "You want this man?"

"No." Cricket somehow felt safe confiding in this woman. "It's my ex-husband who left out of the blue, divorced me, and wouldn't say one word about why."

"The wimp wouldn't talk about anything. He dodged every attempt my friend made to communicate with him and just sent her the papers to sign," Honey clarified.

"Ah." Gillian rocked in her chair, gazing out into the distance. "I had a husband leave. These days, I have one or two nice men I pal around with but being single suits me fine."

"There are all sorts of ways to be happy." Honey gave a firm nod.

The three women were quiet, staring out over the mountains, contemplative.

Cricket's thoughts ricocheted around in her head. Knox spent time crisscrossing the mountainous states in the country, but she knew from his posts that he'd spent time in Asheville. Impulsively, Cricket pulled up her Alpine Girl account and thrust the phone in front of Gillian. "Have you seen this man around town? Knox Boney?"

Gillian peered at the screen and shook her head. "Don't know him."

Cricket found the picture of the laughing men and the shapely calf of the woman in the Scarlet Clouds. "You ever seen any of these guys or the woman with this tattoo?"

Gillian paused, thoughtful. "Don't know the guys, but that tat looks familiar. Let me go to the kitchen and check with Annalee." Taking the phone Cricket handed her, Gillian walked off.

"Good thinking," Honey murmured.

A few moments later, Gillian rejoined them, handing back Cricket's phone. "My sister didn't know the guys either, but the young woman is a local named Meadow. One summer a few years ago, she worked for us in housekeeping, cleaning rooms and making beds. I didn't know her because I was managing renovations with the subcontractors, but my sister handled day-to-day operations and hired her," she explained. "Annalee says Meadow was a hard-working, nice young woman."

Cricket was even more confused now. How did this young woman fit in with Knox and his dashing friends? She glanced at the photo again, enlarging it. Assuming Knox was the photographer, there was some arcing energy between him and the woman in the shot. Cricket had a feeling she was not a waitress passing by, but a part of the group. Meadow was somehow connected to Knox and the rock stars.

Cricket thought of the innkeeper's exact words, blinking as she took it in, stunned. Had Knox started a romance with a woman in her early twenties?

"When you say young, about what age are you talking about?" Cricket asked.

"She'd just finished college." Gillian winced, somehow divining that her news was not good.

Cricket allowed herself to think about Knox with such a young woman and fumed inwardly. What a clichéd move for a man at mid-life. He could have been more original.

Honey must have been thinking the same because she muttered, "Son of a biscuit…"

Gillian held up a hand. "No jumping to conclusions. You'll get the facts this weekend."

A guest walked up, hovering. "Excuse me, Gillian, but can you help us figure out how to get to the restaurant? Our reservation is in twenty minutes."

"Sure," Gillian said graciously and rose. She turned to Cricket and Honey. "We'll be either near or on the main stage at the Expo Center all day. You need any help, just holler." She gave Cricket an encouraging smile. "Hope you get the answers you came for."

"Thanks," Cricket said quietly, touched by the sincerity in Gillian's voice.

That night, Cricket slept fitfully. In one disturbing dream, Knox held a microphone as he acted as the master of ceremonies at a fashion show in which glamorous young women wearing swimsuits, feathery wings, and Scarlet Cloud running shoes high-stepped down a runway. Cricket woke with a start, sweating. After quietly flapping the sheets back and forth to cool down, she finally willed herself back to sleep.

In the morning light, Cricket stood in front of the long mirror on the dresser, gazing at her reflection, wide-eyed. Honey had done a bang-up job in picking clothes that transformed her from small-town dweller to mountain girl.

The light, flexible ripstop pants fit comfortably and looked like something a climber would wear. On top, Honey had gone for a boho glamour look that might not look authentic but was fun. Business on the bottom, party on top.

Cricket kept reaching to adjust her shirt, forgetting it only had one shoulder. She slipped on the indigo blue silk, tie-dyed kimono jacket with bell sleeves that Honey had selected to top it. Her earrings were as sparkly as amethyst sequins. Cricket would have to get used to the clinking sound when she walked. Checking herself out in the mirror one more time, Cricket decided she liked the look.

The best part was the wig from Pearl, an artlessly tumbling-down up-do of ginger locks that came with fringy, clip-on bangs. Honey had helped her scrape her auburn hair into a ponytail, slipped on the wig, and clipped the fake bangs. Cricket laughed with delight. Knox would never recognize her.

Honey stepped beside her to examine herself in the mirror. Her friend had topped her low-cut paisley shirt with a fringy red suede jacket and wore a necklace that looked like it was made of gravel from a driveway. A long hairpin in her mouth, she jabbed another pin into the long dreadlock braids that were the same color as her own shiny golden hair. After securing the last braid, she gave Cricket a mischievous grin. "Well, how'd I do? I was going for aging Coachella girls who've taken up climbing. Do you think we'll fit in?"

"You did a terrific job." Cricket pulled another tendril or two down close to her face, liking how smooth the fake hair felt. "Other than pushing the demographic age of the Clinic up twenty years or so, we could pass for weekend climbers or aging bluegrass groupies."

Honey raised both hands palm up. "That's all we need. We just need to see Knox before he up and disappears into thin air."

"Agreed."

As they clomped down the stairs in the rugged, possibly climber-ish boots that Honey had scored at the S.P.C.A. thrift store, Cricket's palms were clammy. At the doorway to the dining room, she balked. "I'm not eating in that dining room in these getups."

Honey just patted her shoulder. "Whatever you say, girl."

Pausing to grab to-go cups of coffee, they caught the scent of fresh baked goods and screeched to a stop. They admired a platter of oversized bear claws that were drizzled with chocolate icing and topped with slivered almonds.

Honey nudged Cricket. "Let's fortify ourselves for the day."

Wrapping two bear claws in paper napkins, they slipped them into their purses. Blowing too-long bangs back from her eye, Cricket tried not to make eye contact with the other guests.

But as they slipped out, an angelic-looking young waitress in a short skirt and combat boots breezed by with a coffee pot in her hand and a tray on her shoulder. Blinking when she saw them, she beamed. "You must be Cricket and Honey. Annalee asked me to give you this." Pulling a note from her pocket, she thrust it at them and twirled away.

The note read, "Good luck, ladies. We all are rooting for you."

Though it was just a quarter after eight, the parking lot at the Expo Center was overflowing, and people streamed in. A shuttle bus pulled up from the Thunderbird Resort, disgorging a group of scruffy, fit, and attractive young men and women who were burbling with excitement. Cricket and Honey got in line, waiting to pick up their packets.

"What a big crowd," Honey chirped to the young

man behind the registration window as she told him their names. According to the fellow's name tag, he was Caden. His shiny black hair was in a braid bound with a strip of leather.

Cricket tried casually to crane her neck, peering at the back of his head. Did men wear clip-on braids too? She fought the urge to give it a tug. Nerves.

"Sixteen hundred people are expected. We've got sixty-two professional rock climbers coaching participants on both outdoor climbing and indoor. We've got clinics on trad climbing skills, sport climbing, crack climbing, top rope climbing, free solo climbing, and bouldering," he intoned.

Caden had his spiel down pat but had a bored look in his eye that telegraphed he'd rather be talking to two young babes. Sighing inwardly, Cricket had a moment where she missed being young and pretty enough to put a spark in men's eyes.

Honey seemed oblivious to the senior citizen attitude Caden was giving them. "Thank goodness for the bouldering clinic. My bouldering skills are so rusty."

Cricket raised a brow at her, and Honey gave a little shrug.

Caden's eyes flicked over their clothes, looking skeptical. "Are you two climbing today?"

Cricket thought fast. "Oh, yes. We brought our outfits…um, gear…in our bags." Just to be convincing, she patted her purse heartily, feeling the bear claw.

Caden glanced at his computer screen and looked at them, his brow drawn. "I've got your registration, but I don't see that you signed up for any clinics."

Honey's brow furrowed. "I didn't know we were supposed to do that."

"Yeah, a lot of them are already filled. A bunch of half-day and full-day clinics still have spaces open, but you need to sign up soon. Plenty of climbing going on inside." Caden hooked a thumb over his shoulder. "The shuttle buses take you to the outdoor climbing locations." He jabbed a finger at the schedule. "We have a number of off-the-rock activities here at the Expo Center. There are lectures, demonstrations, competitions, films, and a small group of vendors." With his head, he pointed at the hall behind them.

"Perfect," Cricket said briskly.

Caden handed them each a schedule and bag of promotional swag. "Remember, mountain biking and slacklining workshops start at noon, and mountain top yoga at sunrise and sunset. Bluegrass all afternoon and evening. Cookout tonight, and buffet and party tomorrow night with ten craft brewers. Lots of cold beer."

"Oh, goody. We love beer," Honey said, sounding girlishly enthusiastic.

Cricket gave her a discreet elbow jab, and Honey looked penitent. Even in her funky outfit, Honey looked and sounded like a Pinot sipper who had a healthy 401K, belonged to a book club, and owned good pearls.

As they stepped into the crowded Expo Center, Cricket felt a buzz of excitement. She glanced around the crowd, scanning faces and looking for her tall ex-husband with the wide-set eyes, strong jaw, orthodontically-correct teeth, and the two perfect dimples of a Hollywood leading man. Knox's charms had worn off for her. When Cricket used to drop by his office, she'd watched his adult women patients with braces forget their sore teeth as well as their mortification of having metal mouths after the age of thirty. They'd laugh at everything he said. Knox lit up most women. It was just a shame that he couldn't pack up all that warmth and charm and bring it home with him from the office.

To get out of the surging foot traffic, Cricket and Honey found an alcove and studied their programs.

"We could learn about belaying, rappelling, and climbing etiquette." Honey shook her head wonderingly. "This is a whole new world—climbing, being one with nature, and sleeping under the stars."

Cricket rolled her eyes. "And not showering for days? Hanging off rock faces by a slim piece of rope?" Flipping to the third page, she found the pictures of the instructors. Her legs and arms turned watery. "Here he is." She pointed him out to Honey.

Knox was sinewy and ripped, like he was built of solid muscle. In the photo, he was dressed in climbing gear, leaning against a boulder. With a rope slung across his shoulder, he looked as confident and understatedly macho as a smokejumper or a fighter pilot.

"Dang. He looks good." Honey put a hand over her mouth, looking like she wished she could take her words back.

Cricket peered more closely at the picture. "He does," she admitted. "And you know what else? He looks happy."

CHAPTER 16

HONEY PATTED HER SHOULDER. "YOU'RE happy too. You've got a great life going without him."

"I'm ready for this to be over." Cricket squared her shoulders, taking a deep breath to gather her resolve.

Honey studied the clinic schedule. "Knox's program started at nine. He's in the Haywood Room. I'm glad he isn't doing outdoor clinics on the rocks. After a big show-down with him, you'd have to ride back with him on the shuttle to the Expo Center."

Cricket shuddered, glanced more closely at the sched-ule, and pointed out the hand-lettered update. "Knox's program is filled. There's a waiting list."

Looking defiant, Honey tossed her polyester braids. "We'll slip in after his talk, then pounce on him."

"Good." Cricket nodded firmly and took her friend by the arm. "Come on. We've got forty minutes. Let's see the sights." Distraction would help keep her nerves from jumping right out of her skin.

Cricket and Honey tried not to gape as they watched muscular climbers effortlessly scale walls. A young woman found finger holds and toeholds, flying up a wall that looked impossible.

Honey nudged her, whispering, "I could do that."

But Cricket was too distracted to laugh. Soon, she'd be face to face with Knox. She glanced at her watch. "It's almost time. Let's head over to the room."

Honey gave a determined nod. "Let's do it."

Cricket shivered, jittery with worry. "What if Knox darts away? If he slips out the door and into the crowd, we'll never find him."

Honey had a determined gleam in her eye. "I've got an idea." Grabbing Cricket's arm, she scanned the crowd, and they strode off.

At 9:52, the two of them were stationed outside the main doors to the huge meeting room. Cricket glanced at her watch, patting her hairdo to make sure it was still pinned securely on her head.

She sent up a quick prayer. *Please let this go well. Help me let go and stop carrying around hurt.*

Beside her, Honey had her arms crossed and wore the icy "don't mess with me" demeanor of Clint Eastwood from *Dirty Harry*.

Thunderous applause erupted in the room. The doors flung open, and the crowd surged out, talking animatedly about the program. Cricket was laser-focused on the front of the room but heard bits and pieces of the gushing praise from the attendees. They said things like "He was so blaze" and "Did you see how he took down that V7?" Some of the words she heard—like "guppy," "Egyptian," and "highball bouldering"—had to be climbing terms.

Cricket was hardly breathing. Finally, the last of the enthusiastic admirers cleared away from the room. Knox was alone. Gathering the samples of his new, technically improved climbing rope, he put them into his satchel. Looking pleased with himself, he slid his laptop in a bag and gathered his notes. Cricket gave Honey the high sign, and they slipped inside.

Honey kicked out the stop to one of the double doors and closed it. Standing in the doorway, she gave Cricket a thumbs up.

Cricket walked slowly to the front of the room. Her heart was trying to slam its way out of her chest, but she felt a sense of preternatural calm as she approached the podium. Knox wore pants with many pockets and a bright red jersey with a logo that read "Climbing Rocks!" Her ex looked even more vital and handsome than she'd ever seen him look. Cricket checked her reaction to him and lifted her chin, feeling exultant. No fondness, no longing. She was immune to him. Bombproof.

Knox must have sensed her approach because he looked up with an indulgent smile, probably expecting a starry-eyed young female climber fabricating a rock-related question just to get a special word with him.

Cricket stepped closer, gave him a level look, and

pulled off her wig. She watched a flicker of recognition and then what looked like panic cross his face.

She spoke in a clear, strong voice. "We need to talk."

Knox glanced around frantically and sprinted for the exit.

Knocking over a chair, he flung himself toward the back door.

Disgusted with this sorry excuse for a grown man, Cricket trotted toward the back of the room, knowing with a glance that Honey was in her Dirty Harry mode as she manned her post. Her friend was so mad at Knox for Cricket that, even though he had seventy pounds on her and was pure muscle, she could probably take him down. You did not want to mess with Honey when she was mad.

Knox must have recognized Honey under her dreads and hippie threads because he faltered and veered off to the left, toppling over a serving tray loaded with glasses. He gunned it to the two sets of doors on the side of the room, flinging one open and screeching to a halt as he saw a trio locked arm in arm, blocking the doorway.

"We got you covered, Cricket," Gillian hollered, flashing a pirate smile from her spot in the middle of two beefy guys in overalls.

Cricket broke into a grin, and Honey whooped in the background.

Knox raced around behind another section of chairs and skidded toward the last set of doors, but another group of burly, bearded mountain men stood in that doorway—more of Gillian's Stony Gap Ramblers. Knox reeled backward, searching desperately for another exit, but he was out of doors to escape. Burying his face in his hands, Knox leaned against the wall.

Her fury rising like heat, Cricket walked toward him, but she slowed when she saw the raw anguish on his face. Knox began to sob, brushing the tears streaming down his face on his silly climber's shirt. Feeling a wave of pity, Cricket fought the urge to feel sorry for him. Knox was an incredibly selfish man who'd abandoned the marriage and left her tethered to thin air. Now unmoved, Cricket stood in front of him, her hands folded, and waited for his tears to subside.

Finally, Knox looked at her. In a tear-choked voice, he said gruffly, "Let's go outside to talk. There's a beer garden that should be quiet now." Glancing around at her reinforcements, he glowered, flashing them a resentful look.

"You a flight risk?" Cricket demanded, her arms crossed.

Knox shook his head. Instead of good-looking, her ex now just looked like a spoiled, squirmy guy with sweat circles under his arms and a patch of gray stubble on his chin that he'd missed while shaving.

"Y'all go talk, but we'll stick close," Gillian called out, and her henchmen nodded their agreement. "Call us if he's a runner."

Honey beamed, walked over to Gillian and the bluegrass boys, and clasped her hands, her eyes wide with admiration. "Our heroes. You showed up at the perfect time. I think y'all are terrific." Each man either flushed, shuffled his feet, or gazed at her, mesmerized.

Gillian grinned at her pals, and Cricket bet she'd rib them later on for succumbing so quickly to Honey's charms.

Linking her arm in her reluctant ex-husband's arm, Cricket perp-walked him out to the beer garden.

Steering him to a table that sat near the banks of a rushing stream, she let go of him, glancing around to make sure her friends were nearby. She sat beside him.

"Tell me everything."

Knox blew out a gusty sigh. "There's really nothing to tell, Cricket." Shrugging, he looked at her flat-eyed. "We just grew apart, and…"

Leaning forward, Cricket cut him off, red fury rising. She bit out her words. "Do. Not. Even. Start. That. Bull. With. Me."

Knox's eyes widened. "Calm down, Cricket," he said, a placating tone in his voice.

But Cricket did not want to calm down. Her mind was racing, remembering. Growing up, her mother had ingrained in her that angry women were unbecoming, saying, "Pretty is as pretty does. Stay sweet, sugar. If you can't say something nice, don't say anything at all."

Cricket shook her head. Mama's "staying sweet"

had reaped a marriage so distant that Daddy didn't even know she was unhappy enough to leave him. And Cricket did the same with Knox. So many times, Cricket had held back her frustrations or hurt instead of talking to him about them.

Knox looked at her warily.

Cricket watched a hawk circling above the woods that framed the Expo Center. A breeze picked up the hair on her neck. A group of musicians gathered underneath a willow tree for an informal jam session and struck up "Rocky Top," a song her father liked. Cricket watched Knox, feeling tired. This is what they did best—not talk.

Honey breezed over, two foaming mugs in her hand. "Thought you two might need a sip of something cool. Eases conversation." Thumping the beer down on the table, she glared at Knox and pointed two fingers to her eyes before turning them back to Knox's. Then she strolled off, rejoining her group of new mountain friends.

Thinking about her part in the demise of their marriage, Cricket took a sip of cold lager, held up a hand, and took a moment to collect herself. She'd waited years for him to come clean, but Cricket needed to come clean with him too. "I owe you an apology."

Knox took a swallow of beer and stared at her, seemingly struggling to keep the aggrieved expression on his face. "Apology accepted," he said stiffly. But his eyes slid over to hers. "Um…what exactly are you sorry for?"

Cricket leaned back in her chair, her thoughts and

feelings churning. "I should have been more honest with you. I didn't confront you when you wouldn't talk to me. I tried to keep the peace. If I'd been straighter with you, maybe we could have sorted things out instead of glossing them over."

"Maybe," Knox said doubtfully. Emotions flickered across his face. "This is not your fault, Cricket. I always thought you were too good for me." He sounded almost bitter. "I didn't tell you what I was unhappy about because I didn't want to disappoint you. So, I wasn't happy, and I couldn't be that honest with you either."

"Is that why you left? Why wouldn't you at least talk to me about what was going on?"

Looking miserable, Knox scrubbed his face with his hands and took a long swallow of beer.

Cricket just stayed quiet and listened.

"It wasn't just one thing," Knox said, his voice gruff with suppressed emotion. "Losing all that money on Girly Rae's was a real setback. The boys and I had always played it safe. This was the first risk we took, and we got hammered."

Cricket stared at him intently, taking in every word he said.

"Then, my forty-fifth birthday hit me as hard as a load of bricks. I could count how many more years I had left, and I wasn't doing a thing I wanted to be doing." Knox paused, again scrubbing his face with his hands. "Climbing in college was the happiest time of my life. I got obsessed with the idea of climbing again—the quietness, the rush of adrenaline, the exhilaration, and the sense of accomplishment when I sat on top of a rock I'd just climbed. I could just sit on that rock and look out on the world." Knox raked a hand through his hair.

Astonished, Cricket just stared at him. "I had no idea you wanted to do the climbing again."

"It seemed like a silly, irresponsible, mid-life dream of mine," he muttered, giving her a hangdog look. "I also didn't want to be an orthodontist anymore. All those open mouths, and kids who wouldn't brush their teeth or kept breaking their braces eating candy. The revolving door of the clinic staff. My back aching from leaning over people. I just got tired," Knox admitted, his mouth twisting. He rubbed his eyes with his fingers.

Cricket's head was spinning, taking in all this news. "I thought you loved your work."

On the office wall, Knox had specially commissioned a neon sign of happy dancing incisors, and underneath the teeth, the slogan read, "We love making great smiles!!!"

"Why didn't you tell me?" she asked.

"My parents were so proud I was an orthodontist. Remember Mama and my business cards?" Knox gave her a ghost of a smile.

Cricket remembered. Bea would search out people with crooked teeth and hand them Knox's business cards.

This part was starting to make sense. Knox's parents were successful by anyone's standards. They'd raised good kids. They were well-off financially and owned a second home on the ocean at Emerald Isle. But more than once, Cricket had heard Bea say that the biggest accomplishment of her life was that all their sons were successful.

Cricket nodded slowly. "Even when you were in your thirties, your mama would remind people that you were one of only five candidates accepted into the Orthodontic Program at Carolina the year you applied."

Knox bobbed his head, looking relieved that she was following him.

"You didn't tell me you wanted to give up your practice—because you didn't want to disappoint your parents or disappoint me?" Cricket searched his face for answers.

Crossing his legs, Knox fiddled with a lace on his boot. "Both."

Cricket threw up her hands in exasperation. "But I would have told you to do what made you happy."

Knox nodded miserably. "I know."

Crossing her arms, Cricket leaned back in her chair, leveling a stare at him. "Knox," she began, but he wouldn't meet her eye.

He was not telling her something. Something big.

Leaning forward in her chair, Cricket felt a rush of hot anger. "What else do you want to tell me?"

Knox rubbed the back of his head, saying nothing.

Cricket yanked the phone from her purse, found the

picture of the fox tattoo girl, and held it up to him. "Who is she?"

He flinched. "How did you find this?"

"I'm Alpine Girl," she said evenly, enjoying the shocked look in his eyes.

Groaning, Knox covered his eyes. "Meadow is my daughter."

Cricket gasped, scarcely believing what he was telling her. "Tell me everything, and for once, just be honest."

Knox's eyes finally held hers. "I had a brief marriage before I met you—a girl from college named Dawn. My parents would never have approved of her. No one knew. It was impulsive and so stupid."

Cricket shook her head as if to clear it. "You never thought to mention that? And she had a child?" How could she have married a man who had left a child?

"We were married just two months and realized we'd made a huge mistake. We divorced as quickly and quietly as we married. All those years later when I met you, it didn't seem important to tell you. Dawn and I didn't stay in touch after the divorce, and I was relieved about that." Knox gave her an imploring look and explained. "Dawn never told me she was pregnant. She just dropped out of sight and apparently moved in with a sister in Cullowhee," Knox said grimly.

Cricket gaped. There was so much the man hadn't been telling her.

"Two weeks after that forty-fifth birthday, Meadow

friended me on Facebook. She texted me the results of her DNA test and pictures of herself, asking if I might be her father."

Cricket rubbed her eyes, remembering the DNA testing kits she'd bought them both for a Christmas present a few years ago.

Knox shifted uncomfortably in his chair and studied her nervously, like a man who feared he might be walking deeper into quicksand, but he went on. "Meadow had the same exact dimples we all have in the family. She had my eyes, and the math was right. I guessed she might be my daughter, and I had to find out."

"And she was," Cricket finished for him.

He sent her a pleading look. "I'm sorry, Cricket."

Cricket knew where this was headed. "So you bailed on the marriage, reinvented yourself as a climber, and found your daughter."

"That's it." He held out his hands, palms up, like it was the only sensible option. "She and her mama live here in Asheville now. I've been spending time with Meadow whenever I can. "

"Are you involved with Dawn?" Cricket realized she didn't care if he was.

"Nowadays, Dawn isn't interested in men." Knox gave a rueful look. "But I've gotten to know Meadow, and she's amazing." His face lit up, and his mouth curled in a wondering smile. "She's smart. She cares about people, and she's even a rock climber."

"You bought her those expensive red shoes, didn't you?" she asked on a hunch.

Knox's eyebrows raised in surprise. "I did. Late birthday present."

Buying forgiveness, Cricket guessed. But still, it was a nice gesture.

"I love being a dad, and it turns out I'm good at it." Lifting his chin, Knox looked proud.

Knox, a dad! Mulling it over, Cricket had a pang of a lonesome, left-behind feeling. They'd not had kids. There was no defining big talk, no hashing out the pros and cons, and no one desperately trying to convince the other that they needed children. By unspoken consent, they'd just never gotten around to it. Now, he was the Father of the Year. Another important conversation they should have had.

"Between being a dad and being a climber, I feel so… alive. I'm doing what I was born to do." Knox looked as if he was expecting her to congratulate him for finding himself.

But Cricket just stared at him. He kept missing one important part.

"But you left me hanging, Knox. What about me?"

CHAPTER 17

"I KNEW YOU'D BE FINE, CRICKET. Of the two of us, you were always the strong one. And your new business was a success and growing..." He flushed guiltily. "I always told myself I was going to call you the next day to explain, but the days kept stretching out."

The artful dodger. Cricket waved a hand to rouse him from his happy-family, high-altitude euphoria. "You owed me an explanation."

"I did. I do." Knox closed his eyes, rubbing them with his fingers. "I kept putting that off too. I swear, I was going to call you and hash it out, but things just got busy. Every day I didn't call made it even harder."

And then it came to her. "You just didn't want to have to deal with the fact that the grown-up altar boy had failed in his marriage. You'd have to tell your parents that you'd handled things badly, walked away from responsibilities, and left me in the lurch."

He nodded, looking miserable. “If I did come clean, I’d have to admit that I’d caused the marriage to fail.”

“You abandoned it, but I had a part in it failing too,” she said quietly. “Let’s just get on with our lives.”

Knox cleared his throat. “I’ve always been so fond of you, Cricket.”

Cricket raised a brow. Knox was also fond of Labrador retrievers, Booker’s Bourbon, and college football.

Knox took a long swallow of beer. Wiping foam from his mouth with the back of his hand, he gave her a level look. “This isn’t all about me having a midlife crisis. We’re being honest, right? Are you telling me that our marriage was based on a deep love and that we were soul mates?”

“No.” Cricket look directly at Knox, respecting him for calling her on it. “You’re right. We should have just stayed friends and not married.”

Knox looked at her tentatively, now appearing less hangdog and more like the mountain man he now was.

Cricket gave him a wan smile, knowing that the truth they’d just spoken was the key to her finally letting go and moving on. “What did you tell your mama that made her stop returning my calls?”

He looked chagrinned. “At first, when she wondered why she hadn’t heard from us, I just acted like we were really busy. Later, I told her you wanted a separation and kicked me out. Said you didn’t want contact with them because it made you too upset.”

Cricket winced. No point in wasting her breath talking to this conflict-avoiding, mama-fearing man about how he could have handled that one better. "Can you fix that, please? I miss her and your dad."

"I will," Knox promised. Tilting his head, he looked at her. "Can we just go forward from here in a friendly way?"

"I don't see the point. I'll be civil, but I don't want to be friends with you," Cricket tapped the table with her finger. "One thing I do want. Please tell your parents the truth. I don't know why it matters to me so much, but it does." Cricket's voice caught. "I loved them."

"I know. I'll tell them," Knox promised and suddenly looked sad. "Maybe later, we can also remember that we cared about each other. I am sorrier than you'll ever know about the hurt I've caused you."

"I am sorry for my part." Cricket's eyes pricked, and she willed herself not to cry.

A group of musicians started up behind them. Fiddles, guitars, a Dobro, and a harmonica all melded together in a lilting, toe-tapping melody. Couples danced across the grassy lawn. A lovebird pair of climbers waltzed by the lithe fellow, who had soulful eyes, and they twirled and intermittently kissed. The couple beside them hung on each other as they burst into some sort of manic polka.

Cricket grimaced at all the young love and banked passion. *Sweet mother*. She needed to get away from all of it. Rising abruptly, Cricket squeezed Knox's hand, and blinking back tears, she strode away.

Tears streaming down her cheeks, Cricket brushed them away furiously. Not sure where she was headed, Cricket plunged into the crowd. She needed to get away from him and these sickeningly happy couples. Spying a quiet corner, Cricket stepped into the shade of a tree draped with trailing purple wisteria and found her phone.

After one ring, Honey picked up. "Yes, shug?"

In a quavering voice, Cricket said, "It's done. Let's get out of here. I need you, I need Angus, and I want to go home."

Back at the Whispering Aspen, Honey settled the bill and insisted on paying for the early departure, even though Annalee tried to refuse, saying she'd just called a couple on the waiting list who were thrilled to take the room. The two women shed their hippie mountain girl outfits and packed with startling efficiency.

As they rolled their bags on the heart pine floors of the great room and headed toward the door, Gillian hurried out the swinging door of the kitchen, an impish grin on her face. "That man trapping was fun."

Honey threw her arms around her. "There you are! You and your guys were just amazing back there. I could just eat you all up with a spoon."

"Thank you for being bouncers for us, and thank you for being so kind." Cricket swallowed hard, marveling that a woman she hardly knew would extend herself the way Gillian had.

Gillian beamed. "We enjoyed having you wild women staying with us. Come see us again, and we'll call you if we ever get to Azalea." She thrust a cardboard box into their hands. "Here's a picnic lunch for y'all to eat on the road. White meat chicken salad with pistachios and grapes on sunflower bread that my sister baked this morning, caramel topped brownies, and freshly brewed blackberry tea." Gillian turned to Cricket and patted her on the shoulder. "You did good. You remind me of me when I was at a crossroads with my marriage. You keep on down this promising new path you're on." Gillian gave a crooked smile. "Annalee may have left you a note in your lunch box. She does that. She's the deep sister. I'm the musical one." Giving them each one last hug, Gilliam raised a hand and wheeled around toward the kitchen. "Safe travels."

Because they'd cleared out so quickly, it took Cricket a few moments to realize that Honey had gone country. Her friend had ditched the boho dreads, but she had on cowboy boots and wore her hair in a messily wrapped braid like Miranda Lambert wore.

Easing the Camo Caddy out onto the main road, Honey hummed a bluegrass tune as she expertly wheeled down the curving mountain road.

As the miles rolled by, Cricket finally told Honey the whole story.

"For heaven's sake. Well, at least you know the truth." Honey nodded briskly. "Now you can let go all the way."

Cricket leaned her head back against the headrest. "What's my part of this deal? Why would I stay in a lukewarm marriage for all those years?"

"You sure you want to hear my theory?" Honey's voice was gentle.

Picking at a fingernail, Cricket glanced over at her. "Shoot."

"Growing up, you witnessed your parents' distant marriage. You learned that was how relationships worked and that not communicating was normal. Rosemary avoided dealing with Julius by staying on the go. Julius sensed her emotionally distancing herself and hid in his work. Their mess might have gotten in the way of them bonding with you—and with you feeling secure in their love." Honey paused for breath and went on. "Maybe you married a man with whom you'd never have a big love because the intense connection scared you. Maybe you were afraid you'd let yourself love real strongly, and the love might go wrong, or the marriage might fail, or—"

"A spouse might leave me," Cricket finished for her, wincing as she remembered her parents' slamming doors, eating meals silently, hissing conversations with each other, and the heavy air of disappointment that seemed to hang in her house when growing up. "Your theory makes sense."

"Possibly. But you've grown so much. Now you want

a big love. You deserve it, and when you find it, I'll hog-tie you to keep you from running off, waving your arms, and screaming." Honey glanced over at Cricket. "Let's find you a man who really gets you. A kind, humble, real man who knows how darling you are. One that makes you feel safe and makes your heart race."

"I'd like that," Cricket said quietly, but instead of conjuring up a picture of a handsome, kind stranger, she pictured Hank carefully helping her up when she'd fallen, tenderly brushing dirt and tears from her face, and saving her precious Angus from getting run over.

At a scenic pull-off with big mountain views, Cricket and Honey sat on a rock outcrop and unpacked the picnic Annalee had packed for them. At the bottom of the box was a handwritten note. Cricket read it, felt a swell of emotion, and brushed away a tear. Wordlessly, she handed it to Honey. The note read, "Onward, Cricket. No regrets about wasted time. You are exactly where you are supposed to be, moving toward a joyous future. Love and blessings, Annalee and Gillian."

After they descended from the mountain and finally got good cell service, Cricket called her aunt. "Hey, Joy. How are things going there?"

"Lovely. Marvelous," Joy burbled.

"I'll be home later on tonight instead of Sunday." Cricket hesitated. What could have transpired in less than two days to make her aunt sound like her old sunny self? "What have you been up to?"

"Angus and I have taken some nice long walks. That dog is as smart as my Advanced Placement students. He could drive a car or write a novel." Joy chuckled at her own joke. "And I met that poor widower, Jackson. You can tell he's needing tending." She lowered her voice confidentially. "He listens to conservative talk radio all the time."

"My goodness." Cricket tried to sound genuinely surprised. "How did you meet?'

"I introduced myself yesterday morning when Angus and I were out and about, and then I just happened to be in the kitchen making fried chicken, butter beans, and deviled eggs for supper, and I made way too much," Joy explained airily.

Hah. No, she didn't. Cricket grinned. No self-respecting Southern woman would go to the trouble of fixing that nice a supper just for herself.

Joy went on. "So, I decided the Christian thing to do would be to carry part of my meal over to Mr. Purefoy. I just hate wasting food."

"Of course." Cricket was thrilled at the direction she'd hoped this story was going.

Her aunt's voice warbled. "Then, the strangest coincidence happened. As I was walking across Mimosa around five, he was walking over from his side. He had an armload of supper that he'd cooked up to share with me. Can you believe it?"

"Well, then." Cricket tried to keep her voice neutral to hide her delight.

"So, we just stood there in the middle of the road talking. Good thing there was no traffic. He'd brought me the oddest and most delicious meal," Joy mused. "It was ribs, oysters, and Romaine salad, all of which he'd cooked on the grill, of all things. Well, we just combined our meals like a two-person potluck, sat on his front porch on the glider, and had the nicest supper." Joy sighed wonderingly and added, "Do you know he reads the Wall Street Journal? Another coincidence."

"My goodness." Cricket just couldn't stop grinning.

After stopping for gas at a truck stop because their sign on the interstate claimed they had "the cleanest ladies' restrooms in North Carolina," Cricket moved over to the driver's seat and waited for Honey to get back with the cup of coffee she'd wanted.

Honey walked up to the Caddy smiling, carefully holding an insulated travel mug of coffee. She wore a square-ish ball cap on her head with a picture of the grill of an eighteen-wheeler on it. The graphics on it read, "Big Jim's Truck Plaza."

"Like your hat." Cricket grinned as she put the Caddy into drive and pulled out onto the highway.

"Me, too." Honey took it off to admire it. "I have never been in a truck stop. Do you know drivers pay to shower there? And some have sleep-in cabs right inside the truck and bring along their dogs for company. Just the driver, his little buddy, and the open road."

Cricket grinned over at her, guessing not many doctors' wives would find the truck stop experience so fascinating. "You might slow down a titch on the coffee."

"Coffee keeps those truckers awake." Honey held up her insulated mug. "Look! Big Jim's Truck Stop logo on this matches the hat. You need to get a mug to advertise your business." Carefully taking off the lid, Honey blew on her coffee and took a sip.

Cricket had a niggling sense of unease. Her synapses were trying to fire but didn't have the oomph. She had a feeling she needed to make an important connection, but it stayed just out of reach. Trucks? Mugs? Hats? But it was gone. She frowned and tried to concentrate.

A black Toyota with a gold racing stripe and a rumbling motor jerked into the small break between the Caddy and the car in front of her. Cricket stomped on the brake, easing the SUV back smoothly. The Toyota peeled off at the next exit, wheels squealing as it rounded a curve. Crazy people. She began to breathe again.

Honey called Sanders. "Hey, darlin'." A quizzical expression on her face, she listened for a moment and laughed delightedly. "You are something else. Let me put you on speaker so Cricket can hear."

In a halting, decidedly Southern-accented Italian, Sanders said, *"Ciao belle signore. Mi sei mancato tanto. Addio, il mio piccolo pollo."*

Honey put a hand to her heart. “That sounded so romantic, but I don’t know what you said.”

Sanders drawled, “Shoot. I tried to say something like, ‘Hello, my pretty ladies. See you soon, my little doves,’ but I may have called you my little chickens. The boys helped me find the American to Italian translator on the computer, but I think they changed what I wrote when I went to the bathroom. They were snickering and making clucking sounds when I came back.”

“I like being called a little chicken,” Cricket said staunchly.

Honey looked tickled. “You sounded so Italian, honey. You really did.” Ending the call, she gave a dreamy sigh. “He learned those phrases just to impress me.”

“Your husband is the best.” Now that she was finally free of Knox, Cricket thought she’d either find a nice, nerdy, devoted man like Sanders who’d love her to pieces, or stay a single lady and get four or five more dogs.

“Sanders was cool to me when I left because he’d miss me, but the man does self-correct,” Honey said primly, but the corners of her mouth were turned up.

Just outside of Cool Springs, Cricket pulled over to let Honey take a turn at the wheel. Once she’d buckled in, she shot a text to Pearl. *Coming home a day early. How is biz? Anything new?*

Pearl’s response came back fast. *All good, except Ms. Granville’s daughter. Hissy fit over minor staff change. All smoothed over 4 now. Will fill u in.*

Good grief. Cricket realized she was jittering her foot against the floorboard and made herself stop. She should have never taken on that hard-edged woman, even though her mama was sweet and needed them. Next time she met someone like Lila, she'd "Just Say No" to trouble. Pearl could handle whatever came up, but after the emotional churn of the "visit" with Knox, all she wanted was a calm evening.

Back home, her little apartment felt like a haven after the emotionally draining trip. Grinning, Cricket accepted ecstatic hugs from Angus, who acted like she'd been away for years. Before she dove back into the work week on Monday, Cricket needed a peaceful, lazy Sunday.

Maybe she'd laze around with the paper and get back to a book she never seemed to have time to finish. Cricket would make it an early night and let herself sleep in the next morning.

She called and ordered a pizza for delivery. Snuggled comfortably in bed, contentedly in her pajamas with the big dog snoring beside her, Cricket drank a glass of wine, watched re-runs of *Maine Cabin Masters* and *Homestead Rescue,* and fell asleep at ten.

The phone shrilled. Cricket blinked her eyes open, glancing bleary-eyed at the clock. 1:15 a.m. The only calls that came at that hour were bad news. She sprang from her bed, tripped on her slippers, and grabbed the phone.

"Hello," she said breathlessly.

Eugenia Flowers sounded apologetic. "Cricket, I'm

sorry to call you at this hour, but your renters are having another big party. The music is loud, cars are everywhere, and a young man just threw up in my Mr. Lincoln roses." Her voice quavered with indignation.

Feeling a wave of hot anger, Cricket was instantly awake. "I am so sorry, Eugenia. Did you call the police?"

"Not yet. The neighbors on one side are out of town, and the other neighbors can't hear well, but it's driving me to distraction. I was just about to call 911."

"If you give me ten minutes to get there, I'll make the call myself." Cricket just wanted to see this party for herself so she wouldn't be arguing with the tenants about another neighbor being responsible for the noise.

"Of course, my dear." Eugenia sounded surprisingly composed, given the commotion.

Cricket threw on clothes, clipped a lead on Angus, and hopped in the SUV. Soon, she pulled up near Eugenia Flowers's house to watch. The party was in full swing, and her holy couple were indeed the hosts. Angus was on full alert, sitting straight up in his seat and growling softly.

She stuck her phone out the window and began filming, capturing the blaring music and the party guests leaning on the front porch rail, smoking cigarettes, guffawing loudly, and draining beers. Cricket watched a girl toss her beer bottle into the garden and felt a rush of heart-pounding, pulse-racing fury. The crowd laughed uproariously, and more guests chucked their bottles over.

A few guys stood around a bonfire they'd built in Cricket's old asparagus bed. One lurched over, picked up a wooden outdoor table that Julius had made for her one birthday, and tossed it in the fire. Rage blossomed inside her, making the hair of the back of her neck stand up. Fighting the urge to jump out and confront the moronic bonfire boys, Cricket ended the movie and called 911.

In a calm voice, she said, "I'd like to report a very loud party and possible underage drinking at 185 Poplar Drive in the Rosewood neighborhood…"

CHAPTER 18

Back home, Cricket fell into bed at two thirty and slept like a log.

What seemed like a few short hours later, Cricket sat straight up in bed, her heart pounding at the sound of the revving growl of a chainsaw. Flipping her sleep mask to the top of her head, Cricket felt a surge of hot indignation. What kind of inconsiderate person ran a chainsaw at the crack of dawn on a Sunday morning?

Hackles up, Angus leapt up from the bed, barking menacingly as he ran to the window. Cricket scrambled up, peered through the blinds, and her blood boiled. The white truck was in front of the pink house, and that Hank Mayfield was cutting down a tree.

Cricket was just so sick of inconsiderate people. Throwing fleece and sweatpants over her pajamas, Cricket jerked on her Frye boots, stomped down the stairs, and stalked across the street. Waiting until Hank finished his cut, she waved her arms at him.

Spying her, Hank cut off the saw and took off his ear

protection muffs. With blue circles under his eyes and his short hair standing on end, Hank looked haggard.

Her hands on her hips, Cricket scowled at him. "Do you know what time it is?"

"Um, no." Shifting his weight from one foot to another, he looked sheepish. He pointed to her head. "I'm guessing from your sleep mask that it's early."

Cricket flushed and pulled off the Zombie apocalypse undead sleep shade with the open bloodshot eyes that one of Honey's sons had given her for Christmas. She tried to focus on her huff. "It's before seven o'clock in the morning, and it's Sunday. I don't know how you were raised, but most of us who eat grits and biscuits for breakfast do not operate chainsaws, lawn mowers, or leaf blowers before noon on Sundays."

Hank rubbed the bridge of his nose, looking chagrinned. "Sorry, Cricket. Things have been wide open at work, and I need to get chores knocked off here at the house, too. Got here at four o'clock the last two mornings, and I'm going to start coming back here after my day at Mayfield's and work until late." He gave her a sheepish look. "I forgot it was Sunday and got so focused on cutting that I didn't notice the time."

"What's the rush? Are your first group of rowdy alumni coming in to rent the place next week and disturb our neighborhood?" Shooting him a disdainful look, she rubbed her thumb and fingers together. "Wouldn't want you or your frat pack buddies to miss out on any income."

Hank put the chainsaw on the ground, looking white-faced with fatigue. "Cricket, I don't know what you're talking about."

"What?" She narrowed her eyes at him. Was this dodge around the truth like the ones Knox had perfected?

Hank sagged, looking exhausted. "I need a glass of cold water."

Hank did look kind of pitiful, and he swayed a little. What if he passed out? Cricket's righteous indignation ebbed. She might not like him or his ethics, but she could give a wrung-out-looking man a glass of water.

"Come on," she said churlishly and turned back to her house, waving for him to follow her.

Angus didn't even give Hank the low growl and the stink eye that he usually gave new people visiting the apartment. Ungraciously, Cricket pointed to the kitchen table, and Hank slid heavily into a chair. Angus sidled up and put his head into Hank's lap. Cricket rolled her eyes at the dog's faithlessness as she clinked ice cubes in a glass and filled it with water.

Hank swallowed the whole glass in a few gulps. "Forgot my water, and the water at the house isn't turned on yet." Wiping his mouth, he tilted the empty glass up to get the last drops.

Wordlessly, Cricket refilled the glass and thunked it down in front of him.

He drank most of the glass and looked at her gratefully. "Ah, best water I ever tasted."

Not about to be charmed, Cricket gave a curt nod but still noticed the way his damp t-shirt clung to his broad shoulders. His forearms were muscled sinew too. She caught herself staring and jerked her eyes away.

Watching her, the corners of his mouth turned up. Hank took another long swallow of water and gave her a level look. "Did you find your runaway ex-husband?"

"I did. The truth came out. He had an ex-wife and baby he didn't tell me about, was stifled by the marriage, and hated being an orthodontist," Cricket revealed.

When would she develop a filter with this man? Needing to be busy, she grabbed the coffee pot, spooned in fresh French roast, and filled the water reservoir. She needed caffeine.

"Good," he said mildly.

"We were just friends who never should have married. He didn't let on that he was unhappy because conflict scares him, and he didn't want to disappoint his mama."

Cricket's face burned. Why was she sharing? Blowing out a breath, she raised her eyes to gauge his reaction to the whole pathetic story. If he looked at her with pity or disdain, she might accidentally spill a steaming carafe full of hot coffee in his lap.

But Hank just nodded his understanding. "The divorce from my ex dragged on for three years. She left me for another man, but she wanted the house, the money, and even my dog that I'd had before we even met."

Despite her neighbor being a money-grubbing shark,

Cricket still felt a pang of pity for him. "Hope you got to keep the dog," she mumbled, giving Angus a quick but fervent pat.

"I did. Gave her everything else just to get on with my life."

Cricket pushed the brew button again, the one she'd pushed just seconds ago. "Your ex-wife was a dancer, right?" Sliding into the kitchen chair farthest from him, she winced inwardly, picturing a tawdry strip club with grasping men and greasy dollar bills.

Hank tried to hide a smile. "Hearing Mama tell it, you'd think Piper was an exotic dancer."

"Oh, I didn't think that." Cricket tried to keep her eyeballs from doing the liar's zigzag.

Hank stared out the window for a moment. "When I was in the worst of it, Mama gave me this quote she had cut out of the paper from one of the advice columns. It read something like, 'Strong people know when to let go.' I taped it on my dresser mirror so I'd see it every morning."

Cricket was quiet, finding his admission endearing, but she did not want to like him. "Nothing wrong with starting over, especially if it means a chance for happiness." She cracked a smile. "You've got a lot to be happy about, with that pink house I covet and that nice truck."

"True," he said philosophically. "Did you notice I got the fender on the truck fixed? No more duct tape and bungee cords."

"Hmm." Grudges were so much easier to hold onto with men with weak jaws, stringy arms, and beady eyes. "Coffee?"

"I'd love a cup. Black is good." Tilting back in his chair, Hank scratched Angus's head.

Pouring them each a cup, Cricket sat, sneaking glances at him from above the rim of her mug.

Taking a sip of the smoky-scented brew, Hank gave a contented sigh. "So, some women have told me I am not a good listener, that I pretend to listen, nod from time to time, and can't recall the conversation five minutes later."

Knox did that, too. She gave him a sub-zero look. "Are you bragging?"

"No," he said, unflappable. "I just think I must have missed some discussion about alumni party houses and frat boys."

Cricket leaned forward and tapped the table with her forefinger. "Why are you and your richy-rich, old frat brother friends turning that sweet house into a rental for alumni football game partiers? It will be an air lodging just for loud, drunk people. I hate that."

Brows furrowed, Hank held up a hand. "Whoa. Slow down. I've got no richy-rich investor friends and no plans for doing what you're saying."

"That's not what I heard." Cricket squinted at him, waiting to be sucker-punched with a double talk explanation for how he and the rest of the Sigma Alpha Theta Gamma whatevers only wanted to "support wholesome collegiate athletic programs and maintain their lifelong allegiance to higher academics at Somerset College."

Hank was gently pulling out a burr buried in Angus's coat. When he held it up triumphantly, he gave the dog a pat. "You heard wrong. No idea what you're talking about."

"No alumni rental party house?" she persisted.

"No. It's a bad idea, and I wouldn't do that to my new neighbors."

"Oh, thank goodness." Cricket put a hand to her chest, almost weak with relief. She felt like hugging him but made herself stop. "I'm so glad." But then, what he had said sank in. "So...*you're* going to be our new neighbor? You're not planning on renting it or flipping it?"

"Nope. I'm going to live there. Just me and Gus, my eleven-year-old Beagle."

"Well," Cricket said lamely and sipped her coffee.

Her brain whirred as she tried to make the mental shift from seeing Hank as the real estate sharpie who stole her house to a neighbor like Mr. P, or possibly Mr. Rogers. She squinted her eyes to see if she could conjure Hank as the gentle cardigan-wearing neighbor, but it was no good. Hank's eyes were too expressive, his build too solid, his broad shoulders too perfect for melting into...

With a sharp intake of breath, Cricket felt a wave of fierce attraction to Hank. She hopped up and grabbed the coffee pot. "Top you off?" she asked in a too bright voice.

"Uh, sure." Hank glanced down at his almost-full

mug and watched her, a smile playing at the corner of his mouth.

Awkwardly, Cricket held the carafe a full arm's length away as she poured one-eighth of an inch of coffee into his mug. She did not want to feel this heat toward him. Sitting down again, Cricket skootched even farther away from him so the top rung of her chair was pressed against the window.

Hank sipped his coffee, looking amused.

Thank goodness her phone rang.

Pearl said hurriedly, "Cricket, I'm on the way over to pick you up. Lila Merriweather is on the warpath. She claims Marla stole jewelry and said we'd better be at her mama's house in the next half hour or she's calling the police."

"I'll meet you outside in just a few." Cricket ended the call, her alarm tinged with relief at getting away from this too-attractive man. Glancing at him, Cricket quickly averted her eyes. She needed to get a grip. "I need to go, Hank. We've got a work problem."

"Gotcha." Levering himself up from the chair, he gave her a slow, sweet smile. "Glad we got things cleared up."

Feeling a knee-weakening wave of chemistry again, her smile faded. "Me too. Time to get you on your way." Rising, Cricket held open the door for him.

Eyes sparkling, Hank did not look at all offended by being so unceremoniously thrown out. As he thumped down the stairs in his work boots, he called over his shoulder, "See you around, neighbor."

Not if she could help it. When she shut the door, Cricket leaned against it, trying to slow her heartbeat to normal range. Crazy thoughts raced around in her brain. Liking Hank scared her to pieces. How could she keep a distance from him?

Cricket would plant a row of Leyland Cypresses across the front yard. If she fertilized them, they would grow to sixty feet fast. Maybe she'd build a twelve-foot-high privacy fence around the house. She would have to check with the zoning department first, of course. If Cricket re-routed the driveway so she could get to the carport from the rear of the house, she would never have to see her handsome neighbor again. Shaking her head, Cricket found herself grinning as she went to dress.

Running a brush through her hair, Cricket hurriedly threw on a cotton sheath and a blazer. She thought about her gratitude list. It had been much too long since she had practiced them.

Thank you, God, for the honest talk with Knox. I'm grateful for my health. I'd be happy for help with this tricky client. I would appreciate it if Hank Mayfield would stop shaving and brushing his teeth.

As she balanced on the bed and slipped on sandals, she thought about it. He'd probably still look cute as an unkempt man. *Drat.*

Grabbing her purse, she dashed outside. Pearl's car was idling at the curb.

By way of greeting, her assistant muttered darkly, "That snooty Lila is pure meanness."

Sliding into the passenger seat, Cricket impulsively leaned over and gave Pearl a peck on the cheek.

Pearl broke into a grin. "Guessing you got things sorted with that sorry ex-husband of yours."

"I did." Nodding briskly, Cricket buckled herself in. "Give me the story on Ms. Lila."

"She already called once this weekend complaining because Marla had to cancel.

Marla's daughter miscarried Friday, and she needed to be with her," Pearl explained.

"Of course she did." Cricket felt a rush of resentment.

Pearl went on. "So for one day, I sent over Josie, who is as sweet as pie, and when Lila heard that from her mama, she called me and raised a ruckus about "the importance of continuity of care" and our "revolving door of staff."

Cricket was baffled. "That's the first time we've had to substitute anyone, isn't it?"

Pearl's mouth twisted. "Uh-huh. That woman could start an argument in an empty room."

Turning onto Oak Street, Cricket spotted Mrs. Granville's tidy craftsman-style home. Parked in front of it was Marla's dinged-up blue minivan, sporting the white-outlined stick figures on the back window picturing a father grilling, a mother with flipped up hair, the daughter with a soccer ball, and two dogs. Another shiny, luxury-upgraded rental car was parked behind the van.

As they pulled up, Cricket sucked in her breath. Cell phone pressed to her ear, Lila paced up and down the sidewalk, her brows drawn into an angry "V" and her mouth in a thin line. Wearing tight black pants and suede boots with long fringe on the top and side, she gesticulated rapidly with one skinny arm.

As she unhooked her seat belt, Pearl muttered, "She looks like Cruella De Ville."

Cricket bobbed her head in agreement and got out of the car. "No matter how she acts, we'll be calm and professional."

Pearl locked the car door, pausing deliberately to adjust the clasp on her purse, one that Cricket guessed did not need adjusting.

Cricket kept her pace unhurried as she walked up to the house like she had all the time in the world.

Lila glared daggers at them both, ending her call with a stab of her finger. "About time you all got here."

Cricket gave her a neutral smile. "Good morning. How's your mama?"

Lila put her hands on her bony hips and glared at them. "Mother is fine because she's got mild dementia and does not know any better. But I do. One of your helpers has stolen an exceptionally fine diamond broach from her jewelry box." She held an inch of air between her thumb and forefinger. "And I am this close to calling the police."

"Well, my goodness," Cricket said mildly. She had a crazy thought about how she was single-handedly keeping the Azalea sheriff's department hopping lately. She continued her path up the sidewalk toward the house. "Let's go inside so we can sit and figure this all out."

After a moment's hesitation, Lila followed them back into the house, but their façade of calm seemed to make her madder. "There is not one thing in the world to figure out, except how to get your thieving staff to give it back. My sisters and I had all of Mama's jewelry appraised last year..."

Probably to get a jump on plans for the inheritance, Cricket thought meanly.

"And that broach was worth twenty-two thousand dollars. We're talking about grand theft and larceny charges. I just got off the phone with the insurance company, and they're sending me an itemized list of all her pieces so I can see what other jewelry was stolen." Lila cast a withering look at Marla, who was wringing her hands as she stood in the doorway.

Cricket and Pearl greeted Marla. "How's Ms. Cora doing?"

Marla's expression relaxed a bit. "Just fine. She just woke up, and I was about to fix her some bacon and pancakes." She gave Cricket and Pearl a worried look. "I don't know anything about any missing jewelry."

Looking embarrassed, Marla leaned closer to Cricket and Pearl and quietly asked, "What exactly *is* a broach?"

Lila breathed out a huff of disbelief.

Cricket ignored her, making a circle with her forefinger and thumb. "It's a jeweled pin that a woman might wear on her dress, a sweater, or on the lapel of her coat."

Marla shook her head slowly. "I've never seen Ms. Cora wear any pin or broach. These days, I'm doing good if every morning, I can get her out of her nighty and housecoat and into her warm-up suit."

"Don't play naive with me," Lila snapped harshly, giving Marla a disgusted look. "So, for the last time, before I call the police, where's the broach?"

CHAPTER 19

"LET'S NOT JUMP TO ANY conclusions, Ms. Merriweather," Pearl said calmly and turned to Marla. "Have y'all searched the house?"

"We did." The helper gave Pearl and Cricket an apologetic look. "Since I didn't exactly know what a broach was, I just searched for something valuable looking."

"Well, fresh eyes can be a help." Cricket glanced around, sizing up the rooms.

"She's just stalling." Lila sniffed. "You said you did background checks and looked for criminal records. So how did this happen? I hope you are well-covered insurance-wise." Her hands were on her hips now.

Cricket's mind raced. Could Marla or Josie have stolen the jewelry? She couldn't believe it. Marla was a solid, straight-shooter type who had worked for her for two and a half years. The only time she'd even been a few minutes late was when she drove back to Chik-fil-A to return the five dollars' extra change that the young man at the drive-through had accidentally given her. She hadn't wanted to get him in trouble.

Josie came with glowing recommendations and had worked for the Department of Social Services for twenty years before she joined Cricket's Caregivers.

"We do thorough background checks, and both women passed with flying colors," Pearl said in an even tone. "Now, how about if we split up and give the house another once over."

Lila snorted, pointing at them. "You two are probably in cahoots with Marlene. I'll sue you all."

"It's Marla," Cricket said crisply, hearing the blood pounding in her ears.

A floodgate opened. Nobody was going to ever dismiss her again the way Knox had, and no matter how much she needed the business, no one was going to talk to her employees like this.

She fixed the sharp-edged woman with a steely look. "I'm not sure how you talk in Atlanta, but around here, we try to talk politely to people. We don't threaten people with arrests and lawsuits until we know the facts."

Lila's eyebrows flew up to her unnaturally black hairline, and she looked ready to bite out an angry retort.

Cricket held up a hand. "My suggestion is we search this house one more time and get busy solving this mystery."

"I already searched it," Lila hissed. "Twice."

Cora Granville shuffled into the living room, blinking her eyes open and slipping in her top teeth. "Marla, would you be a love and help me…" She trailed off, and her eyes widened when she saw the group gathered in her living room. "Why, Lila, what in the world are you doing here? Is everything all right?"

"Hello, Mother." Rearranging her features, Lila gave what passed as a smile. Leaning in, she pecked her mother on the cheek. "It's Sunday. Remember, I always try to get by to see you every other Sunday."

Cora put a hand to her cheek and looked chagrinned. "Well, that's right. Marla always reminds me the morning you're coming." She touched her helper's shoulder and gave her an affectionate smile. "Some days, I'm clearheaded, and other days, she's my brain. I don't know what I'd do without her."

Marla's features lost that hunted look, and she returned the smile.

Cora turned to Cricket and Pearl. "I know you nice ladies, but I can't recall your names."

"I'm Pearl, and this is Cricket. We're from Cricket's Caregivers, the agency that sends you Marla," Pearl said.

The older woman looked pleased. "Ah. I knew you looked familiar." She gave a gay little chuckle and threw up her hands. "And y'all are visiting me too? I feel like the belle of the ball."

Drawing herself up, Lila seemed to regain her sense of indignation. "Your broach is missing. I called in these ladies to help straighten out the matter."

"What matter? And how do you know my broach is missing?" Cora Granville looked bewildered.

Lila looked away. "I…er… looked in your jewelry box."

Cocking her head, Cora suddenly looked as bright-eyed and alert as a Carolina wren. "Why would you do that?"

Lila wouldn't meet her mother's eyes. "The Heart Ball is next weekend, and I'm chairwoman of the event. I needed a piece of statement jewelry and thought I might borrow the broach."

"Without asking me?" Cora's voice had an edge to it. "I would have preferred you asked first instead of just helping yourself."

Lila shrugged as if it was no big deal, but Cricket watched the red creep up her neck to her face. "I was going to ask you as soon as you got up this morning."

"Ms. Cora, would you mind if we looked through your house to see if we can find your pin?" Pearl asked, looking unruffled.

"Of course not," Cora said.

"I'm sure things will turn up." Pearl caught Cricket's eye and telegraphed an apologetic message to her. "How about you and Lila take the bedrooms and the bathroom, and I can check the rest of the house?"

Lila acquiesced with a quick jerk of her head. As she marched toward the back of the house, even the soft sound of the suede fringe swishing on her boots irritated Cricket.

Marla smoothed the front of her pantsuit and seemed to regain her composure. Turning to her client, she spoke in a soothing tone. "Now, Ms. Cora, how about we get you situated in the good chair with a nice cup of coffee, and you can watch a little TV?" Putting a hand on the woman's slight shoulder, Marla steered her toward her recliner.

In the bedroom, Cricket pulled a small but powerful flashlight from her purse, got down on her hands and knees, and swept the beam underneath the bed. Dust bunny free and no broach.

Lila marched to the closet, pulling out a free-standing jewelry box. She flipped open the lid and began to rake her fingers through the contents.

Fighting an urge to not even speak to the woman, Cricket pulled a clean white towel from the linen closet and spread it on Mrs. Granville's bed. "If you pour everything out here, the light's better." She shone her flashlight behind the dresser, watching Lila from the corner of her eye.

A mulish expression on her face, the woman hesitated a moment but skidded the jewelry box across the carpet and dumped the contents out on the bed.

Mrs. Granville's voice drifted into the bedroom. "Lila, will you bring me my robe? It's hung on the hook on the back of the bathroom door."

Lila's brows knit with irritation at having been interrupted. "Yes, mother." She strode into the bathroom and stepped back out, a chenille robe in her hands and an odd expression on her face. Walking over to Cricket, she thrust the robe at her. "Look."

Cricket stopped running her fingers under the cushion of the pink slipper chair and leaned forward to examine it. At first, she saw nothing amiss. Buttons were missing from the front of the robe, and Cricket saw the glinting sparkle. A bejeweled pin the size of a silver dollar was pinned haphazardly to the robe.

"The broach," Cricket breathed, glancing at Lila to gauge her reaction.

Lila put a hand over her mouth and shook her head, snatching the robe back from Cricket. "Mother," she called and walked toward the living room.

Cricket followed, her knees almost giving way with relief at finding the expensive piece of jewelry and realizing that it wasn't her helper who'd stolen it.

When Lila stalked in, Marla was in the kitchen emptying the dishwasher. Pearl was re-fitting the couch cushions she'd removed from her search. Cora sipped a mug of coffee and watched the morning news. She glanced up as Lila appeared, holding her robe.

"Thank you, sweetheart. This room stays chilly." Cora reached for her robe. Before she handed it to her mother, Lila unclasped the pin and held it up. "Your broach was pinned to your robe, Mama." Her tone was chastising.

"I remember now." Cora put her coffee on a side table with a shaky hand and reached for the robe. "Both buttons fell off in the dryer at the same time. I was going to get Marla to help me sew them back on today, but I needed to close it last night."

Cricket shot a look at Marla, who sank down into a chair, her eyes brimming with grateful tears. Pearl just nodded at Mrs. Granville's explanation as though closing a bathrobe with a twenty-two-thousand-dollar piece of jewelry was a sensible solution.

Marla gently helped the older woman thread her slim arms through the armholes of the robe and handed her back her coffee.

Lila rubbed her eyes with her fingers and blew out a ragged sigh. "May I speak with you all in the other room?"

Cora turned up the volume as she watched the weather, and the four women gathered in the kitchen.

Lila looked at Cricket and Pearl. "I shouldn't have jumped to conclusions. I get so worried about Mama living clear up here in North Carolina, but she will not come live with us in Atlanta. I can't leave my work." She held out her hands, palms up.

Seeing the woman's chin wobble and the color blotch in her cheeks, Cricket felt herself soften. She knew how hard it was for adult children to manage care for aging parents when they lived in another county, much less another state. But the woman had been threatening and hadn't fully apologized. Cricket wasn't letting her off the hook so easily. Also, Lila hadn't even glanced at Marla when she spoke, and the helper was the one she'd treated most rudely.

"We understand." Cricket stepped closer to Marla. "You probably noticed that your Mama loves Marla. She would be devastated if Marla left, and after the way you've spoken to her today, I wouldn't be at all surprised if she quits."

Cricket felt a steely resolve. She needed to right this and hold the queen accountable.

Lila hesitated. Gazing at Marla, she spoke rapidly. "I'm sorry, and I hope that you'll keep working with my mama."

Marla lifted her chin and spoke with quiet dignity. "I accept your apology. I'll be working with your mama for as long as she needs me."

Cricket held up a finger. She wasn't finished yet. "I'm glad Marla forgives you, but if you would like to continue working with us, I hope that you'll speak courteously to our staff. If there's a problem, I hope you'll come to us directly and let us help you handle it."

Crossing her arms, Lila gazed out the window, still bristling at being called on her bad behavior. Her jaw tight, emotions flitted across her face: resentment, anger, and embarrassment. After a long moment, she said, "I'll do that."

"Good," Cricket said mildly. "Now we're going to get

on our way so you all can visit and let Marla cook your Mama a nice hot breakfast."

In the car, Pearl shook her head, grinning. "Uh, uh, uh. Who was that strong lady in there? I sure got a kick out of you. I don't know what happened in the mountains, but it suits you."

Cricket laughed. She'd surprised herself too. "I took back my power up there. Nobody is going to dismiss me, you, or any of our helpers."

"No, ma'am, they're not." Pearl nodded her head so vigorously that her bun looked like it might whirl right off.

Cricket thought about it as Pearl glanced left one more time and pulled into traffic. "As much as I like Ms. Cora, first peep of trouble out of Lila, and she's going to need to find a new caregiver agency."

"I'll give her Gigi's card." Pearl gave her a sly grin.

Cricket cracked a smile and made a quick decision. "Would you mind running me by my old house for just five minutes?"

"Not at all." Pearl changed lanes, looking intrigued.

"My renters had a big ole party last night. I want to pay them a visit while it's nice and early, and they're hopefully hungover."

Pearl began to chuckle. "Good plan. I'll pull in real close and roll down all the windows so I can catch every word."

Cricket shuddered and shot Pearl a sideways glance.

"Confronting people scares me, but I'm realizing I just have got to make myself do it."

Pearl shot her an approving look. "Nothing wrong with speaking your mind or even throwing a hissy fit when it's called for."

At the house, Cricket squared her shoulders and marched up the walkway, her teeth clenching as she saw the broken bottles in the flower bed and smelled the acrid remnants of the bonfire. She rapped hard on the door, and just to be extra irritating, did not stop rapping.

The young wife threw open the door, blinking like she'd just awoken. With tangled long hair and an exquisite face, she looked angelic even with mascara smeared under her eyes.

"What?" she demanded. "What do you want?" A flash of recognition and then fear crossed her face as she recognized her landlord.

Cricket shot the woman a frosty look. "You all threw a big party last night. Lots of drinking, lots of people, and loud music." She thumbed over her shoulder. "Y'all burned the table that my daddy built for me."

The woman spluttered, "Oh, we'd just finished exams, so we had a few people over for a little cookout. We were not loud."

Cricket just held up her phone, hit play, and turned it toward the young woman.

After a moment or two of thumping base and crazy

laughter, the young woman flushed, averting her eyes. “Well, we didn’t go too late…”

Cricket wasn’t going to be talked to like she was stupid. “I was here. It was 1:45 when I called the police. It *was* too late and too loud, and this is the second time the neighbors have complained to me about your parties.”

But the young woman gave her a mutinous look. “Look, I was in law school before I switched to divinity, and as tenants, we have rights. The courts do not look fondly on landlords who harass their tenants.” She put a hand on her hip and gave Cricket a challenging look.

Cricket heard the blood pounding in her ears and made herself speak calmly. “You and your husband need to decide whether or not you want to keep living in my house. If you do, you’ll need to behave like quiet, considerate people. No more parties. You will be reimbursing me for that table, and I will be visiting you to inspect the house for other damage.” Cricket leveled a look at the girl whose lower lip now protruded. An angel with a bad attitude. “You have two strikes against you. At three strikes, you are out. Are we clear?”

Flat-eyed and thin-mouthed, the young woman slammed the door in her face.

Shocked at her tenant’s rudeness, Cricket almost resumed knocking, but she instead spun around and walked back to the car. Slinging herself into the passenger seat, Cricket pulled on her seatbelt. “Can you believe that? She shut the door on me.”

Pearl just raised a shoulder as she pulled away. "Best to let her cool off. You said your piece, and you said it well. Even if she's spoiled and willful, she knows they were in the wrong."

"One would think," Cricket huffed, then gave Pearl a crooked grin. "Do you really think I did good?"

"You did. You pretended to stay calm, you gave her the facts, and you laid out consequences." She gave an approving nod.

"You'll have to help figure out what my next step will be if they keep causing trouble because I think they will." Cricket looked out the window, brooding.

Pearl paused for a long moment and then said slowly, "You've got that fine video clip. Didn't you say their parents were ministers? Seems like those two might not want their folks to see that particular movie." Her assistant's eyes sparkled with mischief.

Cricket put a hand to her cheek, impressed. "You are a brilliant and slightly devious woman. I really like that about you." She tapped her phone. "I'll send this video clip as soon as I track down the parents. That shouldn't be hard."

Looking pleased at being complimented, Pearl nosed the car out onto the busier through street. The Sunday morning after-church crowd was out and about.

When they got closer to Cricket's neighborhood, Pearl pointed. "There's Gigi and that green car of hers."

"She'd been following us the last few weeks. Let's follow her and see what that little sneak is up to." Cricket lifted her chin, still buzzed by adrenaline from this morning's adventures.

Pearl changed lanes, staying a safe distance back from the green car sloping down the leafy streets. Pulling down her visor, she slipped on sunglasses. "Let's keep Miss Smarty Pants from knowing it's us. At least we don't have a lime car and a crazy hot air balloon magnet slapped on the side door. I never understood what that balloon full of women was supposed to mean anyhow."

A van pulled in front of them, and Cricket craned her neck to keep an eye on Gigi's car. "She hooked a right on Elm."

The lumbering van finally turned into the library parking lot, and Pearl pulled around it, stepping on the gas to make up for lost time. Jerking the wheel sharply to the right, she avoided a big pothole.

Cricket gave her a grin. "Go, Danica Patrick."

But as Pearl sped up, they saw Gigi's green car stopped at a traffic light just half a block up. Pearl braked, and slowing the car to a crawl, pulled onto the side of the road. Both women slumped in their seats, worried they'd been spotted. But Gigi was fluffing her bangs and applying lipstick in the rearview mirror.

"A slow-speed chase," Pearl said drily.

The light changed, and Gigi whizzed off, Pearl staying a few car lengths behind.

They were back in the older section of town, near

Daddy's house. The green car pulled into the brick-paved driveway of a stately old Cape Cod-style home. Gigi hopped out and let herself into the house.

Cricket fumed. "That's the Finches' house. That little wench keeps infiltrating my own neighborhood."

"Lordy. How does she do it?"

"I don't know. The Finches are a sweet older couple that used to come to my mama and daddy's parties."

Pearl pulled over on the shady side of the street beneath the leaf cover of a tree and cut off the engine. "Can't imagine Gigi would have an initial client meeting on a Sunday, and I doubt Gigi does any of the actual caregiving herself these days. There's no telling what she's up to. Let's watch her."

CHAPTER 20

"We'll be still as possums." Pearl slumped down further in the driver's seat until the bump of her fancy bun was probably the only sign of her from outside the car.

Ten minutes passed, then fifteen. Surveillance was boring and the car was getting hot. Pearl cranked the engine momentarily, and they let down the windows.

"On TV show stakeouts, a Mercedes Benz will pull up, and men with dark glasses carrying briefcases get out. Here, nothing," Pearl groused. Pulling a pack of Nabs from her purse, she offered one to Cricket.

The two crunched away companionably.

Cricket studied a Nab. "Why do these crackers always taste so good, and why do you think they make them orange?"

Pearl was gazing eagle-eyed at the house. "Bingo." She pointed to the Finches' front window.

A light had been switched on in one of the rooms closest to the street.

Straining her eyes, Cricket could see the back of a computer monitor and the silhouette of a woman that looked like Gigi sit down behind it.

Pearl frowned. "Why is she on their computer? Looks suspicious."

Cricket felt the same way. Something was off. She glanced around. The grass was too high, a few rained-upon newspapers lay in the grass by the mailbox, and the plants in the window boxes looked dead. A chill went down her spine. "The house looks empty."

Pearl's eyes flicked around the property. "Might be, but some older folks aren't much on the upkeep of the outside." Brushing an orange crumb off the side of her mouth, she looked thoughtful as she pointed to the pile of rained upon newspapers. "But most of them want their daily paper."

Cricket agreed. "Could the Finches be visiting family or gone to Florida for the winter and asked Gigi to check on the house?"

"Maybe." Pearl looked skeptical.

The two women slouched further in their seats as Gigi slipped out the door, looking one way and then the other. Slinging her orange Helene bag over her shoulder, she hopped in her car and zipped away.

"That was the shortest intake meeting or four-hour shift I've ever seen." Pearl glanced at her watch. "She was inside just twenty minutes."

What is going on? Cricket racked her brain for answers. "Are Gigi and her girls doing housesitting, too?"

Pearl whipped her phone from her purse, poked it with a finger, and studied the screen, eyes narrowed. "Her website doesn't say a word about it."

Cricket looked off into the distance. "I don't know what's going on, but every instinct tells me it's not all above board."

"I agree." Pearl turned on the engine. "Let's head home. We'll get to the truth." Making a U-turn, she rolled down a few short streets and pulled up at the curb in front of Julius's house.

Cricket gave her assistant a grateful smile. "Thank goodness for you. If you hadn't been with me today, I might have backed out of everything. And the stakeout gave us clues, even though we might not know what they mean right now."

Pearl gave a sideways look. "This job is way more exciting than working at the salon all day." She waved as Cricket stepped out of the car.

Cricket paused to pick up a flyer someone had stuck underneath the windshield wipers of her own car. Glancing at it, she grimaced and held up a hand to stop Pearl before she pulled away. Stepping back to Pearl's car, she held up the flyer for her to see.

A gaggle of smiling women in hot air balloons floated across the page. The copy read, "Trust your mama and daddy to Gigi's girls, the *most trusted* caregiver service in

Azalea." At the bottom of the flyer was a glamour shot of Gigi, smiling confidently with her arms crossed and wearing what appeared to be a doctor's white lab coat. Odd, since during her "let's be friends" conversations at the Kiwanis meeting, Gigi told Cricket that her work experience had been as a teacher's assistant and a clerk in a drugstore.

Pearl rolled her eyes and tooted the horn as she pulled away.

Cricket balled up the flyer as she traipsed to the house, feeling even more determined to win new clients and solve the mystery of Gigi's growing dynasty once and for all.

Monday morning flew by, though the calls came in fast and furious. Cricket tried to talk with Kiara about her concerns that her client might have a urinary tract infection, while Pearl had a hollering conversation with Mrs. Watson, who was going deaf but too vain to wear a hearing aid. After a blaring back and forth about transportation to and from a doctor's office, Pearl gave Cricket an apologetic look and hurried out to the porch to continue her conversation.

At eleven o'clock, the phones went quiet. Pearl gave a little salute as she left to visit a newer client to see how he was doing with his caregiver.

Cricket tried to do the books but kept obsessing about Gigi at the Finches' house. What was that about? Something seemed fishy, but she couldn't put her finger on it. Heaving a sigh, she closed the laptop. No use pretending that she could concentrate.

A quick smooch fest and wrestle with Angus helped lighten Cricket's mood. Exercise. She needed exercise. Changing into comfortable clothes, she examined her foot before she pulled on socks. The bruising on her ankle from her tumble had faded, and the swelling was gone. Good. She gave her ankle an experimental rotation and a back and forth; it seemed better. A little sore, but not bad.

As she gave her foot one last look, Cricket noticed veins on both of her ankles that she hadn't noticed before. She shook her head in disgust. When did all this age-related, un-prettiness come on? Not that long ago, she was wearing sophisticated flats with no arch support or va-va-voom heels on a date with Knox when she was trying to fire up their marriage.

Angus was dancing, weaving around to get her attention.

"Coming, big guy."

Her pulse quickened as she thought about the possibility of running into hunky Hank. She ran a brush through her hair, braided it loosely, and smoothed on a pale peach lip gloss. Clipping the dog to his lead, she traipsed down the stairs with Angus. Slipping on her sunglasses, Cricket looked across the street. No banged-up truck. Snap. And Mr. P wasn't at his usual post on the front porch.

"Just you and me, buddy." Cricket gave Angus a quick pat.

Cricket walked and trotted beside the dog, waiting patiently while Angus staked his claim by lifting a leg on tufts of grass and on every fire hydrant they passed. Breathing in the cool air that smelled faintly of honeysuckle, she stopped to admire the bright, yellow buds of a forsythia bush waving in the gentle breeze.

As they headed home, Cricket felt a fizz of excitement as she spotted Hank's truck in front of the pink house. He was lifting a sawhorse from the bed of the truck, and just the sight of him made her short of breath. Cricket tried to keep her pace steady and look nonchalant.

Angus spotted Hank too and whined as he tugged at his leash.

Hank saw them and broke into a smile. Crossing his arms, he grinned as he waited for them to draw near. "Hey, Cricket." His voice was gravelly and warm, and he gave Angus a good scratch behind the ears.

"Hey yourself." Cricket tried for a friendly, pleasant look instead of what she felt like doing, which was grin so hard that her gums showed. "You're looking spiffy."

Hank glanced down at his khakis and shiny loafers as if surprised at what he wore. "Oh, I've got a meeting at work in an hour, but I needed to swing by and meet the lumber delivery guys."

"Are you allowed to fix up a house you don't officially own?"

"I paid extra and did a buyer possession before closing deal with the owners. They're really ready to unload it.

We agreed that if the deal falls through, which it won't, they'll benefit from any improvements I make and can put the house right back on the market without any reimbursement to me."

"Smart." Cricket thought about it. "What's your hurry?"

"The lease on my condo is up in thirty days." He hooked a thumb toward the pink house. "I want to make this place livable before I move in. The house is rough, though. Years of neglect." Hank raised his eyes to heaven. "It'll take a miracle to get renovations done in that short a time."

"How are you going to do all that by then?" Cricket reached down to stroke Angus's back.

"More late nights, early mornings, and lots of coffee. No more power tools early Sunday mornings, though." Hank flashed a rueful smile. "I've got to run to Charlotte this afternoon for a client meeting, but I'll be hitting it even harder starting tomorrow."

Cricket gave a matter-of-fact nod, though secretly thrilled that she'd get to see him more often. But what exactly did Hank do at Mayfield's Fine Cabinetry? If he was a woodworking cabinet maker, would he attend client meetings? She didn't know, but he sure looked sharp all dressed up. Cricket admired him from under lowered lashes.

Hank pointed at her foot. "How's your ankle?"

"Better." Cricket flexed it one way and then another to demonstrate.

Hank rubbed his chin with his fingers. "I missed you while you were gone. It was too quiet without you giving me a hard time."

Cricket cracked a smile. Gazing at his twinkling eyes and his perfect mouth, she felt a happy, hopeful fluttering in her heart that scared her to pieces.

Hank's phone rang, and the ringtone brought her back to earth. Glancing at the screen, he gave her an apologetic look. "That's the delivery guys. I need to take this."

Nodding, Cricket gave herself a mental pep talk as he stepped away. No irrational hopefulness about a man she hardly knew. No excessive happiness and no gummy grins. Cricket would try for an enigmatic half-smile like Charlize Theron in the perfume commercials or the Mona Lisa.

Hearing cheery whistling, Cricket saw Mr. P walk down his porch stairs, pick up the rolled-up copies of his newspapers, and spring up the steps with a jazzy leg crossing move that Cricket thought she'd seen Gene Kelly use in *Singing in the Rain*.

Her neighbor spied her and beamed. "Speedy!"

Cricket gaped. She'd never seen Mr. P beam before. She gave him a wave.

Hank spoke into the phone, sounding exasperated. "That lumber and drywall were supposed to be delivered by noon. Uh-huh. Uh-huh. Well, what do we need to do to make a delivery happen today?"

Catching Hank's eye, Cricket pointed to Mr. P's porch.

Nodding his understanding, Hank walked off with the phone pressed to his ear. "How about checking with the Gastonia store…"

Angus had also spotted Mr. P, and straining at his leash, tried to wag over to greet his old friend. Pulling him closer, Cricket walked him over to visit Mr. P.

As Cricket came closer to her neighbor, she sniffed, and her eyes watered. Mr. P was wearing a powerful cologne, a spicy bay rum scent with undertones of musk, car air freshener, and maybe a hint of Pine-Sol.

Whoo. Cricket breathed through her mouth.

Mr. P scratched Angus with gnarly, liver-spotted hands. He put his empty pipe in his mouth, slapped the newspaper on his thigh, and gave her a toothy grin. "The neighborhood was quiet while you were gone."

"So I heard." What with Mr. P's beaming, whistling, and quick-stepping, something was up. *Ah, Joy.* Amour was in the air. Trying to hide her delighted grin, Cricket sank onto his front stairs.

"How was Asheville?" Mr. P chomped on his pipe with a General MacArthur air of gravitas.

"Good." Trying to look nonchalant, Cricket stretched out her legs and crossed her feet. "So, you met my Aunt Joy?"

"I did. Extraordinary woman. Stunning-looking and

listens to me ramble on." Looking pleased, he added, "She could be a Democrat, but she seemed to like the ribs that I cooked."

"Well, I'm glad." Cricket let out Angus's leash so he could sniff the tightly closed buds of a coral-colored azalea. "Are you two planning on keeping up with one another? I mean, visiting each other in sort of a friendly way?"

Mr. P rubbed his chin. "Well, if she happens to walk down our street or takes care of that dog of yours again, of course I'd call her over to say hello. That'd be the neighborly thing to do." He looked proud of himself, as if he'd just come up with a swell idea.

"It would," Cricket agreed, her mind racing.

Joy was thrilled about Mr. P, he was thrilled about Joy, and nobody was getting any younger. What was holding up progress?

She eyed her friend. "Mr. P, how about asking her out for supper?"

His bushy eyebrows shot up to his Go Navy cap. "Whoa. That'd be mighty bold."

Cricket raised a shoulder. "Joy said nice things about you. I think she likes you."

"She does?" Looking flummoxed, Mr. P frowned. "A classy lady like Joy wouldn't want an old man like me. I've got bum knees, my hair's mostly gone, and I snore so bad I wake myself up. Plus, I've got partials." He tapped his front teeth with a fingernail.

Cricket hid a grin but was touched by his humble assessment of himself. “Joy probably sees the real you, the smart, sweetheart of a guy who was an excellent father and husband, who served our country, and who still keeps up with world events.”

Mr. P looked thoughtful. “Let me sleep on it before I decide.” He looked off into the distance. “If I ask her out, you might need to give me a pointer or two. I’m rusty.”

“Glad to,” Cricket said staunchly, though 100 percent confident she was a terrible dating expert. Glancing next door, she saw Hank had finished his call. He was headed toward them, smiling. Cricket shivered inwardly, amazed that a man as delectable as Hank seemed interested in her.

Mr. P gave her a knowing look. “I see you met our new neighbor. Hank seems like a good sort.”

“He is.” Cricket was flustered that he’d noticed her own possibly blooming romance. Rising, she reeled in Angus and gave Mr. P’s shoulder a squeeze. “See you soon.” She walked to meet Hank halfway.

But before she could reach him, a marigold yellow SUV with a roof rack cruised up to the curb in front of her house, just close enough that she could read the myriad stickers almost covering the bumper and rear cargo door window. They read, “The mountains are calling and I must go,” “Gravity is optional,” “Mountain climbers like it on top,” and “Rocking out!”

Good gravy. It had to be Knox. Cricket gaped and put a hand to her cheek.

Looking like the ripped, tan, and fit mountain man that he now was, Knox stepped out, slammed the door, and scowled. He'd not noticed them. Crossing his arms, he leaned against the side of the SUV, looking like he wished he was anywhere else but there.

Slumping, Cricket clutched her arms to her chest and looked at Hank. "That's my ex-husband. I don't know why he's here."

Hank looked away, the muscles in his jaw tensing. "Thought you got things straightened out with him up in the mountains."

"I thought I did," Cricket said quietly.

A gleaming new Buick surged into the open parking spot behind the yellow SUV, braking so hard that when it stopped, the car rocked back and forth. The door flew open, and Cricket's ex-mother-in-law steamed out wearing a black skirt, a bulky tangerine pullover sweater, and clogs.

"And that's his mama," Cricket murmured.

"Huh." Hank's face was taut.

Cricket stared across the street at Knox and his mother, perplexed. Why were they here?

"I'll leave you to your company." With a curt nod, Hank strode off.

"Wait, Hank…" Cricket called, but his long legs covered ground fast.

She felt a flare of hot anger. The man sure had an itchy trigger finger about complications. Hank had been through a divorce. He knew nobody's life was complication-free.

Knox spotted her and raised his hand. His smile looked forced, and his lower lip stuck out petulantly.

Bea sent her a radiant smile. "Cricket dear," she called and held open her arms.

Dread making her feet feel heavy as bricks, Cricket crossed the street toward home. This impromptu visit could only mean trouble. In her small kitchen, Cricket poured them each a glass of iced tea and sat, looking warily at Knox and Bea. Knox had tried to call Angus over, but the dog had given him the cold shoulder, turned away, and strolled into the other room. Cricket reminded herself to give the dog an extra cookie later.

Her hand on her heart, Bea launched in. "When Knox told me that you'd walked out on him, it just broke my heart."

Cricket started to protest, but Bea held up her hand to stop her.

"Yesterday, my son told us the truth." Bea sent Knox a scathing look, pulled a ratty tissue from her purse, and brushed away brimming tears. "Honey, I am so sorry my son just disappeared on you. And I'm even sorrier that John and I weren't there for you when you probably needed us the most." Bea looked like she was about to cry in earnest but heaved a ragged breath and tried to gather herself. She reached out her hands across the table, palms up.

Feeling a lump in her throat, Cricket held out her hands to squeeze Bea's. She'd missed her so.

Bea drew in a breath, gathering steam. "All I can say is that I did not raise a boy who would abandon his wife. I don't know where we went wrong, but believe me, Cricket, we are going to fix this." She glared at Knox. "We do not divorce in this family. We soldier on and do the best we can, but we *do not* divorce. The only reason we were able to swallow your divorce was because Knox said *you'd* abandoned *him*."

CHAPTER 21

Knox was flat-eyed and tense. His right eye twitched. Cricket eased her hands from his mother's hands and glanced at him, wondering what prettied-up version of the truth he'd told his mama. She'd bet her ex had only admitted to leaving her and not confessed a word about a former wife and a daughter.

Knox's shoulders were slumped, and despite his height and climber's build, he looked deflated. His climbing clothes that were dotted with sponsors' patches and technical logos now looked like a costume that a skinny, scared boy would don to make himself look big. Cricket felt a pang of sadness for Knox, knowing how his strong-willed mother had cowed him, pushed him, and damaged him throughout his childhood. She slid her chair closer to his.

Knox gave her a beseeching look. Her ex was cowed by his mother. Cricket had the power to make Bea march him back into a re-marriage, and he knew it.

But Cricket didn't want him back. Leaning forward,

she spoke with quiet intensity. "Bea, Knox, and I have talked about this thoroughly, and although we didn't handle things very well, our decision to part ways really is a mutual one, especially at this point."

A spark of hope lit in Knox's eyes.

Cricket sat up straighter in her chair, looking at the crestfallen woman. "Knox and I married for the wrong reasons. We are fond of each other and always will be, but we each deserve more."

Bea began to cry in earnest, wiping her eyes with trembling fingers. "This all makes me so sad."

Cricket handed her a tissue, her heart going out to Bea, but she made herself go on. "Knox and I have seen what a good marriage you and John have. You work well together, you drive each other crazy, and you make each other laugh. Your love is strong." Pausing, Cricket looked intently at Bea. "That's the kind of marriage Knox and I each hope to find one day. But not with each other." Reaching over, she squeezed Bea's hands. "It's for the best."

After more tears and promises to keep in touch, Bea and Knox rose.

Knox pulled his mother into a bear hug, and snaking an arm out, he pulled Cricket in. Glancing over Bea's head, he telegraphed Cricket an intensely grateful look, mouthing, "Thank you."

As she heard their cars start and pull away, Cricket breathed a shuddering sigh of relief. Dropping dramatically onto the bed with Angus, she hugged him. The big dog licked her face.

"I think it's finally done. We did good, baby boy."

Stroking Angus's silky coat, Cricket thought about it. Knox was so afraid of his parents' disapproval that he might never come clean about Meadow's existence, something that would be sad for everyone. If he did tell his family about his daughter, once Bea got over the shock, she would be a doting grandmother. The girl would feel so loved. Maybe Bea might even loosen the stranglehold she tried to keep on her boys. Not her problem, Cricket reminded herself.

Scrubbing her face with her hands, Cricket felt almost weak with relief. One thing she was starting to finally understand was despite Nana, Mama, and Knox departing before she was ready to let go, people didn't keep leaving her. All these comings and goings were just part of life. People were just trying to find a big love, live meaningful lives, and find some joy before they winged away from this earth and on to heaven.

In the kitchen, Cricket picked up the picture of Mama and her and held it up to the light streaming in the window. She sat and stared at it, wistful. Cricket remembered her mother's too-bright smile, her chatter, and her constant need for activity outside the home.

Four years ago, a teenage driver in a pickup truck ran a red light and smashed Mama's car to pieces. Six months later, Julius had asked Cricket to come by and help him sort through Rosemary's things so they could take some of them to the second-hand store. After they'd bagged clothes and personal items, Cricket tapped away at Rosemary's laptop, trying to wipe clean the hard drive before they donated it too. With Julius watching the computer screen from over her shoulder and offering unhelpful advice, Cricket had accidentally opened a file that contained copies of passionate emails between Rosemary and Lars, the Swedish tennis pro.

Her heart slamming, Cricket had desperately tried to close the file, but with a firm hand on her shoulder, her father had taken the mouse from her hands and stopped her. White-faced and shaky, Julius slid into the chair she'd been sitting in and read every word of every note written over the year prior to her accident. His wife was desperately in love with Lars and planning to move to Charleston with him. Cricket and Julius never spoke of it again.

Chin in hand, Cricket sat and studied the summer sprinkler photo. *You were lonely, Mama. I get that. I still don't like what you did or how you did it. And it hurt me that you'd have left me, as well as Daddy. But I understand it and I forgive you.*

Cricket replaced the picture on a higher shelf, where she kept cookbooks she didn't use much anymore. Time to let go and move on.

Cricket went to her laptop and peered at the screen. With a finger that trembled a bit, she opened the

"Household Expenses" file that was the cover for the secret list she'd labeled "Possible Reasons Husband Left Me." Reading it one last time, she firmly hit the Delete key. Lacing her fingers behind her head, she leaned back in her chair, marveling at the feeling of freedom. Cricket had made mistakes, no doubt, but she was done with regrets and self-blame. She was officially letting herself off the hook.

Needing to tell somebody about all her triumphs of the day, Cricket called Honey. "Are you in the middle of something?"

Honey spoke in a hushed tone, sounding enthralled. "I'm at the stable, watching my husband and sons bonding with an Appaloosa named Oakley, a new rescue horse that the owners are rehabbing, so he can be part of the therapeutic riding program. The men surprised me today with a visit."

Cricket was touched, knowing how important this was to her friend. "Oh, how wonderful. I'll call back. I don't want to interrupt you."

"Nonsense," Honey said briskly. "They're learning how to groom a horse, and they're happy as pigs in mud. What's up? Need a psychological consult, I hope?"

Cricket smirked. "Nope. Just giving you updates." She relayed the news of the day.

Honey said, "Ah," "I see," and "*No!*" in all the right places. "This is big. You got even more closure. You know for sure why your marriage ended, you took the high road on a few matters, and you mended fences with Knox's mama."

"I may have messed things up with Hank," Cricket admitted. "Hope I haven't chased off such a nice man just because it took me so long to sort things out with Knox."

"You haven't messed anything up," Honey assured her. "Hank is likely gun-shy, just like you are. Take time to get to know him. No pressure."

Cricket exhaled, liking the advice. "Okay, Hon. Go enjoy those lovely men of yours. I love you lots."

"Love you right back."

Making a kissing sound, Cricket ended the call.

Pulling back the curtains, Cricket peeked out at the pink house. Hank's truck was gone. The truck from the lumber company was just rumbling away, and a stack of lumber was tucked under a blue tarp on his front porch.

Good. His supplies arrived. Tomorrow after work, Hank would have a long night ahead of him. The man might be spooked, but that doesn't mean he was heading to the hills. As soon as Hank showed up the next night, she'd make him talk to her.

Cricket tapped a finger to her lip. All around, it was past time to get cracking and give love a nudge.

Picking up a notepad, Cricket found a pen, thinking about her strategy for getting closer to Hank. Tomorrow night, he'd be starved and tired, and he might well welcome a delicious picnic supper. Cricket cracked a smile. She'd serve supper with sides of apologies, clarifications, and humble pie. Glancing at the clock on the stove, Cricket started her grocery list.

The next morning, Cricket would stop by Bubba's Barbecue and pick up some of *the best barbecue in the state. She'd take home two quarts of Bubba's special diced apple and cabbage* slaw that had a hint of horseradish in it for extra bite. Next, Cricket would swing by Primrose Bakery and buy fresh from the oven Portuguese sweet bread for the sandwiches. The sweetness contrasted nicely with the tang of the barbecue sauce.

Cricket would fix Hank the most mouthwatering sandwich he'd ever eaten. She'd pack a bottle of crisp, effervescent Prosecco to add sparkle to the evening. For dessert, Mama's pecan pie. That was dirty pool because Hank would be putty in her hands after his first forkful. But a girl had to do what a girl had to do.

Pulling a red insulated cooler bag from the hall closet, Cricket glanced out the front window. Mr. P was still sitting on his glider in his Navy ball cap, surveying the street. Though she'd always seen him as a gruff, hearty soul who nodded when Hannity made a particularly good point, he suddenly looked small, old, and lonely. Cricket shivered, picturing herself twenty-five years from now, stoop-shouldered, wearing a faded dress, still ruminating about lost love, and knowing she'd let life pass her by. Cricket pushed her shoulders back.

No, ma'am. No more playing it safe and staying as lonely as she'd been for most of her life.

Picking up her cell, Cricket tapped in her neighbor's number. Peering out the window, she watched Mr. P pick up his phone. With this one call, she'd officially be a meddling Cupid, intent on shooting arrows and spreading the love around. Holding up crossed fingers as he picked up, Cricket launched in before she chickened out.

"Mr. P, I have an idea I want to talk to you about..." After detailing her plan, Cricket ended the call. She just couldn't stop smiling.

Tuesday morning, as she fielded the morning calls, Cricket must have had a lilt in her voice because Randy said she sounded chipper, and Marla said she sounded "jolly as a June bug." So proud of herself that she'd come up with a plan, Cricket felt almost buoyant.

Angus ambled over, rested his warm head on her knee, and gave her a soulful look. He wanted to go outside. Cricket pulled Angus's favorite red rubber ball from his toy box, showed it to him, and took the dancing dog out in the backyard for a celebratory game of catch. Ten minutes later, she was back in the kitchen, panting slightly. She'd forgotten her cell and was worried she'd missed a work call. But when she checked her phone, she noticed a text that had come in at five thirty that morning.

The message was from Deirdre Summerline, her client from the nearby town of Pineville. Somehow guessing it was bad news, Cricket held her breath as she read it.

> *My parents, the Hammond's, will no longer be needing your services. We have made other arrange-*

ments. Will send check for final payment. Thank you.

Sagging, Cricket leaned against the counter, trying to keep from panicking. It was happening again. Another client left with no good explanation. Racking her brain for reasons, Cricket felt a surge of determination. With trembling fingers, she phoned Deirdre, but the phone just rang and rang, finally going to voice mail. Trying for a serene, untroubled tone, Cricket left a message asking the woman to return her call but knew in her gut that she'd never hear back from her. If Cricket didn't get to the bottom of this problem, her business would erode away.

Determined, Cricket called Pearl. Thankfully, her assistant picked up quickly, and Cricket filled her in on the latest development.

Pearl sounded shocked. "Holy smokes. These clients who slip away keep using texts as an easy way to leave and not talk to us."

"I know. But we're going to pay the Hammonds a visit before they've had their second cup of coffee," Cricket said in a steely tone. "How fast can you get here?"

"I'll put the pedal to the metal," Pearl promised and hung up.

Cricket climbed in Pearl's car, buckled up, and Pearl motored through quiet streets. Cricket called Linda, the sunny, calm woman who had worked with the Hammonds for the last year.

"Good morning, Linda. Pearl and I are in the car, and

I've got you on speaker. We just got a surprising text from the Hammonds' daughter." Cricket conveyed the message.

Linda gasped, sounding shocked. "I was going to bring my bread machine over tomorrow. Ms. Bonnie and I were going to bake a loaf of whole wheat bread. And I promised Mr. Jim we'd take a walk around the block in the afternoon while his wife napped."

As Pearl skidded around a corner in an Evil Knievel move, Cricket pushed her foot down on an imaginary brake and shot her assistant a warning look. She went on. "Is there anything you saw or heard that might help us understand why they're leaving?"

"Everything's been going great with those two. Neither of them said a word to me about leaving." Linda sounded choked up, like she might cry.

After a few words of encouragement, Cricket put down her phone and glanced over at Pearl. "So, everything was running smoothly, clients were happy, and then they up and leave. Just like with the others."

Pearl shook her head as she hit a speed bump going too fast, jolting them both into the air an inch or two. "I know, I know," she grumped as she caught Cricket's look. "I just want to get there quick and get some answers."

As she turned down the Hammonds' street, Cricket saw Jim Hammond on the front porch, sitting in the fold down seat of his walker and sipping from an insulated mug. His wife, Bonnie, locked the door and walked beside her husband as he started to make his way down the handicap ramp. Cricket's heart raced.

Pearl stepped on the gas, swerving up to the curb like a police cruiser arriving at a crime scene.

Cricket winced, afraid they'd scare the Hammonds, but they were struggling with the walker that had gotten hung up and hadn't seemed to notice them.

The two of them swung out of the car.

Bonnie Hammond saw them, and her eyes darted back and forth from the house to the car like she was trying to decide if she and Jim could make a run for it.

"Good morning!" Cricket called gaily and waved as they walked toward the couple. "How are you all this fine morning?"

"Good morning," Bonnie said with her innate Southern good manners.

"How are you, sir?" Cricket said to Jim, who looked sharp in a yellow and white seersucker shirt and khakis. With his Velcro shut sneaker, he was poking his toe at the braking mechanism on the wheel.

"Oh, I'm well." Jim gave her a cheerful smile. "This little gizmo gets stuck now and then. I want to put it in 'drive,' and it wants to stay in 'park.' "

Cricket stooped, saw the brake stop was partially engaged, and released it. "They can be tricky. Maybe give it a shot of lubricant later."

"Good idea." He beamed at her like she'd done the cleverest thing.

Trying to keep a calm expression on her face, Cricket decided to just be direct. She gazed at Jim and then his wife. "We got word from your daughter this morning that you weren't needing our services anymore. We wanted to stop by to make sure you were happy with Linda and our services. If we did something wrong, we surely want to fix it."

"I'm sorry, this is just not a good time." Mrs. Hammond clutched her purse to her chest, her mouth taut as a clothesline.

"I'm crazy about Linda." Mr. Hammond shook his head, looking crestfallen.

"She's crazy about y'all too." Pearl shot him a sympathetic look. "Would you mind telling us why you're not going to work with her anymore?"

"I appreciate y'all stopping by, but we've got to meet our Sunday school class for lunch." Mrs. Hammond must have seen the anxiety in Cricket's face because, in a gentler tone, she added, "We heard about your troubles, and we are truly sorry."

Cricket stared at her, confused. "I'm not sure what you mean—"

Mrs. Hammond raised a hand to stop her, giving her a pitying look. "I'm sure you're seeing the light, dear. Jim and I, along with our whole Sunday school class, are praying for you."

Pearl's eyes widened and gave a surreptitious jerk of

her head to the coffee mug Mr. Hammond had wedged in the front pocket of his walker.

Cricket gasped quietly, seeing the dark green insulated drink mug with the hot air balloons floating crazily around it. It was just like the mug she'd seen Neddy Bailey cradling and the one sprouting an avocado seed on Arleen Nelson's front porch.

"So, do you mind telling us why you've chosen to work with Gigi's Girls?" Cricket asked.

Mrs. Hammond drew herself up. "We can't afford to be working with an agency run by a woman who has stolen money from clients. My daughter says that's bad judgment, so we've gone with another agency."

CHAPTER 22

Cricket tensed as if expecting a blow. "Who stole money?" she croaked out.

Mrs. Hammond compressed her lips, looking like she was weighing whether to speak honestly or not. "Cricket, we know your daddy, and both Jim and I think he's a fine man. I'm sure he's all torn up about your arrest."

Since Cricket was momentarily speechless, Pearl stepped in. "My goodness. That sure is not true. Who told you that about Cricket?"

"A woman named Gigi paid us a friendly visit last week," Bonnie Hammond stated cautiously.

Mr. Hammond held up his coffee. "Gave us two of these mugs that keep drinks hot or cold and a hundred-dollar gift card for the R & W Cafeteria. I love that place." He shook his head, looking like he was thinking fondly of chicken fried steak, gravy, and mashed potatoes. "She's going to help us with our bill paying, too."

"I'm sure she wasn't trying to speak ill of you, Cricket,

but she did let slip that you'd been charged with embezzling money from clients." Mrs. Hammond shot her a pitying look. "We were so sorry to hear about that. Once you serve your time, you'll have a chance to start fresh."

Cricket gaped, finally starting to grasp the depth of Gigi's ruthlessness. The woman *had* been following her and Pearl. Could Gigi have been systematically visiting Cricket's clients and spreading lies about her, lies that could spell disaster for Cricket's Caregivers? She rubbed the bridge of her nose.

Holy smokes. Unbelievable.

Pearl spoke in a mild but firm voice. "Mr. and Mrs. Hammond, I think you've been given bad information. Cricket has never, ever stolen money from anyone and has surely never been arrested."

Mrs. Hammond looked skeptical and angled her husband's walker back down the ramp. "Come on, honey. We need to get going." With a brittle little smile, she said, "Girls, it's been nice talking with y'all, but we must get going."

As Mr. Hammond wheeled cautiously down the ramp, he looked at his wife. In a querulous voice, he asked, "Well, why would that nice lady, Gigi, tell us something that wasn't true?"

Bonnie Hammond put a steadying hand on her husband's back and quietly said something to him. They slowly made their way to the car.

Pearl pulled the car away from the house slowly. She

glanced over at Cricket, her brow knit in concern. "You all right?"

"Besides my embezzlement charges?" Breathing shallowly, Cricket felt light-headed. Drawing in a deep breath, she blew it out slowly. "I can't believe it."

"I can." Pearl looked disgusted. "Are people like Gigi allowed to just make up lies and ruin peoples' reputations?"

Her thoughts careened around. "It's just our word against hers though, and clients' kids want to protect their parents, so they'll drop us like hot potatoes if there's even a hint of a question about our honesty."

"Isn't talking trash like that against the law?" Pearl persisted, her chin thrust out stubbornly.

Cricket thought about her resolve to never let anyone dismiss her again. She needed to get hold of herself. A woman as small and sneaky as Gigi was not going to get the best of her and Pearl.

Cricket grabbed her phone. "I'll call the attorney that handled my incorporation and see how she thinks we should handle this."

"That's the ticket." Pearl gave her a thumbs up.

"Good morning. This is your client, Cricket Darley. I've got a bit of an emergency," she began and summarized the situation.

Peyton was in a client meeting, the paralegal told her, but he took the message and promised to convey the urgency of the need for a callback. Cricket exhaled as she ended the call, looked over at Pearl, and held up crossed fingers.

Back home, Cricket promised Pearl she'd call her as soon as she heard from the lawyer. Trudging up the stairs, she felt both rattled and stupid for being naïve for so long. She was still trying to take in the bombshell news that she was being deliberately sabotaged. At the kitchen table, Cricket was coiled tight with restless energy and feeling helpless. Drumming her fingers, Cricket willed Peyton to call her back. Gigi had to be stopped, but she didn't know how.

Chores might occupy her mind. Cricket emptied the dishwasher, refilled the salt and pepper shakers, and threw away iffy food from the refrigerator, but she still didn't feel much calmer.

Dad, she thought, and texted him. *Have a minute? Need advice. Trouble on business front."*

The phone rang, and Cricket gave a whooshing sigh of relief as she snatched it up.

"Daddy," she called, tearing up. But all she heard was static on the line. "Hey, Daddy."

His booming voice cut in and out with a bad connection. "Hello, sweetheart…in…mount…Grand Can…"

Cricket touched her forehead, frustrated as she remembered the text he'd sent earlier in the week. After his cheery travelogue update, he'd warned that he would be in Arizona for a few days riding the Grand Canyon Railroad and that cell service would be spotty.

"Dad? Dad," she called.

Just when she'd thought she'd lost him for good, his voice came through the line as clear as if he sat on the other side of her kitchen table. "What's going on, Cricket?"

Talking fast in case the call dropped, Cricket's words tumbled out. "A competitor is stealing our clients, and she's telling people I'm an embezzler."

Her father harrumphed. "That's slander. Check with an attorney, but I believe…civil offense not a criminal…"

The call was in and out again. Cricket walked toward the window, hoping to magically clear the connection by getting closer to the great satellite in the sky.

"I can't hear you, Dad," she said plaintively.

Now, his voice came through clearly. "May want to do more digging. If you can prove she's done this kind of thing before, you may have more ammunition." He paused a moment. "Cricket, you have the brains and the good judgment to fix this problem. I trust you'll figure it out and do it well."

"Thanks, Daddy," Cricket said, buoyed by his words.

"Need to go, hon…winding, steep…love you…" The line went dead.

The phone rang again, and Cricket snatched it up.

Peyton said brusquely, "I have four minutes before another client meeting. Tell me what's up and tell me fast."

Talking quickly, Cricket relayed the story of Gigi's treachery.

The attorney rattled off her answer. "Okay. If the

woman's doing what you say she's doing, that is slander, but that can be difficult to prove. You'd have to have clear documentation about what financial damage she caused your business. You'd have to drag in older clients as witnesses, and most wouldn't want to go through that stress." Pausing, Peyton blew out a noisy breath. "I can send her a cease-and-desist letter. We'll put her on notice that you'll sue her if she continues maligning you or your business."

Cricket could barely contain her relief. "Thank you, thank you, thank you."

Peyton gave a bark of a laugh. "Don't worry. I'll bill you. Now, I need to scat." She ended the call without saying goodbye.

Her shoulders sagging with relief, Cricket sat for a moment, mulling over Peyton's advice and her father's words. Pursuing a slander charge would be a big sinkhole of time and money. The warning letter from Peyton might work, or Gigi might ignore it. She and Pearl needed a Plan B, and it needed to be a strong one.

Cricket's thoughts sped around in her head. Pearl did all the background checks on potential hires with a program they subscribed to, but that required the written permission of the person whose background they were investigating. Fortunately, Pearl had developed some excellent online snooping skills.

Picking up the phone, she called Pearl. "You're good at investigating. Can you see if you can dig up any dirt on Gigi? Also, check for any Better Business Bureau complaints, any bad reviews, and other things of that nature on Gigi's Girls."

"On it," Pearl said brusquely and ended the call.

Cricket gave a nod of satisfaction. Tucking her shopping list in her purse, she grabbed a light jacket and locked up. Cricket wasn't going to sit around wringing her hands until she forced Gigi to back off. She and Pearl could and would manage Gigi as soon as she got her facts together. But for now, Cricket was going to round up supplies so she could bring supper to a good-looking man and orchestrate amour with Aunt Joy and Mr. P.

Cricket's spirits rose as she walked to the car. She gave a wave to Mr. P, who was at his usual community watch post on the front porch. But as she turned the key in the ignition, Cricket had a thought and cut the car off. She trotted across the street.

"Hey, Mr. P. You looking forward to tonight?" she asked.

With a crooked grin, Mr. P pretended to preen, smoothing back what was left of his hair with both hands. "I am."

"Good. I'll drop the food off around five thirty." Cricket hesitated. "Quick question about the neighborhood."

"Yes, ma'am," he said, looking serious.

Cricket gazed at her neighbor. "You know the Finches,

right? Do you know if they're home or if they're out of town?"

Mr. P's face fell. "Neither. About a month ago, Faith had a heart attack and passed away, bless her. Myers went four days later. They say he died of a broken heart."

Cricket put a hand to her mouth, remembering their smiling faces from her parents' parties. "I'm so sorry. They were real nice people."

"They were," he said softly. Frowning, Mr. P rubbed his forehead. "They have one bad-apple type son who never came around. He didn't even show up for the funerals."

Though she'd not seen the Finches in over twenty years, Cricket felt a pang of sadness. But her thoughts were racing. If the Finches had both passed, why would Gigi be in their home? Had the ne'er-do-well son contacted her to help put the house in order, or was Gigi helping herself to the older couple's possessions while no one was in charge? Her brain whirred, but glancing at her watch, Cricket saw she needed to get a move on.

"See you soon, Mr. P. Tonight's going to be a good night." Cricket gave him a reassuring smile, raised a hand, and hurried back to her little SUV.

A little while later, Cricket inhaled and groaned happily. Her car smelled like a foodie's dream. Tangy barbecue scent wafted from the white bag with the happy pig on it, and the yeasty scent of freshly baked bread drifted from the Primrose's bag.

Wheeling into the Shoppers World Grocery in the older part of town, Cricket hurried down the aisles, gathering the last few items she needed for their supper. As she wheeled into the ten-items-or-less line, she made a mental list of all she had to do when she got home.

The silvery-haired woman in front of her in line unloaded her cart like she had all the time in the world. Her wrinkled hand bedecked with serious rings, the older woman smiled at Cricket and then at the plump, tired-looking cashier with the comb-over hairdo. Holding up the see-through pint container for them to admire, she drawled, "These oysters just looked so pretty. I couldn't resist. And the seafood fellow said they were harvested yesterday in southern Louisiana, which is supposed to be the best. It's still an R month, right?"

Both Cricket and the cashier nodded helpfully.

"So plump looking." Giving the container a little pat as she placed it on the belt, she turned to her new besties. "I love this store to pieces, but I came by last week, and I had to wait in line for almost twenty minutes. I need to remind myself not to shop on the day that our Social Security checks arrive." After paying, she beamed at them and gave a little wave as she waltzed off. "So good to see you both. Now, take care."

On the way home, Cricket's palms were clammy, and her heart was beating double time. She was part excited and part terrified about that evening. If Hank had decided she was a come-here-go-away manipulator, the evening could be mortifying and excruciating. Mama's pie wasn't going to fix that one. This could be the worst idea she'd ever had.

Her shoulders slumped as her spirits sank, and she remembered the ease with which Knox had left her. She couldn't be that compelling. Maybe she should just call off the whole thing.

Cricket gave herself a talking to. *Calm down and don't set your expectations too high.*

If all she managed to do tonight was get back on good footing with Hank, even on a smile-and-wave-at-your-neighbor basis, she'd call that a win. No matter what, Cricket at least wanted Hank as a friend. Even if Hank gave her the cold shoulder, she needed to practice having fun, talking to men, and making friends. Everything was going to work out fine.

After she'd put up groceries, Cricket riffled through mama's recipes and quickly put together a beautiful pecan pie. Breathing in, Cricket sighed with pleasure as she picked up the sweet aromas of the caramelizing brown sugar and the browning pastry. Pulling the pie from the oven, she slid it onto a wire rack to let it cool.

After a quick shower, Cricket slipped on a sage green cotton dress that she hoped accentuated her curves and a strappy pair of soft bed sandals that she'd found on the ShoesToGo website. Applying a calming cream to her hair, she pulled it through a curved brush, blowing it dry until it gleamed. Pulling it up into a loose updo, she secured it with the four-inch-long hairpins that Pearl had assured her were "what the professionals used." With light foundation and a poof of loose powder, Cricket looked in the vanity mirror and felt good. Not bad for a woman who was already getting mail from those go-getters at AARP. With a slick of claret-colored lip gloss and a spritz of something lemony, she turned away from the mirror, feeling a squadron of butterflies rev up in her chest.

Cricket slipped a silver ice pack block into each of the already-packed red cooler bags, inserted the Prosecco bottles, and for a celebratory touch, carefully added two delicate flutes wrapped in dishtowels in each bag. Slipping the note she'd written Hank into their red bag, Cricket zipped both picnic suppers.

There. Cricket gave each bag an affectionate pat, like the woman who'd patted her oysters at the grocery store.

Angus nudged her. Looking pitiful, he reminded her that he'd not yet been fed. Giving him an extra generous scoop of kibble, she pulled back the curtain and peeked out. It was almost five thirty, and Hank's truck had already been at the pink house for over an hour. Hopefully, he'd be hungry soon and more receptive to her surprise visit. Glancing next door, Cricket saw Mr. P pacing on his porch wearing a coat and tie.

Go, Mr. P, she thought with a smile.

A text came in, and she hurried to read it.

Pearl wrote, *Pay dirt! Dug around and called an old friend who is with the Sherriff's Department. We had a nice chat. GG has convictions, 4 bad checks, credit card fraud. Left South Carolina to come here 4 clean start. Still digging. Be back in touch in AM.*

Cricket put her hands on her head, grinning as she sent up a fervent thank you. With this new information, they could get Gigi to stop maligning them. But for now, Cricket needed to get a move on.

Sliding the now-heavy red cooler bags from the counter, she gave Angus a quick pat. "Wish me luck, buddy."

As she approached, Mr. P looked at her, bright-eyed. "You look real nice, Speedy."

She broke into a smile. "And you look like Harrison Ford."

"When you ask an angel out for a surprise picnic, you need to clean up." With gnarled hands, Mr. P straightened his tie. "I wasn't sure what duds to wear. It's my first date in decades."

Cricket realized what a big deal this evening was for him. She hoped the night turned out well for them all. Cricket handed Mr. P one of the packed red cooler bags.

He took it, and his bushy brows flew up. "Heavy. What's in it?"

"All sorts of goodies." Cricket grinned and put a hand on her hip. "So, how did you get Joy to come over?"

"I told her I needed help hanging pictures." Mr. P looked proud of his ruse.

Cricket clasped her hands together. "I love it. That was so clever."

Her neighbor was warming to the idea of his being a clever man about town. "I also told her not to eat because I had leftover lasagna that I needed to get rid of before it went bad."

Cricket rolled her eyes. "Joy must really like you because that was a pitiful meal invitation."

"I kind of froze up," Mr. P admitted.

"Hey, she said *yes*. That's all that counts." Cricket patted him on the shoulder. "Now, where are you taking her for your picnic?"

"We're going to Azalea Lake." Mr. P said proudly. "There's a bluff that folks don't know about because it's down the dirt service access road. I'm bringing an old quilt so we can sit and eat on the ground." He gave her a shrewd look. "I was going to take the plastic tarp I use for leaves but thought the quilt would work better."

"Good thinking." Cricket tried not to smile. "She'll love it."

Her neighbor rocked back and forth on his heels. "Now, you've got plans of your own, right?"

"I do." She held up crossed fingers. "But I'm not so sure Hank likes me."

"What's not to like?" Mr. P said gruffly. He waved her off with a calloused hand. "Go get him, Speedy, and thank you. Never would have gotten the guts to ask that glorious creature out, much less do the whole romantic picnic deal, unless you'd given me a shove in the right direction."

Impulsively, Cricket leaned over and gave him a peck on the cheek. Her heart rocketing around, she walked next door to the pink house.

CHAPTER 23

Feeling as gawky and unsure as she did in high school when they made her sell chocolate bars for the glee club trip, Cricket pushed the doorbell. She heard the whine of a saw, and as she rubbed away dust from the sidelights, Cricket saw Hank Mayfield cutting a board. Not sure if the paint-encrusted doorbell worked, she waited until he'd finished sawing and rang it again. But he didn't come to the door. As he picked up the next board and adjusted his protective glasses, Cricket rapped firmly on the door.

Hank pulled his glasses up on his head, a look of impatience flickering across his face. Catching a glimpse of her through the dirty glass, he frowned as he swung open the door.

"Yes?" He looked at her like she was a stranger.

"Hey, Hank." Cricket's voice came out unexpectedly squeaky, and when she saw his closed face, she flushed. He was mad all right.

"Cricket." Hank leaned against the doorframe and gazed at her coolly.

Thrown by his cool reception, Cricket was also having a visceral reaction to Hank that left her wordless. With broad shoulders, what looked like washboard abs under his t-shirt, long jeans-clad legs, and those eyes, he was a beautiful man. The silence spun out.

"I see you're sawing," she said and cringed inwardly. That's the best she could come up with?

"I am," Hank brushed sawdust off his face with a muscled forearm. He pretended to peer behind her. "No ex-husband this evening, or did you leave him back at your place?"

"That's over for good," Cricket said, trying to sound calm while her insides were churning.

Eyes narrow, Hank shook his head slowly. "Doesn't seem over. You chase him up to Asheville, and he chases you back down here."

"It's not like that." Cricket held out her hands, palms up. "That get-together you saw was his mama's idea. She dragged him down from the mountains by his ear and forced him to meet with me." Lifting her chin, Cricket gave him a level look. "My former mother-in-law is a strong woman who loves me and believes in staying married no matter what. She wanted to talk us into trying again, but it's over."

He raised a brow. "You sure?"

"I am."

Crossing his arms, Hank shot her a skeptical look. "What if you decide you want him back? Is it one of those hot and cold running relationships because I had my fill of those with my ex-wife."

"I am not your ex-wife," Cricket said firmly and was annoyed that her eyes filled up with tears. She brushed them away quickly. "The marriage is history. We're divorced for good, with no reconciliation possible."

"Uh-huh." Hank nodded, but his face was implacable.

Cricket just stared at him, anger searing her heart. What was wrong with men? Why was she always chasing them down? She was so sick of it. Cricket picked up the red bag cooler picnic and thrust it at Hank so hard that she pushed him a step back as he took it.

"I brought you supper." Whipping around, she stalked off toward home. Her face burning, tears coursed down her cheeks, but she didn't care. She'd lock the door on the world, pour a glass of wine, and hole up with sweet Angus.

And that's just what Cricket did. Shucking her clothes, she slipped into her most comfy sweats, put on her Minions slippers, and took a cool washcloth to her face. She talked to Angus, who appeared to be listening hard and looking concerned as she rattled on. "That's it for me, buddy. No more men. They are way too much trouble. Jerks who don't listen."

Angus slumped onto the floor of the kitchen while she poured herself a glass of wine.

Cricket curled up on the couch, still stinging from rejection. Pulling Angus up beside her, she covered them both with a fleecy throw. Taking a manly size sip of wine, she desultorily flipped through channels. *The Bachelor, Married at First Sight,* a Hallmark movie about a hunky widower falling in love with a sassy schoolteacher.

"All these stupid shows about love. Why?" she asked Angus, but his eyes were closing.

An impossibly slim and striking chef was making pasta in a rustic outdoor kitchen, with what looked like the hills of Tuscany behind her. Perfect. Cricket adjusted a pillow under her head and rested her legs on the warm dog.

A knock sounded at her door, and Cricket groaned softly. The visitor had to be her neighbor, and she had nothing to say to him. Angus growled, his ears perked, and he stared intently at the door.

"It's okay, guy." Cricket patted his head to calm him.

The knock sounded again, louder and more persistent that time.

Slipping out from under her warm cocoon, Cricket gazed out the peephole. *Yup.*

Hank Mayfield, looking as hunky as ever, even with the distortion of the peephole.

"Go away," she called loudly. "I don't like you."

"I don't care. I'm going to stay out here and knock until you let me in," he said pleasantly. "I've got all the time in the world, and I'm a strong knocker." Hank gave a loud staccato rap just to showcase his skills.

Shaking her head, Cricket sank back on the couch and turned up the volume. The glamourous chef kept tossing back her sable hair.

Cricket frowned. Shouldn't she be wearing a hairnet?

The chef smiled into the camera. "We're adding earthy flavor to this pasta by mixing homemade pesto to the flour and salt before we crack in the eggs..."

The knocking continued.

Cricket lowered the volume. "You're irritating. Go away," she hollered to him.

"Not going away." Hank sounded downright cheerful.

Cricket cracked open the door, keeping the deadbolt chained. She glowered at him. "What do you want?"

Hank raked a hand through his hair and gave her a beseeching look. "Cricket, I just want to talk to you. Just for a few minutes."

She said nothing and gave him the fisheye.

"I want to apologize." He held up the red bag. "I've brought you an extra-special picnic."

Cricket rolled her eyes but had to smile. She slid back the chain and let him in, careful to keep several feet of space between his lanky loose-limbed hotness and herself. "You've got three minutes," she said.

Stepping inside, Hank put the bag on the table and jammed his hands in his pockets. He shook his head wonderingly. "That supper you packed was...amazing. But the best part was your note." Hank held it out to her so she could see her own scrawl.

> *Sorry for being so grouchy and thinking the worst of you. I like you, Hank Mayfield, and that scares me. But I think you're a good guy and I'd like to start over with you. Do over?*
>
> *Your friend, Cricket.*

Hank rubbed his chin with his fingers. "I may have overreacted in thinking you were a back-and-forth manipulative type, just like my ex-wife. Seems like you might be easy to spook too."

She hesitated and then bobbed her head grudgingly. "Do you believe me about the marriage being completely over?"

"I do." Hank nodded slowly. "Would you like a glass of bubbly? I brought over a fine little bottle."

Cricket cracked a grin and uncrossed her arms. "You are a thoughtful guy."

"Many say I am." Shrugging modestly, he pulled the bottle and glasses from the bag.

Cricket sipped the fizzy Prosecco and sighed happily at its effervescent loveliness. She sat cross-legged on one end of the couch, and Hank was on the other.

"Just for the record," she told him, "my ex-husband and I could have reconciled, but I turned him down. He would have done it to make his mama happy, but I was 100 percent sure I didn't want him."

"I'm glad," he said quietly.

"Me, too." Cricket decided to come clean about all the details. "My ex walked out of my life without one word of explanation. He was big on lies of omission. Little things, like a previous marriage he never told me about. Turns out he has a daughter."

"Hunh." Hank's look was steady. "I don't care for your husband. Can't stand a liar, and he left you and wasn't man enough to talk about it." He scowled. "He's also fit and rugged-looking."

Cricket grinned.

Reaching inside the red bag, Hank pulled out the supper she'd packed, groaning aloud with pleasure as he unwrapped the fragrant sandwiches and sides. "My, my." He passed her a paper plate and a sandwich and peered deeper into the bag. "Let's see what other nice things I brought you."

Cricket bit back a smile. Suddenly, she was ravenous. Taking a swallow from her flute, she found herself relaxing. Cricket studied him from underneath her lashes. "Tell me more about your marriage."

Hank finished the first bite of his barbecue sandwich and groaned aloud. "This is the best supper I've ever had in my life," he said reverently. He took a sip of Prosecco. "My ex, Piper, danced with the Charlotte Ballet and was talented. But she had a fall and tore the meniscus in her knee. It took two surgeries and a year of physical therapy before it began to heal. As she was recovering, Piper fell again. She was out of the running for a prima ballerina role at any dance company and lucky to be able to dance at all."

Cricket was fighting feeling sorry for Piper. She didn't want to like his ex-wife. "Then what happened?"

"We bought a dance studio in Cornelius, and Piper made a real go of it. I was proud of her, but she fell for one of her student's dads. He started an at-home meal delivery business like HelloTasty, but it was for clients with special diets." Hank rubbed his thumb and his fingers together and grimaced. "Big bucks." His mouth twisted. "So, Piper left me for him. Then she'd beg me to take her back, but two days later, she'd go back to him. She'd show up in the middle of the night, crying and saying she couldn't live without me, then leave again a couple days later."

"Wow." Cricket was starting to understand his skittishness.

"It went on for too long." Hank took a bite of slaw and furrowed his brow at the memory. "I'd finally had enough and ended it. Then the great divorce wars started, but I'm past it now. I moved back to Azalea, where I was raised, and got my life back on track. Nice and calm and normal. No drama."

Cricket took a bite of her barbecue and chewed it slowly, savoring the spicy sweetness. "Knox and I were just the opposite. We avoided conflict—and any meaningful talk about the problems in our marriage—until it was too late."

Hank took that in as he swallowed and got a determined glint in his eye. "Life goes on and we move on. I've been working on letting things go and heading to a happier future instead of dragging loss around with me."

"Smart." Cricket couldn't believe she was having a conversation with a man that had emotional depth. This would take some getting used to.

Hank picked up his Prosecco and raised it. "Let's drink a toast to a happy future." Fixing her with a look, his eyes held hers.

Barely breathing, Cricket couldn't look away. Her arms and legs had turned to water. What did his toast mean? Was it just a general one Hank pulled out when a cork popped? Cricket swallowed loudly. No more guessing, and no more skirting hard topics to talk about.

"Just to be clear," she said. "Are we talking about dating and the possibility of a future between the two of us?"

"I'm hopeful about that." Hank had a half-smile on his face, but his eyes were dark and his gaze intense.

Cricket remembered all the loneliness, sorrow, and pain that was caused by marrying a man who was so wrong for her and closed her eyes at the memory. Never again. She held up a hand, knowing she risked losing him by speaking so clearly, but she just had to. "I like you, Hank."

"You told me in your note." Humor gleaming in his

eyes, he patted her card that he'd folded and stuck in his shirt pocket.

Cricket had to smile. "I *do* like you, and I'm hopeful about the possibilities with you too." Warily, she watched to see if he showed any signs of sprinting out the door, but he was staying put. "Can we just take things really slowly? Can we just get to know each other and spend time to see if we're even a good match?"

"A snail's pace suits me fine." The corners of Hank's mouth twitched, and his eyes lit up. "Remember, trying to finish this remodeling so quickly means I'll be here, but I'll be working flat out. Not much time for candlelight suppers and long walks in the rain. I'll be tired and ornery until I finish."

Cricket was almost giddy with relief that he wasn't going to be petulant or push her away. "Good."

"Deal." His voice was low and gruff, and when Hank gazed at her, his eyes were glittering with intensity and longing. Sighing regretfully, he rose. "I need to get back. My drywall guy's coming tomorrow, and I've got to replace a bunch of the rotten boards before he can do his part."

He pulled Cricket to her feet, and she tingled at his touch.

Trying to wipe the fatuous smile off her face, Cricket picked up the cooler bag and thrust it at him. "Take this home. You apparently baked a pecan pie too. You'll need your strength if you're working late." Cricket busied herself gathering the paper plates and napkins. "And I might bring you another sandwich sometime soon."

"Man, oh man." Hank shook his head. "After too many microwave burritos and frozen mac and cheese, you'll spoil me." He gave her a slow, sweet smile. "For the record, I like you, Cricket. I can't wait to see where this goes."

Hesitating a moment, he stepped toward her and folded her into a long hug that felt both safe and dangerous at the same time. Tipping her chin back with his finger, he kissed her slowly, then hungrily.

Cricket sank into his embrace and kissed Hank back. As she reluctantly let go, she sniffed him again. Yup. Hank still smelled as delicious as he always did. Suddenly stepping away from him, Cricket grinned and waved him away with the back of her hands. She shooed him out the door just like she'd once seen her nana do to two chickens who'd accidentally wandered into the kitchen from the yard. If she'd had a broom handy, Cricket would have used it.

"Bye, Hank."

Not seeming to mind being shooed, Hank flashed her a smile. "See you soon, girl," he called as he clomped down the stairs.

The next morning, Cricket floated around, scarcely believing that last night had really happened. She daydreamed about Hank and had many slow-motion reruns of that intense, toe-curling kiss. She shivered. Cricket was going to need to drum up all her resolve to keep the slow pace that she'd preached about last night. But she'd do it. She had to. Cricket peeked out the window at the pink house, knowing Hank wasn't there yet, but still feeling connected to him and comforted just by looking at his house.

Mr. P was on the porch. She'd call him for a quick date report.

Her neighbor picked up the phone, and Cricket cut right to the chase "How did the picnic go last night?"

Mr. P sighed so deeply that Cricket got worried. "It went swell. Joy was surprised, and we got along just like two old shoes."

She blew out a whooshing sigh of relief. "I'm so glad. When are you going to see her again?"

He gave another drawn-out, lugubrious sigh. "I'm not."

Cricket sat down hard in the kitchen chair, glancing out the window at him, wondering if she needed to go next door and give him a shake. "Why in the world not?"

"Speedy, I feel guilty, like I stepped out on my late wife. Alma was a good woman, but she was the jealous type. I was as loyal as a good dog, but she always worried other women were angling for me. That evening with your aunt was…pure magic." Mr. P hesitated. "But I think my Alma would be upset about me taking up with Joy."

Cricket took that in, thinking she probably wouldn't

have liked Alma. "Your late wife wouldn't want you to be happy?"

"Not as happy as Joy might make me," he admitted.

"I understand." Cricket sighed as she ended the call, disappointed for him and for her aunt.

She'd bring it up again later and see if he might change his mind. Cricket shuddered, dreading her having to break the bad news to Joy.

She glanced at the clock, realizing she'd need to get moving if she was going to make Angus's vet appointment. She threw on some clothes and rounded up the dog.

"Come on, buddy. Time you got spruced up." She herded a reluctant Angus into the car and motored off to the vet's office for his six-month checkup.

The big dog trembled the entire ride to Azalea Animal Hospital, despite Cricket's efforts to soothe him.

On the drive home, Angus was mellow and calm.

Cricket smiled over her shoulder at him and passed him a few cookies she'd picked up from the jar at the vet's office. "That wasn't so bad, was it? Now you're good and healthy, and the vet techs all talked about how handsome you are."

But Angus was ignoring the pep talk, busy crunching the cookie and sniffing the car cushions to hoover up any crumbs he'd missed.

Nearing home, Cricket was about to turn right but impulsively hooked a left. She'd drive by the Finches' house one more time. Slipping on her sunglasses as she turned east into the morning sun, Cricket turned it over in her mind again. An important part of the Gigi-the-schemer puzzle was still missing. Maybe a drive by the Finches' place would jar the thought loose.

Slowly, she cruised by the sad-looking house. Busy rubbernecking, she almost sailed through a yellow light that had turned red. Cricket stepped hard on the brake. Eyes wide, Cricket checked to make sure Angus hadn't been jolted from his seat, but he was fine.

With her sudden stop, a crumpled scrap of paper had rolled out from under the front seat. Her shoulder pulling against the seat belt, Cricket leaned down to nab it. The receipt must have fallen from the bag after yesterday's grocery store run. Could it be? Pulling over, Cricket's breathing was shallow as she examined the receipt, checking the date.

All the pieces that had lurked just out of reach of her awareness began to fall into place. She thought about the chatty older woman with the oysters and her comment about the long lines on the day Social Security checks got deposited. Cricket threw back her head and laughed, so excited she felt breathless.

Pulling over, she reached for her phone. "Pearl, can you come by as soon as you can? I think I may have figured out Gigi's deal with the Finches. Does your sister, Agate, still work downtown?"

Pointing her car toward home, Cricket grinned.

Get ready, Gigi. The chickens are coming home to roost.

CHAPTER 24

Afterward, Cricket and Pearl sat on the rockers on Daddy's front porch and sipped their iced tea, marveling and still a little stunned that they'd conveyed their concerns to Pearl's sister, Agate, who worked at the Social Security Administration. The facts that they had dug up about Gigi Gallagher's background made it hard to fathom how she'd been allowed to work with vulnerable older people at all.

Pearl fished the lemon wedge in her glass of tea and gave it an extra squeeze. "Do you think she really has been stealing the Finches' social security? Stealing money from dead people is as low as you can go." Looking disgusted, Pearl shook her head.

Cricket couldn't believe it either. "They'll find out. If Gigi had a helper working at the Finches' house before they passed, she could have easily gotten access to their bank accounts and diverted money every month when the checks came." Though Pearl's sister had been tight-lipped as she listened to their information, she did tell them that stealing Social Security checks could result in heavy fines and even imprisonment.

Pearl rocked and sipped her tea. "Glad we told Agate about Gigi's offering to help the Hammonds with their bill paying. If she's dipped her fingers into any other of her clients' bank accounts, they've got the folks who could find out."

"We've done our part. If we're wrong, they'll find that out." Cricket looked at Pearl and mused aloud. "But if we're right, we just handed off this heavy anvil of worry to the right people."

"Agate is smart as a fox." Pearl gave her a crooked grin.

As they swallowed the last of their tea, they rose.

Pearl slipped her purse onto her shoulder. "I need to get home. This has been a whopper of a day." She eyed Cricket, and the corners of her mouth twitched. "We are dynamic lady detectives. Rizzoli and Isles, Cagney and Lacey, or…" She hesitated.

"You ran out of names of lady detective duos." Cricket smirked, and feeling a swell of gratitude and affection, she reached over to hug Pearl. "Thank you so much. I couldn't have done this without you."

"No need to be without me. I'm not going anywhere." Pearl colored at the display of affection but looked pleased. "Glad to help, and I got a kick out of it." With a wave, she headed toward her car.

"Have a good rest of your day." Cricket thought more

about her need to lower a few walls, and she blurted out, "Pearl, is Dalton moving any houses anytime soon?"

Turning back to look at her, Pearl gave a sideways smile. "He's moving an old bungalow tomorrow."

Opening her mouth, Cricket shut it again, her thoughts racing. Was she being intrusive? Did Pearl just view her as a boss to be tolerated for the paycheck? But she made herself forge ahead.

"Can I come watch? I've never seen anything like it and think it would be cool." Cricket rubbed her forehead with her fingers. "I mean, if that's okay. I won't get in the way or anything..."

Pearl broke into a slow smile. "Sure. It's *very* cool. They start at five in the morning, so bring your coffee. I'll text you the address." With a little wave, she headed off.

Upstairs, Cricket got into comfortable clothes and started a load of laundry. Her phone rang, and she saw Joy's number. Bracing herself, she picked up. "Hey, Joy. How are you?"

"Amazing, wonderful, happy. That about covers it." Her usually reserved aunt giggled like a teenage girl. "Jackson and I have so much in common, and he's smart and makes me laugh." Joy gave a swooning sigh. "Well, have you seen him, and did he say anything about the evening?"

Cricket groaned inwardly. "I did talk to him, and he had a great evening. In fact, I believe he said it was a *magical* evening, but he..." There was no way to sugar coat this, and her words came out in a rush. "He's worried that seeing you again might upset his dead wife, who was apparently the jealous type."

"Goodness," Joy mused and was quiet for a long moment. Then, in a brisk voice, she said, "I believe I need to pay that man a visit and talk some sense into him. When God hands you a gift, you don't just say, 'No, thank you.' Wish me luck, sweetheart."

"I'm rooting for you." Cricket's heart lifted as she ended the call.

Cricket saw a voice mail message from Hank that she'd somehow missed. Her smile faded as she listened to his message.

Hank sounded curt. "Hey, Cricket, this is Hank. I'm calling to cancel Mama's helper for tomorrow. We won't be needing your services any longer—"

Cricket stabbed the end button before she heard the whole message and hurriedly hit redial. Her mind raced. Had Gigi gotten to him too, and what if he believed her lies? When she heard his hello, rising anxiety made it hard to breathe.

"Hey there, Hank."

"Hey, Cricket." He paused. "You sound out of breath."

"Just busy," she said, trying to sound casual. "I wanted to come talk with you about your voicemail."

"I just got to the house. I'm in the kitchen. The door is open. Just walk on back." He sounded cool, distracted.

"Don't go anywhere. I'll be right there." Racing across the street, she tried to compose her face.

In the kitchen, Hank knelt on the newly tiled floor, mopping up a large pool of water. The cabinet doors under the kitchen sink were open, and a wrench lay on the floor. "Hey there. Give me a minute. Plumbing problems."

Cricket exhaled. His cool tone might have had nothing to do with her.

A few soggy bath towels later, Hank gave the cutoff valve one final twist and rose. "Averted a small disaster, and I've got a plumber on the way." He cocked his head. "You look tense."

"I am tense." Cricket held her hands behind her back so she'd stop wringing them. "Did a woman named Gigi Gallagher recently pay a visit to you or your mama?"

"Don't know her." Hank leaned against the counter, managing to look elegant in his khakis with the wet knees.

"Oh, thank goodness," Cricket breathed, sagging with relief.

Hank's brows creased with concern. "Everything okay?"

"Fine, fine," Cricket said, trying to sound casual and relaxed.

"Wish you'd gotten here sooner. Mama's gone," Hank said in a regretful tone.

"Gone? Already gone?"

Tears sprang to her eyes. Gloria had seemed so alive just a few days ago. Cricket felt a rush of sympathy for Hank. But why was he so concerned about a plumbing problem when his mother just died?

"How did she go so fast?" she choked out.

Looking baffled, Hank rubbed the back of his head. "Southwest Airlines. She got a direct flight to Sarasota."

"Sarasota?" she asked weakly, trying to make sense of it all.

Hank gave her a level look, an amused expression on his face. "You didn't listen to my whole voice mail, did you?"

"No," she blurted, feeling foolish. "I thought you were firing us because you'd heard about my alleged embezzling."

The corners of his mouth twitched, and Hank rubbed his chin. "Gosh, you stay busy."

Cricket smiled, weak with relief. "And I thought you just told me your mama passed."

His eyes widened, and his brows flew up. "No. My Mama's still way too much of a live wire to pass." Hank gave her a reassuring grin. "In my message, I said she went to visit her sister in Florida for a few months."

Cricket smiled, relief flooding over her. "I'm so glad. I like your mama a lot."

"Me too." He shook his head, his eyes getting a nice crinkle around the edges when he smiled. "Mama would be tickled to know we are spending time with each other. She was determined to be a matchmaker for us."

"Speaking of that," Cricket said. "Remind me to tell you about a little matchmaking I've done recently."

"So many talents. Running a business, embezzling, matchmaking." Hank shook his head admiringly.

Cricket burst out laughing, maybe too hard for what he said, but it felt so good.

Hank was serious now. "I'd never believe anything bad about you, Cricket." He glanced at his watch. "But if I don't leave now, I'm going to be late for the board meeting."

"Board as in board of directors?" Cricket asked slowly. "That's a great company that invites all their employees to the board meeting."

Hank's mouth turned up. "They'd better invite me. I'm one of the owners."

Cricket frowned. "But your mother said you were a carpenter."

"Mama always says that." Hank looked chagrinned. "It's an inside joke in our family, but there's truth to it. Family members are required to spend a lot of time in the shop and on the ground floor before moving up into management."

"Well." Cricket blinked, gazed into his caramel brown eyes, and took it all in. Hank might be a big mucketymuck and not a carpenter who could use her flash cards to pass the contractor's licensing exam, but when she looked at him, Cricket still felt the same knee-weakening and pulse-accelerating connection since she'd landed in his lap in the African restaurant.

Watching her reaction, he broke into a teasing grin. "You liked me when I was a blue-collar guy. You still like me if I'm not?"

Cricket's eyes fixed on his and pressed her palms lightly against his cheeks. "I'd like you no matter what you did for work. I just want you to be happy."

"I'm happy every minute I'm with you," he said in a low, husky voice. Pulling her into his arms, he brushed her lips with his thumb and kissed her long and deep. Pulling back, Hank smoothed her hair with both his calloused hands and looked at her almost reverently. "I found myself a sweet, smart, gorgeous redhead. How did I get so lucky?"

"I'm the lucky one," Cricket murmured, her voice cracking with emotion. Skimming her fingertips along his strong jawline, she put her arms around his neck and pressed her lips to his, feeling a rush of crazy attraction.

When they finally broke off the kiss, Hank held her tightly, and Cricket sighed, letting herself relax into the solid warmth and solace of his embrace.

After Hank left for his meeting, Cricket went home and slipped into cotton shorts and a favorite T-shirt that had been washed so many times that it felt like gossamer. Pouring herself a glass of ice water, she sat at the kitchen table as Angus curled up under her feet. Cricket felt a sense of peace and possibilities wash over her.

Glancing over at Mr. P's, she grinned as the familiar blue Volkswagen bug pulled up. Wearing a pink velour tracksuit and a determined look on her face, her aunt stepped out and walked toward Mr. P's house. Ah, love was in the air, and Cricket had a strong feeling that letting Joy into his life was going to make Mr. Jackson Purefoy a happy man.

Out of habit more than anything, Cricket slid in front of the laptop and pulled up the ShoesToGo site. She might just heat up the Visa card and order herself the suede moccasins or the patent leather Oxfords she'd been eyeing. Buying shoes out of hopefulness rather than loneliness was a new thing for her.

Cricket looked down at her scuffed boots—the ones with the slightly worn-down heels and the tooth marks where Angus had nibbled on them. Her boots suited her fine. Cricket didn't need fancy new shoes to bring her a happy life. With a firm click, she closed the site and then her laptop.

Rising, Cricket whistled up Angus before grabbing a windbreaker, a bottle of water, and the life vests from the hall closet. Skipping lightly down the stairs with Angus thundering down beside her, Cricket stopped when she got in the yard. Hands on hips, she breathed in the clear, cool air. Pulling Angus close so she could lay a hand on his handsome head, Cricket admired the dogwoods flowering a delicate pink. The azaleas lining the yard were putting on a show, having burst into vivid, colored blooms—fuchsia, violet, and scarlet.

With low humidity, a cloudless sky, and sparking sunshine, it was a gift of a day. Cricket paused to send up a thank you.

For beauty all around, new love blooming, work that I love, and dear friends, my life is full of contentment and promise.

With Angus beside her, Cricket strode to the garage. She'd load up the kayak and head to Azalea Lake, where she and Angus could get on the water and glide, loll, and drink in the sheer loveliness of this achingly beautiful spring day.

Dear Readers,

I so hope you enjoyed reading my latest book, *Pecan Pie for Breakfast (An Azalea Lake Sweet Romance Series Book 1)*! Please help me get the word out about *Pecan Pie* by leaving a review on your preferred online retail site.

Also, please share my Facebook posts about the book and/or post your own review of the book. Readers love to read book recommendations from friends.

https://www.facebook.com/authorsusanschild/

Follow me on BookBub to get early word about my next releases and upcoming sales:

https://www.bookbub.com/authors/susan-schild

ARRIVING SEPTEMBER 2021

A Front Porch Sunday

(An Azalea Lake Sweet Romance Series Book 2)

One other thought. Isn't it time we saw more

heartwarming movies and television shows about interesting women after 40 who are having adventures and falling in love? So many of my over-40 readers write to tell me about fresh starts, wonderful new marriages, or falling in love with their husbands all over again. One of my readers is a new bride at 80! Wouldn't it be amazing to see more of *our* stories, featuring older heroines like you and me, in fun and uplifting movies?

Which movie star(s) would you cast to play your favorite character(s) from this book or any of my other books? Message me on Facebook to share your thoughts!

I'm so grateful for your support!

Best,

Susan

ABOUT THE AUTHOR

USA Today Bestselling author Susan Schild writes heartwarming novels about heroines over age forty having adventures, falling in love and finding their happily ever afters.

A wife and stepmother, Susan enjoys reading and taking walks with her Labrador retriever mixes, Tucker and Gracie. She and her family live in North Carolina.

Susan has used her professional background as a psychotherapist and management consultant to add authenticity to her characters.

BOOKS BY AUTHOR SUSAN SCHILD

Love and Adventures after 40

AN AZALEA LAKE SWEET ROMANCE SERIES

Pecan Pie for Breakfast (Book 1)

USA Today Bestselling Author Susan Schild writes heartwarming romances all women can enjoy, about heroines over 40 having adventures and falling madly in love.

After a rough divorce, 45-year-old Cricket has built a new life for herself in the charming small town of Azalea Lake, North Carolina. With her caregiving business taking off and a possible new romance brewing with a handsome neighbor, Cricket's life is looking up. But before she moves ahead, she must deal with unfinished business from the past, namely her ex-husband, Knox, who abandoned her without a word of explanation and has become a famous rock climber.

Cricket and her best friend Honey decide to track down the elusive ex and discover why he left. Posing as wannabee rock climbers, they find Knox and learn the truth. Finally able to stop blaming herself and let go of the past, Cricket realizes how much promise her new life holds and embraces her budding happiness.

Join the many readers who have fallen in love with Susan Schild's charming small-town romances. You won't regret it.

"Cricket is such a spirited and engaging heroine—the best friend we all wish we had! You'll root for her as she boldly seeks answers about a past heartbreak and you'll celebrate as she discovers new truths and navigates her reimagined future. A delightful story about a woman who finds herself and much more. I loved it!"

–Barbara Josselsohn, award-winning author of *The Bluebell Girls, The Lilac House,* and *The Last Dreamer*

A Front Porch Sunday (Book 2)

ARRIVING SEPTEMBER 2021

Follow me on BookBub to get early word about this next release:

https://www.bookbub.com/authors/susan-schild

THE LAKESIDE RESORT SERIES

Christmas at the Lakeside Resort (Book 1)

Forty-two year old Jenny Beckett is dreading the holidays. Her fiancé has just called off their Christmas wedding, and she's been evicted from her darling chicken coop cottage. When her estranged father dies and leaves her eight rustic guest cabins on Heron Lake, Jenny seizes the chance to make a new life. She packs up her dogs, her miniature horse and her beat up Airstream trailer and moves to the lake.

Short on time and money, Jenny and her contractor, widower Luke, work feverishly to renovate the cabins in time for the festive holiday event she's promised her very first guests. When an unexpected blizzard snows them in and jeopardizes the resort's opening, Jenny and Luke work to save the event and, along the way, find true love… and the magic of Christmas.

Summer at the Lakeside Resort (Book 2)

Forty-three year old Jenny Beckett has just renovated eight rustic guest cabins on beautiful Heron Lake, North Carolina. Brand new to the inn keeping business, she is struggling to make The Lakeside Resort profitable. Wrangling guests like The Fighting Couple, persnickety attorneys, and the curvy gals from the Fabulous You Fitness Week keep her on her toes.

Jenny's business isn't her only problem. Her mother and stepfather have just moved in for an extended stay. Startling developments with her possible fiancé, Luke, make Jenny question his commitment to her. An all-gal camping trip in her old Airstream lifts her spirits, but Jenny still has doubts about whether she and Luke can make their love work. After all the heartache she's had, can Jenny learn to trust love again and finally find her happily ever after?

Mistletoe at the Lakeside Resort (Book 3)

Join forty-three-year-old newbie innkeeper Jenny Beckett at the Lakeside Resort on beautiful Heron Lake. Jenny's dreading Christmas. With almost no cabins booked for the holidays, she's accidentally made promises on social media about dazzling Christmas festivities happening at the Lakeside Resort. Trouble is, the holidays are fast approaching, Jenny's not begun to finalize plans, and she keeps running into roadblocks.

Stretched tight, Jenny scrambles to book a decent Santa Claus, a horse-drawn wagon for Currier and Ives-style sleigh rides, and the Christmas choirs she's so enthusiastically described online. To complicate matters, Mama has a frightening fall, Charlotte and Ashe are at odds about their upcoming wedding, and Jenny's getting the jitters about marrying and building a cabin with her fiancé, Luke.

When Jenny shares her fears with Luke and her best girlfriends, she starts to feel the wonder of the season. Friends gift her a new vintage camper, Mama and Landis make a startling announcement, and friends and family pitch in to help her deliver the dazzling Christmas she'd promised. Jenny realizes she already has all she needs for a magical Christmas and a happy future.

With cozy romance, classic carols, horse-drawn sleigh rides, and happily ever afters, Christmas joy is always on tap at The Lakeside Resort.

Wedding at the Lakeside Resort (Book 4)

When it comes to love, forty-four year old Jenny Beckett's track record isn't great, but she's finally found Luke Hammond, a kind, down to earth man who adores her. And she's marrying him!

But Jenny has no time to moon about the big day. With the Lakeside Resort's busiest season fast approaching, she's busily preparing for guests coming to stay in her tiny cabins and vintage campers.

When Luke is called away on business, Jenny must singlehandedly manage the resort, oversee construction of their new cabin, and plan the wedding. But she's also dealing with more troubling events. A late-night trespasser is destructive, and a developer is intent on building condominiums right next door. Jenny and Luke must scramble to protect the serenity and beauty of their beloved resort.

With love over 40 blooming all around, a plus-sized heroine, and relatable characters, come join your friends for a June wedding and stay awhile at the Lakeside Resort.

A WILLOW HILL NOVEL SERIES

Linny's Sweet Dream List (Book 1)

Set in the off-beat Southern town of Willow Hill, North Carolina, Susan Schild's moving and witty novel tells of one woman who loses everything—and finds more than she ever expected.

At thirty-eight, Linny Taylor is suddenly living a life she thought only happened to other, more careless people. Widowed for the second time, and broke, thanks to her cheating late husband, Linny has no house, no job, and no options except to go back home. There, in a trailer as run down as her self-esteem, Linny makes a list of things that might bring happiness. A porch swing. A job that nourishes her heart as well as her bank balance. Maybe even a date or two.

At first, every goal seems beyond reach. But it's hard for Linny to stay in the doldrums when a stray puppy is coercing her out of her shell—right into the path of the town's kind, compassionate vet. The quirky town is filled with friends and family, including Linny's mother, Dottie, who knows more about heartache than her daughters ever guessed. And as Linny contemplates each item on her list, she begins to realize that the dreams most worth holding on to can only be measured in the sweetness of a life lived to the fullest...

Sweet Carolina Morning (Book 2)

Life down South just got a whole lot sweeter in Susan Schild's new novel about a woman whose happily-ever-after is about to begin... whether she's ready for it or not.

Finally, just shy of forty years old, Linny Taylor is living the life of her dreams in her charming hometown of Willow Hill, North Carolina. The past few years have been anything but a fairy tale: Left broke by her con man late-husband, Linny has struggled to rebuild her life from scratch. Then she met Jack Avery, the town's much-adored veterinarian. And she's marrying him.

Everything should be coming up roses for Linny. So why does she have such a serious case of pre-wedding jitters? It could be because Jack's prosperous family doesn't approve of her rough-and-tumble background. Or that his ex-wife is suddenly back on the scene. Or that Linny has yet to win over his son's heart. All these obstacles—not to mention what she should wear when she walks down the aisle—are taking the joy out of planning her wedding. Linny better find a way to trust love again, or she might risk losing the one man she wants to be with—forever…

Sweet Southern Hearts (Book 3)

Welcomes you back to the offbeat Southern town of Willow Hill, North Carolina, for a humorous, heartwarming story of new beginnings, do-overs, and self-discovery…

When it comes to marriage, third time's the charm for Linny Taylor. She's thrilled to be on her honeymoon with Jack Avery, Willow Hill's handsome veterinarian. But just like the hair-raising white water rafting trip Jack persuades her to take, newlywed life has plenty of dips and bumps.

Jack's twelve-year-old son is resisting all Linny's efforts to be the perfect stepmother, while her own mother, Dottie, begs her to tag along on the first week of a free-wheeling RV adventure. Who knew women "of a certain age" could drum up so much trouble? No sooner is Linny sighing with relief at being back home than she's helping her frazzled sister with a new baby…and dealing with an unexpected legacy from her late ex. Life is fuller—and richer—than she ever imagined, but if there's one thing Linny's learned by now, it's that there's always room for another sweet surprise…

Made in the USA
Columbia, SC
31 January 2025

53035384R00200